HAYNER

Renegade

Renegade

J. A. Souders

TOR
TEEN

A TOM DOHERTY ASSOCIATES BOOK

NEW YORK

RENEGADE

Map by Jon Lansberg

Design by Mary A. Wirth

A Tor Teen Book
Published by Tom Doherty Associates, LLC
175 Fifth Avenue
New York, NY 10010

www.tor-forge.com

Tor® is a registered trademark of Tom Doherty Associates, LLC.

Library of Congress Cataloging-in-Publication Data

Souders, J. A.
  Renegade / J. A. Souders.—1st ed.
      p. cm.
"A Tom Doherty Associates Book."
ISBN 978-0-7653-3245-5 (hardcover)
ISBN 978-1-4668-0095-3 (e-book)
   1. Undersea colonies—Fiction.   2. Secrets—Fiction.   3. Memory—
Fiction.   4. Genetics—Fiction.   5. Science fiction.   I. Title.
PZ7.S7246Ren 2012
[Fic]—dc23

                                                        2012024424

First Edition: November 2012

Printed in the United States of America

0   9   8   7   6   5   4   3   2   1

To Ben, for being my
knight-in-not-so-shining armor.

And to the memory of my Uncle Rick,
for giving me my wings.

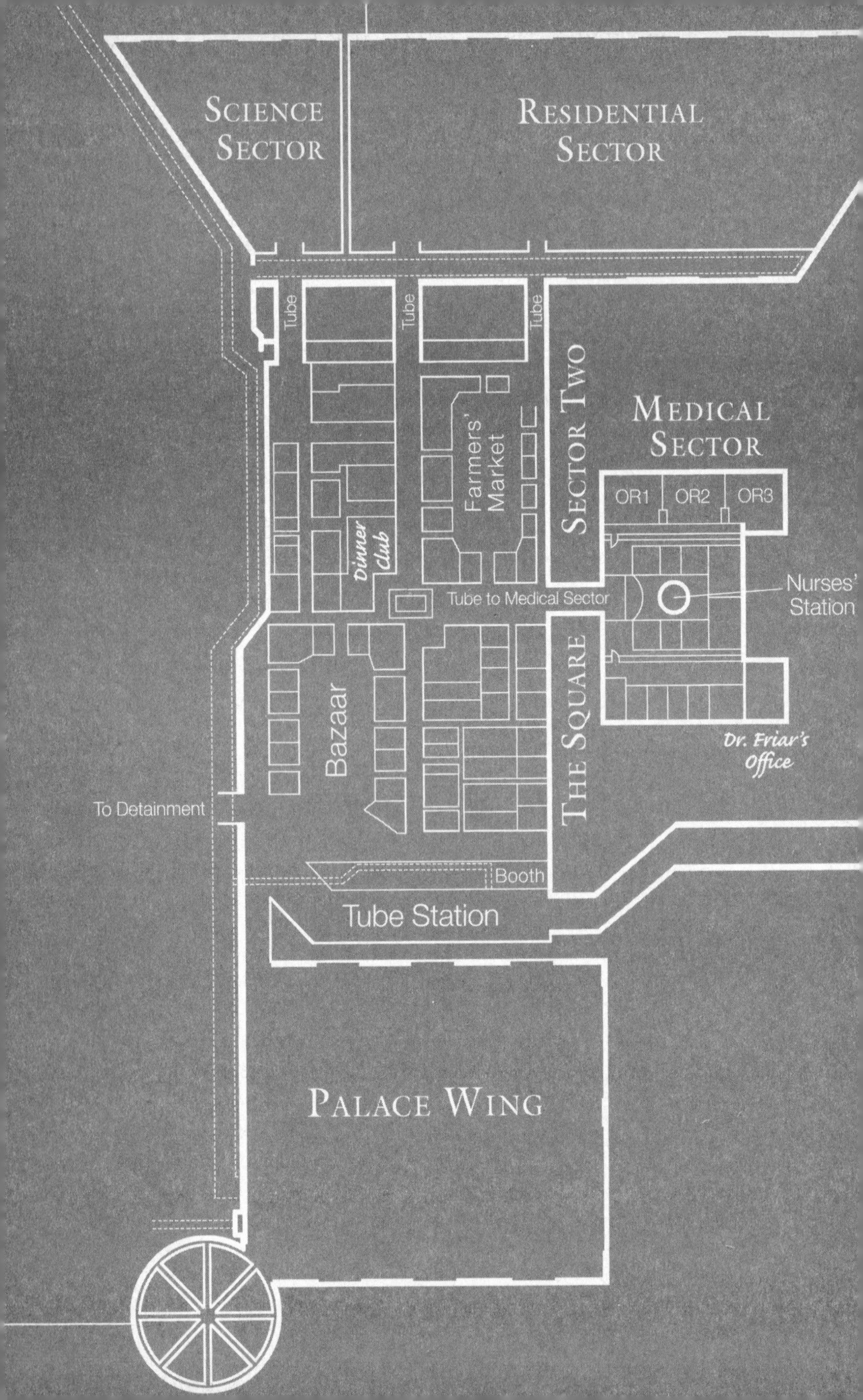

Science Sector
Residential Sector
Tube
Tube
Tube
Sector Two
Medical Sector
OR1
OR2
OR3
Farmers' Market
Dinner club
Tube to Medical Sector
Nurses' Station
Bazaar
The Square
Dr. Friar's Office
To Detainment
Booth
Tube Station
Palace Wing

ELYSIUM CITY PLAN

UNDEVELOPED TERRITORY

SECTOR FOUR
(AGRICULTURAL)

Tube Station

Booth

SECTOR THREE
(MECHANICAL)

UNDEVELOPED TERRITORY

*Please note: Due to irregularities in underwater terrain,
not all sectors on the same plane.*

Renegade

CHAPTER ONE

Sacrifices must be made for the greater good.
—CITIZEN'S SOCIAL CODE, VOLUME VI

M*y life is just about perfect.*

Every morning Mother has the Maids wake me at precisely ten. Then it's time for a light breakfast followed by a mandatory visit with my Therapist. *It's nice to have someone to talk with.*

After, I am free to do as I wish until it's time to perform one of the duties Mother has requested of me. This morning I sit in my garden, quietly doing my cross-stitching. The garden is so peaceful in the morning, especially when the sea life outside the glass dome passes by.

The Surface could never compare. Not that I've ever seen the Surface. It is forbidden, even for me.

Which is fine. *My life is just about perfect.*

The scent of roses, gardenias, lilies, and countless other

flowers fill the air. Compared to the rest of the facility, the sunlamps make the air here feel sultry. Between that and the continual buzzing from the bees pollinating my lovely flowers, I often find myself falling asleep. The wind chimes my friend Timothy made for me tinkle in the current from the oxygen recyclers.

Timothy is from Sector Three. His father is a metal worker and his mother a child-care worker, but he's been allowed residence in Sector Two because of his status as my favored Suitor. Due to his genetics he's been chosen as a potential match for me. *It will ensure only the best are born in Elysium.*

Of the three Suitors chosen for me, I like him the best. He is the most understanding of my . . . eccentricities. A warm feeling tingles in my stomach and I press a hand to it and smile. Yes, Timothy is my favorite.

A butterfly flits in front of me, distracting me from my thoughts, and lands in the blueberry shrubs, which are filled with the white blossoms of spring. I love that spring has come, and with it longer days, and that summer is just a few months away. My garden will be even warmer and the lights will be on even longer, allowing more free time to play among my flowers.

Music plays in the background. A soft, enchanting number that relaxes the mind and spirit.

There are Guards stationed around the room, but they don't bother me. They're just a fact of life. The cost of peace.

With that thought, I decide to take a walk in my gardens.

My fingers fiddle with the pleats in the skirt of my dress. I cross over the concrete paths that separate the plantings in wheel-spoke fashion, leading from a path that rings the outer wall of the garden to the pond, which is dead center.

My life is just about perfect.

I'm drawn to the roses—besides my violin, they are my most prized possession—as if their scent has literally pulled me to them. They remind me of something—a fragrance that rests at the far edge of my memory. It's too elusive to remember, but not enough to forget completely. My fingers brush the rose pendant resting in the dent of my collarbone.

It is the one thing Mother has allowed me to keep from my childhood, before she adopted me and named me Daughter of the People. Though if she knew what I use the necklace for, I am fairly certain it would disappear.

I stare at the roses for another moment. I can't resist—just a touch. It is what I walk these gardens for.

Mindful of the thorns, I pluck a rose from the bush and bring it to my nose. I inhale its heady scent and hope it, along with the pendant, will bring forth my memory.

The pendant to recover what is lost. The fragrances to fill the empty spaces.

A vision of a woman and a much younger version of myself forms in my mind.

My breath comes fast through my teeth as the pain starts to bloom in my brain—and then a sharp stab in my finger pulls me back into the present. I glance down to see blood welling on the tip of my forefinger. A rose lies on the ground a few centimeters from my feet. I stare at it, wondering how it ended up there.

"Evie," Timothy says from beside me. When did he get here? "Are you all right? Here, let me help you." He pulls a first-aid kit from one of the metal beams that frame the windows, separating my gardens from the Atlantic, and then bandages my finger. His grin lights up his face as he looks down at me.

"There you go. All set." He pats my hand and I'm overwhelmed with conflicting emotions. Part of me wants to yank my hand away, while the other part relishes the warm tingle of his hand softly melting into mine. The latter is a comfortable feeling—not new. Not as if it were the first time.

"Wouldn't want you to get sick now," he continues.

"No," I say, trying to remember why his touch is so familiar. "Wouldn't want that." A breeze from the recyclers blows by and I catch a whiff of Timothy's scent. Memories roll under a deep fog in my head, but nothing is clear. I can't even remember what I've been doing. Wasn't I . . . somewhere else?

"Are you all right?" he asks. His blue eyes fill with worry as he watches me.

I nod. *"My life is just about perfect."*

He smiles, but there's sadness in his eyes. "Good. I'm glad. I was worried"—he glances to the Guards—"you were sick or something, the way you were staring off into space."

"How are your parents?" I ask, more from politeness than out of an actual interest. Although guilt tickles at me because

I know I should care—that something changed between us, not too long ago, but I can't remember what.

Timothy frowns. "I don't know. They didn't come for our traditional Sunday dinner yesterday and they haven't been answering any of my messages, which is strange because Mom was waiting for me to tell her what your"—he stops with a glance to me, then sighs and continues—"how you're doing. I plan on going over to Three today to check on them."

"I see. Well, if you require assistance, please don't hesitate to ask." How nice of his mother to ask about me.

"I will. Thank you," he says.

We both realize at the same moment that he is still touching me. My eyes meet his quickly, heat spreading from my toes to my face. This isn't the first time, I think again. My heart beats furiously and I'm gasping for breath. Because touching him is impossible. I would remember if we touched. Unless . . .

I drop his hand quickly, and we jump apart from each other, glancing around to make sure we weren't noticed. We are not Coupled, and skin-to-skin touching is strictly forbidden.

He glances around, as I had just done, but then to my surprise, he pulls something out of his pocket and holds it out. "I found this for you," he whispers, leaning close.

I keep my hands where they are, but knit my brows together, trying to see what it is.

"It's for your"—he glances around again—"collection."

Immediately I get a buzz and shove my hand out, eagerly awaiting the possible Surface object. He drops a silver-colored metal disc into my palm. And I study it carefully. It has strange markings on it. A picture of a head on one side, and some kind of . . . creature on the back.

" 'In God We Trust,' " I read. I look up at Timothy. "What do you think it means?"

He shrugs, but I'm too excited to care. I've never seen anything like this before and I can't wait to study it closer, but here's not the place. I'll have to ask Mother later. When Timothy isn't around. Mother is indulgent of my curiosity about the Surface, but I doubt that tolerance would be extended to Timothy. I shove it into the pocket of my dress as Timothy bends to pick up the rose from the ground. Carefully he removes the thorns and hands it back.

"For you, Miss Evelyn." His smile now is shy. My face still burns from the memory of his touch, and I lift the rose to my face to hide it.

The rose's heady scent triggers some memory in the back of my mind. But before I can think on it further, Timothy wanders over to the small pond a few meters in front of us.

The blue glimmers under the lights like tiny diamonds floating on the glasslike surface. Unlike in Sector Four—the Agricultural Sector—this water is fresh instead of reclaimed, and pumped directly from the desalination tanks. It's filled with lily pads and other water flowers.

I follow him. He points to a bluish flower with oval-shaped petals resting on top. "Will you tell me what this one is again?"

I smile. He always knows how to make me feel better. "It's an Egyptian Lily. We use it in many of our medicines. It is used as a sedative, but it is also an aphrodisiac."

The rose slips from my fingers.

Today is Request Day. I have many responsibilities as Daughter of the People, but this is my favorite one. It's also the most important of my many duties. It shows Mother trusts me. I am the Citizens' voice, and they look up to me to make sure they have everything they need and want.

Elysium is a family, and it's important that the heads of that family listen to its members, so that all may be happy.

Mother allows me to host the requests wherever I like, but I prefer to use what I've called the Request Room. It's fairly large with one wall-sized window in the back, and pink marble walls and ceiling. In the front are two doors. One is the door Citizens will enter from. The other is where they exit, unless they need to see Mother. In that case, they'll use the door to the left of my chair—which is in the center of the room—to take them to Mother's receiving room.

I settle myself into the chair, crossing my legs at the ankle, like Mother has taught me, before straightening my favorite silk skirt so it covers my knees. It's a little short, but the blue brings out the color of my eyes, and Mother usually lets me get away with it.

I glance at the Citizens standing behind the velvet ropes before nodding to one of the two Guards next to me that I am ready to start. The line is short today, thank Mother. As much as I enjoy my duties, it can get quite overwhelming.

The first Citizen who steps forward is slightly older than my own sixteen years. He twists his hands together as he walks toward me, and there's a slight shake to his legs when he kneels in front of me and bows his head.

When he only continues to kneel without looking up, I realize this is his first time here and he is nervous.

"Speak, Citizen. What is your request?"

He glances up, and while his hands still shake, his eyes aren't as wide as they were before. "I wish to request a Coupling License, Miss Evelyn."

My smile grows. This is why Request Day is my favorite. "And who is the lucky girl?"

He waves a hand and a girl my age rushes to his side. She's careful not to touch him, but kneels next to him and bows her head. "I'm Alice, Miss Evelyn."

I signal for the Guard to get me my Slate. "What is your current designation?"

"Child-care worker."

I take the Slate from the Guard and place my hand over the glass screen, waiting for the computer to read my print and boot to the main screen. "So you've already been approved for breeding?"

"Yes, Miss Evelyn," she says, and then places her hand on the screen when I hold it out to her.

I take a few minutes to study her file and nod approvingly at what I read. She is an excellent candidate for breeding.

After verifying the man's file, I approve them for coupling on a contingency basis, pending genetic testing, and send them to the Medical Sector. They have two weeks from today to complete the necessary testing before they'll have to report to Mother—she has the final say on whether or not they'll couple.

I can see they're nervous, but from what I can tell from their records, they don't need to worry. Mother should happily grant them their final approval.

The next few people pass through without incident, asking for the typical things: a request for Mother to visit a newborn child for her blessing. A larger stipend and quarters for the soon-to-be parents of twins. I make a note in Mother's calendar to set up a celebration for when the children will be born. Twins are such a rare occurrence, I'm sure she'll want to do something. There's even a sweet request from the parents of a little girl who wants to see my gardens.

All will have to be approved by Mother, but I have no doubts she'll approve. Especially the request from the little girl. Mother enjoys my humanitarian efforts.

But my mouth is dry from all the talking. I would really like to have a drink, but I still have Citizens to attend to. I know if I ask my Guard to get a drink for me, he'll go, but it's not exactly his job to get me a drink and it doesn't feel right to ask him. I'll just wait until I'm done.

When the sixth person in line approaches me, I smile and ask him what his request is. His hands tremble, but he bows his head and says in a shaky whisper, "I want to know what happened to my wife."

"Excuse me?" I ask, sure I didn't hear him correctly.

"I want to know what happened to my wife." He looks up with bloodshot eyes. "She wasn't home when I got back from working yesterday. I've looked for her everywhere."

"Name?" I ask, my hand hovering over my slate.

"Renee Davis."

I skim the Citizen Roster, confused. "Can you spell that for me?" I ask. He does, but my Slate still shows no one by that name. I purse my lips as he continues to watch me with pain and hope mingling in his eyes. "I can't seem to locate anyone by that name," I say.

From the corner of my eye, I see an Enforcer step out of the shadows, and I have to stop the shudder that threatens every time I see one. Like all Enforcers, she's wearing the customary black dress with pleated skirt that stops just above her knee. The tops of her black boots are hidden underneath the skirt. Her black gloves go all the way to the middle of her biceps and she's wearing a hooded cape that covers all other exposed areas of skin. I've always found it strange that Enforcers would wear dresses, but Mother believes that no matter their duties, ladies should dress like ladies.

The Enforcer pushes her hood back, revealing the blank face they've all perfected. She's the one known as Veronica.

All Enforcers make me nervous, but this one is the worst of them all.

I tense, my heart beating faster. I find myself wanting to run as far away from her as I can. And it's not just me. The handful of Citizens still in line have stopped talking and fidgeting. They hold their collective breath and step farther away from me. It's as silent as a tomb now.

However, the moment passes and the Enforcer makes no other move, staying silent and vigilant just this side of the shadows. The icy tension in the room will just have to be dealt with. The Citizens look to me as an example of how to behave, so I must swallow my unease. I take a deep, calming breath and force a smile.

"As I was saying"—I shoot one more glance at the Enforcer—"place your hand on my Slate. Perhaps there was some sort of bookkeeping mistake."

He drags his gaze from the Enforcer, then nods and places his hand on the glass. When it beeps, I look at the information and frown. His file states that he is Single, never been Coupled. There had been a Courting Application filed late last year, but the woman in question, a Renee Davis, had died from unknown causes during the testing process. It's a pity Mother's genetic matching program still can't prevent such anomalies from happening. This Renee was clearly too weak for breeding.

My heart breaks when I realize what's happening. I wish Mother was here to help me, but she is not. I decide to break the news to him gently.

"I'm sorry," I say quietly, "but, according to her file, she died last year. I'm very sorry for your loss."

Feet shuffle behind the man and someone coughs as the man stares at me with a confused expression. The Citizens mutter among themselves and a few have angry expressions. How inappropriate, I think. This is not his fault; his broken heart is confusing his mind.

"I will have order!" I say, and immediately the room quiets again. The angry ones glance toward the Enforcer before lowering their gazes to the floor.

"That's not true," the man in front of me says, so softly I almost can't hear him. "She was with me yesterday morning. We had breakfast in the Square. As we do every morning."

"I'm sorry, Citizen."

He looks up at me again, his eyes flashing with anger. "She's not dead. Your Slate is wrong."

The Enforcer advances, and the room becomes quiet again as chills race up and down my spine.

"Mother handles the death certificates—"

"Then Mother is wrong!" the man says, and steps forward, tears streaming down his cheeks.

"Hold your tongue, Citizen!" I shout, but immediately I regret it. The Daughter of the People must never lose her calm.

The Enforcer is watching me closely, obviously waiting to see how I handle the situation, and I can't help but feel I'm not measuring up to whatever she expects from me. And that she's delighting in that fact. That makes me more nervous than I want to admit, and I swallow the lump in my throat.

I gesture for the man to step closer. "You will have to speak with Mother, then, if that is what you believe." The Guard moves toward the man, but the Enforcer beats him to it.

When she steps closer, unlike the respectful Citizens, she first meets my eyes before bowing her head. There is no life in those cold blue eyes, or in the unmoving set of her mouth.

"I'll escort him, Miss. Your Guard is needed here, with you." Her voice is quiet and breathy, and shouldn't be any more frightening than the ladybugs in my garden, but it makes my skin crawl. I nod and she grabs the man.

"No," he whispers, and there is a strange understanding in his eyes, but he doesn't fight as the young Enforcer pulls him toward the door on my right, then disappears with him.

I glance around, trying to determine if another Enforcer has replaced the one that just left, but it's useless. I'll never be able to see her.

The room remains quiet as I rub my arms to remove the chill from my skin. I'll have to ask Mother later what happened. The Guard next to me leans down. "Are you all right, Miss Evelyn?"

"Yes, I . . ." I straighten my shoulders and force my hands to rest in my lap. "I'm quite well. Bring me a soy chai latte."

"Yes, ma'am."

He turns and is halfway to the door before I remember to say, "Iced."

"Yes, Miss."

I focus on the next person in line. "Next?"

Mother and I sip our afternoon tea in her sitting room. We enjoy having tea together. It is really the only time we have to recount our days to each other and just talk. Just us girls. I smile when I see she's using my favorite tea set: the gold-rimmed china with the large English tea roses on the side. Flowers from my gardens sit on the table between us.

Today, only two Maids are in the room with us, waiting patiently to serve us whatever our hearts desire. Two Guards stand by the door, but they aren't the same ones that were in the gardens earlier. It is unusual for me not to have the same Guards. I may not know their names, but it is slightly disturbing not to recognize a familiar face. My life revolves around familiarity.

Mother sits across from me, her attention completely focused on her tea. Her wheat blond hair gleams in the light of the overhead crystal chandelier. It amazes me, as it always does, how beautiful she is. *She is the epitome of excellent culture and breeding. What every lady should strive to be.* What *I* strive to be.

Today she wears a bloodred dress suit that enhances her small curvy body, but not enough to tempt the men around her. *A lady should be like a flower under glass, beautiful yet untouchable.*

It's quiet. Pleasantly so, and I stare over her shoulder to the window behind her. The outside lights make the water a gorgeous blue and a school of colorful fish swims by. Very faintly I can hear the low moaning of a whale.

"Evelyn," Mother says, tapping her nails on the tabletop to draw my attention back to her. I love the pink marble of the table. It reminds me of my roses.

"Yes, Mother?" I say.

"Do you have your speech prepared for Festival?"

"Yes, Mother. I submitted it to your assistant this morning for your approval."

She nods and takes another sip of her tea as I spin the metal disc in my hand.

"Mother?"

She looks over at me and lifts an eyebrow. I hold my hand out to her, with the metal disc in the center of it. "Do you know what this is? Ti—" I cut myself off, not wanting to get Timothy into trouble. "I found this. When I was in Three yesterday, checking on the mining. Remember? I don't know what it is, but it has the most unusual markings on it." Her beautiful peaches-and-cream face pales, and the dusting of freckles across her nose and cheeks stand out clearly against it. She plucks the disc from my palm and studies it carefully, but I continue. "On this side, it looks like that's one of the birds from the Surface. And the other has some kind of head on it. Is it from the Surface?"

She nods slowly. "Yes, I'm afraid it is."

I bite back a smile, trying not to show how excited I am about it. "And the words? 'In God We Trust.' What do they mean? What is it, Mother?"

"It is death, Evelyn." She looks from the disc to me. Her eyes bore into mine; their gray striations standing out against the sapphire blue. "This little disc—they call it a coin—is half responsible for starting every war there has ever been on the Surface. And that saying? It's the other half. You must never touch this thing again, Evelyn. I won't have you corrupted by its power."

Despite her warnings, I'm still curious. How could such a tiny little metal object be responsible for so much destruction?

She narrows her eyes at me and folds her hand over the coin. "This curiosity you have with the Surface is unhealthy, Evelyn. I must insist that it cease. Immediately."

I sigh, but bow my head. "Yes, Mother."

"And to make sure of it, I'm going to have your little fountain dredged for any more Surface contraband."

No! Not my collection!

I look up sharply, but her face is dark and I know better than to argue. "Yes, Mother."

She watches me for several minutes before she takes another sip of tea.

"By the way, Evelyn, I heard a disturbing rumor this morning as I was taking my morning constitutional." She lifts the delicate teacup to her mouth, but pauses. "Do you know to which rumor I am referring?"

Rumors are not uncommon among the Maids. If there is ever anything you wish to know, the Maids are sure to know it. They were unusually quiet this morning after my time with

Timothy. But this couldn't be about him. Mother approved of him.

"No, Mother."

She places her cup in its saucer and purses her lips. They are the same color as her dress. "I'm surprised. Since this rumor mostly revolves around you and a particular Third you're fond of."

So this *is* about Timothy. Though that doesn't explain what rumor would be so important Mother would concern herself with it, or why she would talk to me about it.

"Still don't know?" Her eyes are hard and cold.

"No, Mother." I suppress a shiver. I don't like that look. It reminds me of one of the sharks that sometimes swims outside my gardens.

"According to the incessant mutterings of the Maids, he touched you this morning. In plain view of the Guards and an Enforcer."

"Touched me?" I think back to the garden. "Oh, no, Mother. He didn't touch me. A thorn stuck my finger and he bandaged it for me." I smile and sip my tea, pleased with myself for remembering. *Today is better than yesterday. And yesterday was better than the day before.*

"The Guards report this to be true," she says, her lips still pursed, "but they also say he didn't let go right away."

"It was an accident. He asked if I was okay and, when I said yes, we both realized he was still touching me. It won't happen again."

Mother's face turns hard and she nods. "You're right. It will not happen again. Guards!" She claps her hands with the command, causing me to jump in my seat and slosh tea out of the cup.

My eyes widen when two Guards enter, carrying Timothy between them. His face is bruised and bloody. A black eye is already forming and his slack jaw reveals several teeth are missing. I barely realize when my teacup slips from my limp fingers and shatters on the marble. Two more Guards are suddenly at my side, holding me down.

"What's happened?"

Mother clicks her tongue. "Evelyn, Evelyn, Evelyn. I thought I taught you better than that. Touching before coupling is an impropriety. Punishable under the law."

I swallow hard as she continues to stare at me, then close my eyes. She is right. I must resign myself to it. The law is the law, after all. *It is what keeps us safe. Keeps us from being like the Surface Dwellers.* "Very well, Mother. What is our punishment?"

"Oh, no, my child. *You* are not being punished. It isn't your fault. It was *he* who touched *you*. *He* who tried to defile *your* innocence. His punishment is death."

My eyes fly open. "What? No! It was an accident. This was my fault, not his! Please, Mother—" I'm cut off when she slaps my face. Hard. Rage tears through me in a sudden jolt, but fades as quickly as it came, leaving only panic. I stare aghast at her as I curl my fingers into my palm.

"You do not talk back to me. Ever." She straightens the skirt of her dress, then her hair. She makes a gesture with her hand and an Enforcer—Veronica—steps from the shadows. She holds a Colt .45 equipped with a silencer in her gloved hand.

Before I can blink, she pulls the trigger. Once. Twice. Two bullets rip into Timothy's chest, hitting both lungs. He collapses to his knees as the Enforcer steps back into the shadows. Her face is completely blank—there's not even a spark of emotion in her eyes—and the Guards let him fall.

The Guards on me have held me tight, but I haven't even moved; my body is still frozen in shock. When they finally release me, I run straight to Timothy's side. I don't care if Mother punishes me. He's dying and it's my fault. Because of my carelessness. Because I hadn't remembered until it was too late.

He gasps for breath and blood pours from his mouth just as quickly as it comes from his wounds.

He looks up and into my eyes. "I'm sorry," he gasps out before his eyes close. "I thought I would be different. I thought I could"—he coughs, splattering blood across my chest—"save you."

I try to stop the flow of blood, but it seeps over my hands.

"No," I whisper. His breath shudders out one last time before his chest becomes still. I turn to Mother. "How could you? I'd chosen him. He's the one I *wanted*." My voice cracks with each word.

Mother walks over and places a hand on my shoulder. I think she'll say she's sorry, but instead she says, "Now this is a pity. His genetics were . . . promising."

Her words only barely reach my ears. She walks away, her heels clicking on the marble.

A Guard steps over and something cool presses on the skin of my arm. I look over in time to see him inject something into me. Immediately the room spins and I collapse onto Timothy.

No!

His blood warms my cheeks as darkness swoops over me like a shroud.

CHAPTER TWO

The War has corrupted the Surface Dwellers. They have been consumed with hate and violence, and should be considered extremely dangerous. Any Surface Dweller who attempts to break into Elysium should be shot on sight.

—ENFORCER STATUTE 104A.1

M*y life is just about perfect.*

Every morning Mother has the Maids wake me at precisely ten. Then it's time for a light breakfast followed by a mandatory visit with my Therapist. *It's nice to have someone to talk with.*

After, I am free to do as I wish until it's time to perform one of the duties Mother has requested of me. This morning I sit in my garden, quietly doing my cross-stitching. The garden is so peaceful in the morning, especially when the sea life outside the glass dome passes by.

The Surface could never compare. Not that I've ever seen the Surface. It is forbidden, even for me.

Which is fine. *My life is just about perfect.*

The scent of roses, gardenias, lilies, and countless other flowers fill the air. Compared to the rest of the facility, the sunlamps make the air here feel sultry. Between that and the continual buzzing from the bees pollinating my lovely flowers, I often find myself falling asleep. Wind chimes tinkle in the current from the oxygen recyclers.

The sound reminds me of something, someone, just at the far reaches of my memory. Absently, my fingers reach up to play with the charm around my neck.

The pendant to recover what is lost.

I stare at the chimes for a long time. They twist and sway in the slight breeze, the silver and purple of the metal glinting like knives in the light. For some reason, my heart races. I can't stop myself from reaching out to touch the cold, smooth metal. Without warning, a flash of memory—pain and blood—causes me to jerk my hand from the chimes, but I continue to watch them spin. I touch a hand to my temple as a tremendous sense of loss sweeps through me.

Tears sting my eyes, but I blink them back. I don't know why I should react this way to wind chimes.

Mother steps up next to me. "Is there a problem, Evelyn?" She watches me carefully, as if I am a snake and might strike out and bite her.

An odd feeling of guilt pulls at me. "No. I thought I knew something about the wind chimes."

Her eyes narrow. "Really? And what would that be?"

Don't tell her, a voice whispers in my head. I glance over at her and slowly say, "I don't know."

Her face softens. "It is nothing, my child." She runs her own finger down a chime. "These have been in the gardens since your father had it constructed for you. However, if they bother you, I can have them removed. I found the most talented metal Artist today. I would be more than happy to have him commission something for you to replace these old things."

"No, that's all right." While they carry a hint of sadness and guilt, I find I don't want her to take them away.

"Are you sure? How about a new dress? The Dressmaker reports she has made a lovely purple silk she thinks will look exquisite on you."

"A dress would be wonderful, Mother."

"Very well. I'll make an appointment for her to come after lunch so she can measure you." She glances around the garden and her nose wrinkles. "I don't understand why you want to play in the dirt, Evelyn. Such a messy business. You should spend more time playing your violin. It's really the only thing you do well." She lifts a blue silk-covered shoulder. It isn't quite a shrug, because ladies don't do that, but the gesture is meant to be the same. "Your Therapist will be here at noon. Please make sure you are ready for him."

Inwardly, I sigh. I always feel so peculiar after seeing him. No. That's not true. *It's nice to have someone to talk with.*

"Yes, Mother, of course."

She smiles and pats my cheek before clicking away. I stand where I am, unsure of what I was doing before she came. The corners of my lips lift when I remember. I was gathering Egyptian lilies for the Healers and Scientists.

I slip out of my kitten heels and into the water. It is shin deep—only a few centimeters below the skirt of my dress—and warm as bathwater. I hum while I collect the delicate flowers, taking care to make sure the hem of my skirt does not get wet, and think that my best friend, Macie, will be pleased with this latest bunch. They are quite a bit larger than the last batch.

A low moaning pulls me from my thoughts and I walk swiftly to the windows that separate my gardens from the millions of liters of seawater that is the Atlantic Ocean.

Because my garden juts off the side of the buildings that make up our underwater city, I have an almost three hundred and sixty-degree view of the ocean. Even the ceiling is made of the thick glass. As often as I am in my gardens, it never fails to amaze me how clear and undistorted the water looks.

A blue whale passes by the window, and from the pattern of the scars by his eye, I'm pretty sure I've seen this particular one before. The thought pleases me. I touch a hand to the cool glass and his eye fixes right on me. He moans again, and it's as if he's talking to me.

He's large, considering how small I am in comparison, but he's small for a blue whale—maybe only twenty meters or so—and from research, I know he's probably only a few years old, probably just reaching sexual maturity. He's gorgeous, with his blue gray mottled skin and pale, ridged underbelly. I hope he'll sing for me today. The songs always sound sad, but they're lovely.

Then he rolls, showing off another of his pod. Since it's slightly larger and appears to be flirting with him, I wonder if she's his mate. She comes close enough to the glass that I'm sure, if the glass didn't separate us, I could touch her.

Her large eye studies me carefully for a long time, and I stand there, watching her back. Though she can't really smile, I can see it in her eye. She makes a loud moaning sound and the first whale joins in her song.

It always amazes me when they come to visit. I'm not sure why exactly, since fish life is abundant where we are. It's rare not to glance out the window and see schools of brightly colored fish. Or a manta ray. Sharks. Jellyfish. Our city sits in a trench, our buildings dug into the walls. All except Sector Three—I have to press a hand to my stomach when the thought of Three causes flutters there—which is settled on the trench floor because we use the geothermal energy from the lava tubes to power our facility.

The warmer water attracts plenty of pretty things. The water is mostly blue, and highlighted because of the outside lights that shine during the daylight hours, but if I tilt my head just right, I can detect a hint of orange closer to the bottom. It's strangely intriguing.

For almost an hour, I watch out the window until my friends bid me adieu with a flick of their tails as they disappear into the blue.

No sooner are they gone than running footsteps sound behind me, quickly followed by the alarms from the DNA cameras. It's unusual to hear, and I immediately tense, spinning to face the door directly across from me. It's not so much the alarms—they're easy to set off, though they make my ears hurt with their high-pitched screech—but the running. Sometimes the Maids will walk a bit faster if they are behind in their duties, but running is almost unheard of.

I peer around the hemlock bush that blocks my view, and my eyes widen when a very dirty boy around my age runs through the doors leading into my gardens. He slides to a halt just inside the doors, looks in all directions, and then darts off to my left.

Within seconds, Guards rush in and head straight for my own two Guards, who've barely paid attention to me since I got here. They confer quietly for a moment before one turns to me.

"Miss Evelyn. You must go back to your room right away. There is a Surface Dweller running around."

I wonder how they have missed the fact that one just ran through the door.

Normally I would agree to their request—it's just easier to do what they ask and it's usually only a minor inconvenience—but the boy looked more scared than anything. Not savage, as I'd always been taught. I wonder if he's a Surface Dweller at all. Maybe the DNA alarms are just malfunctioning. But even if he is . . . I've never met a Surface Dweller before.

I fight the urge to turn my head in his direction. "I am safe here," I say, straightening my shoulders and lifting my head. "There is only one way in and one way out." I make sure my voice is loud and clear so the young man can hear me, wherever he's hiding. "I wish to continue my gardening duties. I won't be long."

The Guards exchange a look. They probably want to argue with me, but the last time one did so, Mother did not take kindly to it. After a long moment, they nod and go to watch over the doors.

I pretend to walk my gardens with nothing on my mind other than removing dead heads of the flowers I pass, but I'm really looking for the boy and keeping an eye out for Enforcers. They aren't usually in my gardens, but I don't want to take any chances.

I hum softly under my breath, hoping I appear normal to anyone watching. They're used to me acting oddly, but I wonder how closely they're watching me.

Never did I expect my . . . condition to be of use to me.

When I finally find him, he's hiding underneath the table used for cuttings. He's holding my shears in one hand and glaring at me. Inwardly I tense; he is an armed Surface Dweller after all, but I refuse to show how nervous he makes me.

He's shaking, but I now doubt it is from fear. He doesn't look afraid. He looks sick. His skin is pale and pasty. His hair is stringy and partially covers his eyes, which are bloodshot.

But he's strong. The lines of his chest are visible through his shirt, which—along with his pants—is torn and, although covered in mud, clings to his skin. There's a spray of something red across the front. It's dark, and I think I smell something rusty.

A memory pushes its way front and center.

He's dying and it's my fault because of my carelessness.

He gasps for breath and blood pours from his mouth just as quickly as it comes from his wounds.

With a gasp, I cross my arms over my chest, hugging myself and shaking the memory from my head. I'll work on figuring that one out later. Right now I need to figure out what to do with the Surface Dweller in front of me.

I kneel, careful not to get too close. He's quite obviously a Surface Dweller and therefore unpredictable.

"Hello," I say softly. "I won't hurt you."

He shrinks away from me and narrows his eyes, but adjusts his body, bracing his legs. It's obvious he's positioning himself to run again.

"Yeah, right." His voice is scratchy, as if he's swallowed too much saltwater.

I try again, using a smile this time—*a woman's best weapon is her smile, unless there's a loaded Beretta 9mm nearby.* I frown. What an odd thought. "I don't blame you for not trusting me. You don't know me, but I assure you, I mean you no harm. My name is Evelyn Winters. I'm the Daughter of the People."

"Gavin Hunter," he answers warily.

I smile again, a real one this time, and he blinks, as if surprised.

"Gavin. It's a pleasure to meet you."

His eyes widen and then narrow, but there is something else in his expression. Hope, maybe? He shakes back his hair, revealing his eyes. His pupils are so dilated it's almost impossible to see the color of his irises, but they're gray. I've never seen anything like them.

"I'm not sure if I can say the same." His voice is different than I'm used to. He has an accent, but Mother hasn't taught me enough about accents to locate where he's from. It's slow and lazy and he draws out his vowels. It's strangely beautiful.

My heart gives a little flutter and I scoot closer. "Are you really a Surface Dweller?"

His eyebrows wing up. "A what?"

"Do you come from the Surface?" I point above our heads, to the water through the glass. A school of brightly colored fish swims by.

He glances around and his eyes land on the fish. They widen and there's a hint of amazement before they meet mine again.

He gives a slight nod. "I guess I am."

I glance around to see if anyone has noticed me kneeling here, but when I don't see anyone, I lean closer. "Are you the one that set off the alarms?"

He looks at the ground and his hands clench over the shears. They snap shut, startling me. His teeth press tightly together and his jaw flexes with the effort.

"Not me. My friend."

"There's another like you?" I take a quick look around, wondering how I missed him. I'll need to find a way to get both of them out of here and somewhere safe. If Mother finds them, she'll have them shot. *Surface Dwellers have been consumed with hate and violence, and should be considered extremely dangerous. Any Surface Dweller who attempts to break into Elysium should be shot on sight.*

My duty is to report them—turn them in to the Guards—but he's . . . different. I'm curious about him. Curious about the Surface. If it's really as Mother says, or if Father's accounts are more accurate.

But I mustn't think of Father's stories. Our little secret. Nothing but bedtime stories.

Gavin glares at me. "Not anymore," he says, hate peppering his voice. "Y'all took care of that."

Before I can ask him what he means, I'm jerked back and shoved behind my Guards, who block my view. That tingle of panic I felt when I touched the wind chimes tickles my nerve endings and, for a second, fury curdles in my belly.

Anger is a poison and will eat away at your beauty.

Dizzy, I sway as the words swirl through my mind, erasing the anger. Biting my lip, I stand on tiptoe to peer over the Guards' shoulders.

Others yank Gavin out from underneath the table, hitting his head in the process. Blood trickles from the small gash on his forehead and into his eyes. He struggles to pull away, but they're holding him too tightly. I bite the inside of my cheek to prevent myself from coming to his rescue. It will only make things worse if I do.

An Enforcer steps from the shadows with her blank face

and dead eyes and aims her pistol at Gavin, awaiting orders from Mother, whose shoes click on the concrete as she approaches. It makes me nervous that despite my vigilance an Enforcer was still able to remain unseen. It appears, even here, Enforcers can hide in plain sight.

It didn't take long for the Guards to call Mother, I think as she pushes her way past them and straight to Gavin, muttering, "I don't have time for this. First Three and now an SD. What else could go wrong?" Then she takes his chin in her hand and studies him, asking him questions about how he got in and who else is with him, but he ignores her.

His attention is on me, and he's not happy. He glares at me, but there's something beneath the surface—something more than just the feeling of betrayal. There's still a glimmer of hope, and I can't let it die out.

Knowing what his fate will be if he refuses to answer the questions, I elbow the Guards out of my way and step forward, refusing to even glance at the Enforcer. "Mother, before the Guards placed their hands on me," I say, and watch as she tenses, "I was getting the Surface Dweller to answer my questions. If I had a few more minutes with him, I could get all the information you are requesting."

She moves her attention from Gavin to the Guards and I know I've effectively distracted her for the moment. "The Guards touched you? Without permission?"

"Yes, Mother," I say, and the Guards squirm. I squash the little worm of guilt burrowing itself into my stomach lining.

"Which ones?" She stares coldly at them as they avoid looking at either Mother or me.

I pause. I shouldn't say. I can't remember why exactly, but I'm sure it would be a mistake. "I'm not exactly certain. It happened very fast."

She glares at the Guards. "No one is to touch Evelyn again. Ever."

Gavin raises his brow—it seems to be his way of asking questions without saying a word—but no one else responds. They haven't been given permission.

Mother turns her attention back to me. "The Surface Dweller was answering your questions?"

She seems honestly curious, which gives me the courage to keep going. "Yes. He seems to trust me."

"Not anymore," he mutters under his breath. We ignore him.

"You have your appointment with Dr. Friar soon, Evelyn. But I suppose . . ." She gives Gavin a considering look with her lips pursed. "Very well. I will permit you to postpone your session for now. This will be the perfect opportunity to see how your training is coming along." She turns to the Guards. "Take him to the Detainment Center. On full lockdown. If he tries to escape, kill him."

Chapter Three

. . . Peace is not free. For some the cost is too steep. But for the enlightened—for the peoples of this city, those who choose to start anew—peace is worth every sacrifice. To secure the safety of our families, we will pay the cost willingly. No, my friends, there is no cost too high. . . .

—Mother, Founding Speech

They have placed him in the deepest, darkest part of the Detainment Center, which is in Sector Two on the bottommost level, set into the trench wall. Water drips down the walls to form small pools on the concrete floors. It's dark, dank, and dreary. The exact opposite of everything I'm used to. Most of the time, we have no need for the Center, so it's not taken care of like the rest of the facility. But Mother delayed me by instructing me on the questions she wanted answers to, and now I have to travel the route by myself.

Some kind of animal—a rat, perhaps?—darts across my path. Mother will not care to hear more rats have found a way in or that maintenance has allowed them to continue breeding. They eat the food supply.

Since it is of no concern to me at the moment, I ignore it.

The click of my shoes echoes back to me and the yellowish lights flicker as I pass. Several times during the trip I pass DNA cameras and turrets set into the wall. Worry tickles my nerves as I pass each one. While rare, it is not completely unheard of that one might go off without provocation. That's why there are none in the Palace Wing—wouldn't want one to accidentally go off and shoot Mother, Father, or me.

I finally enter a large room that is divided in half by a glass wall. The half I'm in has a control panel on the wall, but the other half—the one Gavin is in—is completely empty except for a toilet in the corner.

Though it's fairly large, it makes me feel claustrophobic. I'm used to the openness my ocean-view garden provides me. Even in the other Sectors there's always some kind of view. There is none here. Not even a tiny glimpse.

The Guards who watch Gavin's cell straighten when they see me. I breathe easier when I see there is no Enforcer. Gavin, on the other hand, does not even acknowledge my presence, though I'm sure he knows I'm there as he was looking straight at the door when I walked in.

The burliest of the Guards allows me entrance, but locks me in. This, of course, makes me instantly wary. If they are unconcerned he'll hurt me, what have they done to him?

Even though the floor is the same as outside his cell, the sound of my steps is muffled, which means the cell is soundproofed. A quick glance shows a camera in the far right corner. Anyone who is watching will be able to see everything that happens in the room, even if they can't hear what we're saying.

Gavin sits in the far corner, his eyes closed. He doesn't so much as flinch when I go to him. Something in my chest tightens at what they've done to him in the few minutes since I saw him last.

One of his eyes is blackened and swollen shut. There are cuts all over his face. His shirt is bloody and torn, practically into rags. His right arm hangs uselessly by his side. I wonder if it's broken. However, the skin is split and bleeding over one of his knuckles.

I smile grimly. At least he fought back.

"What do you want?" he asks. His voice is strong, at least. "If you're going to kill me, can you just get it over with?" His body trembles like before, but he doesn't open his good eye.

I raise an eyebrow. "Most people don't beg for death this early."

That gets his attention. His good eye opens and focuses on me. "How would you know?"

With a cautious look to the camera, I extend a hand to touch his forehead. It's hot to the touch and I pull my hand away. "You're running a fever. You didn't get that from what they did to you. What happened?"

Gavin keeps his mouth shut and his one good eye on me. It's dilated and bloodshot. Whatever happened to him was bad. He needs medical attention.

He watches me warily as I get up to go to the door and wait for one of the Guards to notice me. I ask for medical supplies and a cleaning kit. I'm not as good as the Healers, but I can do some basic first aid. It appears my humanitarian duties as a volunteer in the Medical Sector will come in handy.

The Guards exchange a look. "Medical attention hasn't been authorized."

I smile sweetly. "Neither was the beating this prisoner has endured. Mother requested certain information. I don't suppose she would be very pleased if the prisoner died before I was able to obtain it, do you?"

They glance at each other again before the younger one shrugs and volunteers to retrieve what I've asked for.

"Thank you," I say, and smile at him.

He blushes and leaves, while I wait patiently for his return. When he does, I slip back into the cell. Gavin watches while I set up my supplies, but says nothing. His trembling is getting worse.

I pull a pressure syringe out of the box and go to take his arm, but he yanks it out of reach. "Stay away from me."

"I'm trying to help you. You're sick. If I don't treat you soon, you could die."

"So? Y'all are just going to kill me eventually anyway." He looks away, but not before I see a shadow cross his face.

I'm certain he's right; Mother wants to kill him. But . . . I don't want that to happen. "I know you don't trust me. I don't blame you, but I really do want to help you."

Gavin leans forward with his eyes narrowed. "Just so you can get answers."

"The answers are what's keeping you alive until I can figure something else out. But go ahead and be stubborn." I shrug and pretend I'm absolutely okay with leaving him to rot in the cell. "It's of no concern to me." I start repacking the med kit.

He curses under his breath and I scowl at the language, but don't say anything. He reaches out a hand to stop me. "Why do you want to help me?"

I've been wondering the same thing. "I don't really know."

He's quiet for a few minutes as he studies me, but finally he says, "Okay."

"Okay what?"

"Okay, you can help me." He leans back and rests his back on the glass wall.

Irrational relief passes over me and I pull the syringe out again. "This is going to sting. I'm sorry."

"What is it?" He tries reading what's on the silver canister.

"It's a medication made with willow bark and meadowsweet, along with a few other things the Healers have created. It'll reduce your fever." It also has some poppy seeds in it for pain relief, but I don't tell him that.

When Gavin nods, I inject him and although he hisses, he doesn't fight.

With a scrunched nose, I wash out his wounds as well as I can. He really is filthy. Then I pull out the mending wand.

His brow furrows. "What's a flashlight going to do to help me?"

I almost have to laugh. "It's not a flashlight. It's a mending wand. The blue light acts as a catalyst to stimulate the skin to heal itself. Just keep still as much as possible. It won't hurt, but it will probably itch."

He watches me as I work, which is a little unnerving.

"How do you know how to do this?"

"It was part of my training." I wince on the inside. I should not have said that.

"Training? For what?"

I don't answer, and he sighs. "My friend and I were gathering food for our family. It's fall, so the animals are getting fat for the winter. Perfect time for hunting." His voice is so soft I can barely hear it. I have to lean forward to listen, and still what he said makes no sense.

I frown up at him. "I'm sorry?"

He looks up to the ceiling, clearly frustrated. "You wanted to know how I got here, right? Well, I'm telling you. I get how this works."

I'm not entirely certain what he means, so I silently continue working on his wounds.

"It started to storm so we took refuge in a cave. Or what we thought was a cave. As we explored it to make sure we weren't going to be sharing it with something we didn't want to, we found some tunnels. The tunnels eventually led us here."

I glance up at the cameras again and then lean even closer, just in case. "You found the entrance from the Surface?"

Gavin shrugs. "One question. One answer. Your turn."

"My turn?" Furrowing my brow, I start working on the wounds on his torso.

His shirt is so torn and dirty I remove it. Despite everything I've seen during my Medical Sector duties my breath catches and my heart aches when I see the damage to his back. I'm not sure what has caused the wounds, but they are deep and, from the look of them, a few days old. Green pus leaks from some of them. The antiseptic I have won't be enough, but there is clove in my gardens. I will need to go and retrieve it. For now, though, the antiseptic I have here will have to do.

He groans when I gently spread the cream on his back. More pus weeps from the wounds. Disgusting. I fight the urge to express my distaste aloud. It's not becoming of a lady.

"I answered your question. Now you get to answer mine," he says as if it's the simplest thing in the world. "I want to know more about you and you want to know about me. Fair trade."

I stop what I'm doing and glance up at him. "Why do you want to know more about me?" He only stares at me with an infuriating little grin. "What do you wish to know?" I finally ask when I realize he isn't going to answer me until I answer him. It's not that I want to tell him anything, but it seems to keep his mind off what I'm doing. If I play along, I will be able to get some of the answers I need to keep him alive.

"You said you had training. What kind of training?"

I decide to let the antiseptic on his back do its job while I work on his arm. It's more important to fix that first, and then worry about the strange wounds. I relax when I see it's only out of joint.

I look into Gavin's eye and can tell from the way it can't quite focus on me that the poppy seeds are doing their job. Thank heavens for small blessings. "Your arm is out of joint. I'm going to pop it back in, but it's going to hurt. A lot. I want you to try not to scream. I'm not sure if the Guards will hear it, but it is better if they don't. Okay?"

He nods and grits his teeth. Bracing myself, I tug as hard as I can and feel a pop as it slides back into place. He gives a whimper, but doesn't scream, though sweat pops out on his forehead and he slumps a little.

"All right?" I ask. He nods, but his pupil is wider than it was before. I wonder if I should be worried about blood loss. Not to mention shock from the pain and the infection I'm sure is in his blood. "I need more supplies. I'll be back as soon as I can."

Brushing the dirt from my skirt, I stand and then wrinkle my nose. I'm in a state, aren't I? *A lady must not be seen as anything other than perfect.* This is unacceptable.

"You never answered my question."

I'm startled by his voice, and turn to look back down at him. He's staring up at me again.

For some reason I'm embarrassed of my answer, like he would look down on me for it. I don't know why—it's our most prestigious designation. *A privilege. An honor.* "I am being trained to be the Daughter of the People."

"What's that?"

"One question. One answer."

He smiles grimly. "I had a feeling you were sharp." He pauses. "What do you want to know?" He throws my question back at me, and for some reason, I'm enjoying the banter.

"Why are you really here? The emergency escapes are almost impossible to find and it's more than two days' walk from here to the Surface." Or so Mother tells me.

"Sharp," Gavin mutters. He narrows his eyes and then shrugs as if it doesn't really matter. "I'm here trying to see if this is where my people are." He smiles when I open my mouth to ask another question. "My turn. What's the Daughter of the People?"

I stare over his shoulder. I don't want to answer, but I feel that if I don't, any of the tentative trust he has for me will disappear, and I have a feeling I'll need it. I'll need him. I just don't know for what yet.

"I'm being groomed to rule the city after Mother can no longer do so." I look down at the ground. "To protect my Citizens from Surface Dwellers. At any cost."

Not looking at him, I wait for the Guards to release me from the room. I pause as I exit, looking straight ahead to the hallway. "I need more supplies for your back. I will return shortly."

When I return from gathering the herbs, he is in the exact same position as he was when I left, only asleep. The Guards let me in and the door closes softly behind me. I make my way over to him.

So I don't disturb him, I try to be as quiet as possible. I'm a little disappointed we won't talk, but there is no need for him to wake; he'll be in considerably less pain if he stays asleep.

A chill down my spine and a movement out of the corner of my eye alerts me to the fact that there is another person on the other side of the glass. When I turn around, I find myself being studied by an Enforcer.

A shudder rips through my body before I can stop it as the young girl meets my eyes. The Guards stand at attention next to her, but they shift their weight from side to side as she talks to them, never once taking her eyes off me.

I force myself to turn around and do what I came to do, but I have to close my eyes and take deep breaths.

I'm doing nothing wrong. I'm doing nothing wrong. I'm doing nothing wrong.

When I open my eyes, it surprises me to see Gavin watching me.

He doesn't seem bothered by the revelation I expressed before I left. Only mild curiosity shows in the tilt of his head and slant of his eyes before he too notices the Enforcer beyond the glass.

"Why is that little girl looking at me like that?" he asks, his gaze moving back to mine.

I debate on whether or not to tell him the truth, but he'll find out anyway, and it's best he be prepared.

"She is an Enforcer. A . . ." I pause as I try to recall the

Surface term Mother taught me. "A police officer? She makes sure people follow the law."

"Earlier you said that you would protect your Citizens from Surface Dwellers at any cost. Are these Enforcers part of this . . . protection?"

I nod, refusing to meet his eyes.

"And what exactly does 'at any cost' mean?" I don't answer, but he apparently doesn't need one. "What happened to my friend, that's what you mean, isn't it? And my other people? The ones that disappeared after going into the woods. We saw their stuff in the cave. They're dead too, then. That's why they haven't come back." He looks at the Enforcer, who is still watching him. "She's an assassin!"

"Enforcer," I correct. "And you are the only Surface Dweller I've ever seen."

"But she kills people on your orders."

"Not mine. Not yet." For some reason it's important for me to make that distinction.

"What is a little girl doing being an assassin?" he asks.

"Enforcer," I correct again, oddly relieved he's more curious than frightened. I kneel next to him and adjust my skirt so it lays flat on my legs, and when I glance back up, he's watching me intently. I realize he's still waiting for my answer. "All Enforcers are female. They are the only ones selected for the designation."

"Why?"

"Because females have endurance and dexterity that men lack." I pull out all my materials and lay them in front of him in the order I will use them. The clove leaves, Egyptian lily petals, the bottle of water from my pond, and my mortar and pestle for grinding all that together into a paste. "Mother tried men, but they never withstood the training."

"What happened to them?"

My eyes flit to his before focusing back on my task. "They died."

He watches as I set it all up. His eyes follow each movement of my hands, as if not completely trusting I won't slip something in there that doesn't belong. While it should bother me that Gavin doesn't trust me, the intensity of his gaze has my stomach fluttering with nerves and the heat of a blush creeping up my throat to burn my face.

"But she's just a kid!"

"Mother also tried older women, but again the training failed. So she just kept trying younger and younger girls until she found an age that worked."

"Besides Surface Dwellers, why would y'all possibly need assass— Enforcers here anyway?" he asks. "I can't imagine we're a threat very often. Especially not when you have to fall off a damned cliff first."

His eyes give too much away and I don't want to know what he's thinking, so I keep my eyes focused on my task.

"Because that is the cost of peace. Everyone must follow the law. If you do not, you are a traitor and will be treated as such."

"So you kill people who don't follow the law?" His voice is filled with disgust.

I finally meet his eye. "If it is necessary."

He shivers, but then his brow furrows. "How does being the Daughter of the People help you treat my wounds?"

"You have asked five questions since you last answered mine."

He makes a sound like a growl in his throat. "Fine," he spits out. "Ask away."

Crushing the leaves and petals, I mix little drops of water into the bowl of the mortar. "You said you were hunting? Why?"

Gavin gives me a look of disbelief. "For food. And fun. How else do you get meat?"

"Well, you grow it, of course." He starts laughing, and a smile cracks my lips. I'm pleased his disgust isn't directed at me. "What?"

Still smiling, he says, "You can't grow meat. It's not a plant."

I laugh a little. "I suppose the correct word is raise. You *raise* cows and chickens. Goats. Pigs. All sorts of strange creatures. So I have read. We don't have animals here. All our protein comes from vegetables, like soybeans and beets. Fish."

He frowns, looking disgusted again. "No real meat?"

"We have a whole Sector devoted to raising crops. We can grow almost anything. Because of the dormant volcano that created this trench, we have some of the richest soil in the world. And our scientists have developed ways to make the crops even more nutritious. Plus the fish are plentiful here. Raising domestic animals causes too much waste and requires too much space," I explain. "We have excellent nutrition, and the cooks are quite talented."

He doesn't look convinced. "If you say so. Anyway, we have livestock, but not everybody has the money for it. Besides, fresh game can bring a lot of money. Like, we caught a peacock the other day and we were able to trade the meat for flour, lamp oil, fruit, even some meat from the butcher. I even traded some of the feathers to get a bolt of fabric for my mom."

I stop crushing the paste and tilt my head to look closer at him. "But if you got meat from the butcher with it, why didn't you just eat it in the first place?"

He gives me a strange look. "Because for the half pound of peacock I gave him, I got enough meat to feed my family for a month, if we're careful."

I still don't understand. That seems like a really long and complicated circle. "Why don't you just buy it outright then? Is there no stipend? Do you not have designations? Does the Governess not compensate you for contributions?"

Gavin laughs sharply and leans back against the wall, crossing his arms behind his head. "What Governess? We have a sheriff that makes sure no one kills one another, and a mayor sent from The City who gets paid to sit on his ass in his office and look pretty, but otherwise there's no one to give us money. We trade and barter for whatever we need. For instance, my mom makes clothes and trades them to the general store for the things we need from there." He pauses. "You have someone who gives you money?"

"We receive our allotment of credits based on our designations—"

"Designations?"

"Our occupations. Everyone is given a position in our community based on their genetics."

He lifts an eyebrow. "So, you don't have a choice of what you do? And you don't have a problem with that?"

"Why would I? *Sacrifices must be made for the greater good.*"

"O-kay—" he drags out the "O" sound. "So. You get a designation and then someone pays you?"

"Yes. Mother."

He gives me an incredulous look. "Your mother pays everyone? Wow, she must have a money tree."

I cross my arms over my chest and narrow my eyes. "I'm not an idiot. There's no such thing as a money tree."

He chuckles. "It's just an expression. Sorry."

I'm not completely convinced, but I continue. "Mother is the Governess. She compensates everyone by his or her designation. We're allotted quarters, a certain amount of food, and credits to spend based on that and whether we have a family or not."

"If you're given food and shelter, why do you need money—credits?"

I sigh. "For the extra things. Like clothing, amusements, the Bazaar where the Artisans sell their wares. Not everyone is given money by the Governess, you know." I think he may feel more comfortable if I can use his language. "Like you said, she doesn't have a money tree." The corner of my mouth tilts up in a half smile.

He returns it. "Okay, so who isn't compensated and why not?"

"Well, just the Artisans really, because they sell their wares and earn money that way. Mother says they create more beautiful things when they have to worry where their cred— money is going to come from. Otherwise . . . I guess we're not so different from you. We trade our services for the things that keep us alive. And you hunt and trade the meat and skins for other things."

"Yes."

Not so different. The opposite of what Mother always says. We look at each other. But something else is bothering me. Something that *is* different. "And for . . . fun?" I ask.

He nods and his eyes glaze as if remembering something from long ago. "Yes. Sometimes my brother—he's the one who usually hunts with me—we make a game to see who can get the most kills."

With a surprised gasp, I place my hand over my mouth. The mortar slaps onto the concrete floor.

Gavin glances over, confused.

"That's horrible. You're killing all those animals for *fun*?" I look away from him, pick up the mortar, and go back to the paste, but I don't do anything with it. I just sit with it in my lap. I look back up at his face and shake my head. "Mother *is* right. You are a bunch of barbarians." This is why I shouldn't be helping him, but I find myself still mixing the herbs together to make a paste. As repulsive as I find this behavior, it's also fascinating.

He leans forward. "Yeah, so what? You have assassins. Now that's barbaric." He looks relaxed, but there's a tension to his body that wasn't there before. As if he's preparing for a fight.

"They're not assassins, they're Enforcers! There's a huge difference between killing for fun and killing to protect peace."

Gavin rests his hands on the floor between us so he's eye level with me. I squirm, but he ignores me. "How is it better to murder human beings just for breaking some rules? At least we use everything the animal offers, even if we make a game out of it."

I grip the mortar tightly between my fingers. So tightly, it's a wonder it doesn't crack. "But we must keep the peace," I spit out. *"Sacrifices must be made for the greater good."*

His eyes flash. "And some sacrifices must be made so we can eat and live!"

Seething, I take the paste and smear it on his back. He grunts, and I have to force myself to apply it more gently. I refuse to say anything to him, but part of me realizes there is a certain truth to what he is saying.

We kill to maintain our way of life. They kill to remain living. Which is more barbaric? I have to admit it's probably us. At least they eat the things they kill and make use of the creature. What do we do? Turn the bodies into ash.

This is not what I expected to learn. But it gives me plenty to think about.

When his back is completely covered in the medicinal paste, I pack my things and then glance at the Guards. The Enforcer is gone. While I'm relieved, I have to wonder why she was here in the first place. If it wasn't to help the Guards, what was the real purpose? I move so my body blocks Gavin's from the cameras. *You can never be too careful. It is better to err on the side of caution.* Mother taught me that.

I hand him the second first-aid kit and lean down to whisper in his ear. I am confident my position looks like I am surveying the work I've done on his back. He jumps a little when he hears my voice.

"This is filled with nonperishable food. It's not the best, but it's all I could get without Mother noticing," I say. I move to leave, but he grabs my hand. Little tingles zing up my nerve endings and cause a fluttering in my stomach. I snatch my hand away as panic swirls through my body, causing my heart to hammer in my chest. *Touching between unCoupled people is forbidden.*

This must be why unCoupled people shouldn't touch each other. It feels funny. And yet, it's slightly familiar. I'm not sure why. Even when one of my previous Suitors accidentally touched me, it hadn't felt like this.

"Are you breaking the law by giving me this stuff?" His voice is soft, but I'm sure it's only because he doesn't want me to get in trouble. If I die, there will be no one to help him further. He doesn't seem like a stupid person, even if he is a Surface Dweller.

I stuff my items back into the little pack I brought them in, trying to ignore the tiny flutters still tickling my stomach. "No, but I do not suppose Mother would be pleased, either."

His eyes move to meet mine. "I appreciate everything you're doing for me. You could have left me here, as sick as I was. I probably would've given you the answers you needed, eventually."

"I know." I pause for a second, then decide to finish my sentence. "I want to help you."

He watches me carefully. "Why?"

I take a deep breath. Why *am* I helping him? Charity doesn't extend to Surface Dwellers, does it? "I don't really know. I just . . . want to."

Before he can reply, the door to the cell opens and a Guard gestures me over. Mother is waiting. Her presence can mean nothing good. She'd never risk a walk by the turrets.

Before turning back to Gavin, I make sure any trace of fear is erased. I don't want him to know anything is wrong. "I guess my time is up. I will be back when I can."

He nods, but there is disappointment in his eyes.

I step out and carefully close the door behind me, taking the time to calm myself before turning to face Mother.

Chapter Four

Mother stands before me, or rather her hologram does. I can see now what I hadn't been able to see from the cell: the wavy lines of the projection and the concrete wall behind her semitransparent body. She hadn't risked a walk by the turrets after all. This should make me feel better, but it doesn't.

She has eyes only for me. And those eyes are filled with a rage I've never seen before.

"Just what do you think you're doing?" Her eyes bore into mine, as if she can see all my secrets. Her voice is tinny and echoes around the room.

"I don't know what you mean." I struggle to keep my eyes on hers and not squirm under the scrutiny of her stare.

"Why are you treating his injuries? You are supposed to be getting information."

"I am, Mother. B-but he was very sick. He couldn't answer. Besides, I needed to regain his confidence. He didn't trust me after the Guards beat him."

She only asks, "What did he tell you?"

Obviously that bit of information didn't have the effect I'd hoped for and again I struggle to keep my eyes focused on hers. I'm about to smudge the truth and it will be disastrous if she senses I'm lying. She'll never forgive me. Again I question why I'm even helping him, but I can't answer myself.

"Only that he came through one of the emergency exits."

She narrows her eyes and then turns her head. Unable to stop myself, I follow her gaze. She's focused on Gavin, who glares at her.

"Does he remember how to get there?" she asks. Her eyes are blank now. None of the anger I'd seen previously is visible. No emotions are. It's worse than if she was angry.

I swallow quickly, which is almost impossible, because my mouth has turned to sand. "No," I finally manage to say. "He said everything was a blur after his friend set off the DNA camera." I have no idea if he does or not, but any other answer puts him at risk.

"Turret," she corrects me. "The other one set off a turret." She continues to study Gavin. "Is that all you've gotten from him?"

"Yes. He's not very lucid between his infection and the medicines I had to give him."

Mother purses her lips. "It is of the utmost urgency we get answers from him. There comes a point where the danger he presents outweighs the import of his answers. If he was able to get in, others may do the same. Besides, I don't want my one and only daughter hurt." She smiles at me and I relax. "Surface Dwellers are manipulative, and you are so naïve." She waves me off, her attention focused back on Gavin. "Your Therapist is waiting for you."

I hurry away, breathing a quick sigh of relief, but I don't even dare look at Gavin as I leave. I just have to hope Mother doesn't take it upon herself to start where I left off.

Guards flank me as I make my way toward Dr. Friar's office in Sector Six—the Medical Sector. If I wasn't with my Guards, I'd stop and chitchat with several of the shopkeepers who are scattered around in organized chaos in Sector Two along the Bazaar, or the Square.

Like all the other Sectors, Sector Two is in its own building, connected to the other Sectors by glass tube hallways. Sector Two itself is the largest of our Sectors, with the Square being its largest part. Although it's only one floor, it's several stories tall. The domed ceiling and three of the walls are entirely made of glass so the ocean is visible at all times—just like in my gardens. Mother says the Square was designed to replicate what the Surface city streets used to look like before the War, complete with alleys and dead ends. While it looks like there's no pattern to any of it, Mother has arranged the shops to make it easier for people to get from one side to the other and get what they require quickly. There are also areas next to trees and the central fountain for recreation, like picnics or birthday parties and such.

When not working, Citizens are allowed to do whatever they wish—as long as they don't violate the law. The Enforcers make sure of that. I know from Mother's teaching that there are only two-dozen Enforcers to police the two thousand Citizens, but they have the eerie ability to appear at a moment's notice, so they seem to be everywhere. Even as the Daughter of the People, I can't be sure how many are watching me now.

Today the Square seems busier than usual, which makes sense since tomorrow is Festival, the day we celebrate the city's founding. The Citizens are already preparing. I want to join them, but sadly, my Guards are accompanying me and I have no time for niceties. I continue through the Square without making eye contact with anyone, but despite that, the Citizens bow as I pass.

Just past the sushi bar, I turn right and walk through the tubular glass walkway that leads to the reception area of the Medical Sector.

I've always thought Dr. Friar's receptionist is one of our prettier women. Even though all Citizens have blond hair and blue eyes, there is something exceptional about her—*though not as exceptional as Mother, of course.* I smile my thanks as she waves me through to Dr. Friar's office.

I pause at his door and wonder, as I always do, why he chooses to have his office in a room without any windows.

Surely, if he wanted it, he could just ask Mother. Given his position, she'd grant him anything he wanted.

Dr. Friar is waiting for me with his customary smile: one that both soothes and makes my hackles rise. I'm never sure why I have such strong, yet opposing, feelings about him. Today, however, I notice his teeth are stained a rust color. I know it's only something he ate, but it gives me an uncomfortable feeling. He's wearing his normal attire of a dove gray business suit with a bright white button-down shirt and maroon tie, his thinning blond hair smoothed back. His watery blue eyes are surrounded by thin lines, as is his thin mouth, probably because he smiles so much.

He's sitting behind his rosewood, double pedestal desk, which has a glass piece over the top of the desk surface. It always looks precisely the same—a stapler, pen holder, intercom telephone, Slate, and dark brown leather blotter placed just perfectly. His clasped hands rest on the blotter.

"Well, now, Evelyn, are you prepared for our session today?" He gestures for me to sit.

I sit in the leather wingback chair in front of his desk. "Yes. *It's nice to have someone to talk with.*"

Dr. Friar's smile widens. He's obviously pleased with me. "Very good. Do you know why Mother has asked for you to visit today?"

"No."

He nods as if this is what he's expecting, then stands and goes to a cabinet on the sidewall. It's painted to resemble the weathered wood of the room's walls, making it appear as if it's only a set of built-in bookshelves instead of a freestanding cabinet. He opens a drawer and pulls a metal box from it before returning to sit on the corner of the desk.

"Mother tells me you've been tending to the Surface Dweller," he says.

I eye the box. It is familiar to me, but I can't quite place it. "Yes. He was quite sick."

"And did you not think of the consequences?" He taps the box.

I move my eyes to meet his and then adjust them so I focus on the wall behind him. *It's impolite to stare a man in the eyes.* "Consequences?"

His smile widens again, as if he knew that's what I was going to answer. "You said yourself he's sick. He could give you something. Do you not remember about the epidemic from your studies?"

"Oh." My gaze travels back to the box, where Dr. Friar caresses the case as if it's his pet.

"Besides, he's only a Surface Dweller. Not worth wasting our precious resources on, or being waited on by the Daughter of the People. On Festival's Eve of all days."

This time I don't say anything.

"What have you learned from him?" he prompts.

I take a deep steadying breath and play with the hem of my skirt. "Just that he entered through one of the emergency exits."

"Did he tell you why he came?" He strokes the box and I swallow. Little rivulets of sweat slide down my back to pool at the base of my spine, though I don't know why I should feel so uneasy.

"He said he stumbled upon a cave when he took refuge from the rain."

There's a shadow crawling over the box and I have no idea where it came from. I take a quick glance around the room, but there's nothing I can see that's causing it.

"I see." Dr. Friar's voice stays that happy, cheerful tone that should put me at ease, but it only makes the sweat all over my body turn to tiny little ice cubes. "And what did he say his designation was?"

I can't stop staring at the box. Whatever's in there, I don't want to know what it is. I don't even want to be in the same room with it. It makes my skin crawl. "N-no. H-he doesn't have one." I wet my lips, and Dr. Friar purses his. The move is so like Mother's when she's angry that it makes spiders of fear skitter along my nerves.

"None?" He looks disappointed. "Surely he must do something to bring money for his family?"

"He said they don't get money from the Governess."

Dr. Friar leans forward. "He did, did he?" He studies me carefully, his eyes taking a full journey from my face to my feet. He stops once on my chest, making me want to cross my arms, before continuing the journey. When he's finished, he opens the box. Inside, nestled in black velvet, is an old-fashioned syringe.

"You'll need to take your medicine so you don't get sick,

Evelyn. We can't have the Daughter of the People getting sick, can we?"

A memory of pain comes to mind and I cringe away from it. "No. I feel fine. I don't need that."

He snaps his fingers and my Guards step next to my seat. The room feels like it's shrinking around me. The walls I'd just admired feel like they're going to crush me at any minute.

Dr. Friar sprays a little stream out of the needle of the syringe. The air starts to smell like alcohol and a mixture of familiar and terrorizing scents I can't place, but make my heart go wild and my breath catch.

"Don't struggle, Evelyn. This will only hurt for a minute. You'll never remember it."

"No, please, no," I whisper as fear clogs my throat.

He gestures again and two of the Guards take my arms, holding me in place. I struggle, knowing I'm not stronger than them. I can't pull away. The Guards are chosen for their strength and fear has apparently robbed my own muscles of theirs. I can't escape. No matter what I do, I'm trapped in the leather chair.

Dr. Friar advances on me as I struggle. Whimpers come from my mouth as he steps next to me. His breath warms my neck.

The needle slides into the skin of my neck, just behind my ear. I cry out as my whole body seizes. The pain is excruciating, as if they are holding a lit match to my skin. Nerves twitch all over; it feels like insects are crawling over me—insects that are made of fire and burrow into my skin—and I'm trying to shake them off. Besides the tremors, I'm frozen in place. Eventually the pain is too much and, when it comes, the darkness is a blessing.

But it doesn't last long.

Soon I'm wide awake. Voices swim in and out as if I'm underwater. One voice in particular is familiar, yet not.

"Evelyn," it says, "why have you decided to help the Surface Dweller?"

I don't want to answer, but it's as if my body has stopped listening to my brain. "I was drawn to him." My voice sounds strange. It's slow and slurred.

"No, Evelyn, you were repulsed by him."

"Yes. I was repulsed by him."

"You won't try to help him in the future."

"No. I won't help him."

"He deserves his fate for breaking our laws."

"Yes. He deserves it."

"After everything Mother has done for you, you should be more grateful for her generosity and obey her without question."

"Obey without question."

The voice stops waiting for me to respond.

Surface Dwellers are manipulative and dangerous. Nothing more than heathens who'd just as soon kill you as look at you.

He's the worst of them all.

Why am I protecting him? He means nothing to me.

He would not do the same had our roles been reversed.

He is not my friend. I'm only here for answers.

His kind is the reason for the fall of man and our exile to the ocean.

I will share all of my knowledge with Dr. Friar and Mother. Why would I not want to? They are only trying to protect me.

Surface Dwellers are manipulative and dangerous. Nothing more than heathens who'd just as soon kill you as look at you.

He's the worst of them all.

Why am I protecting him? He means nothing to me.

He would not do the same had our roles been reversed.

He is not my friend. I'm only here for answers.

His kind is the reason for the fall of man and our exile to the ocean.

I will share all of my knowledge with Dr. Friar and Mother. Why would I not want to? They are only trying to protect me.

After some time, the voice says, "Very good, Evelyn. Time to wake up."

"Very good, Evelyn. Time to wake up," I repeat as another sharp pain stings my arm. Then darkness bleeds in.

CHAPTER FIVE

*Idle hands lead to an idle mind. Therefore all Citizens will be
given designations to benefit their city more effectively.*
—CITIZEN'S SOCIAL CODE, VOLUME V

My *life is just about perfect.*

Every morning Mother has the Maids wake me at precisely ten. Then it's time for a light breakfast followed by a mandatory visit with my Therapist. *It's nice to have someone to talk with.*

After, I am free to do as I wish until it's time to perform one of the duties Mother has requested of me.

After the delightful talk with Dr. Friar about my flowers, Mother instructs me to go back to the Detainment Center. I'd rather play my violin. The soft, dulcet tones are the perfect balm to my soul. For some reason, each and every one of my muscles and joints hurt. As does my throat. Maybe Mother was right and I'm coming down with the flu. It's a good thing she made me take my medicine.

But she wants more answers from Gavin. Although . . . I'm not sure what I am to say to him. Or what to ask. I do not wish to be near him. He's a contemptible Surface Dweller. Why had I ever thought to protect him? *Had our roles been reversed he would not have done the same for me.*

No answers come to me, but I follow my orders. The sooner I get answers, the sooner I get back to the way things are supposed to be.

Two of my Guards lead the way while the third walks behind me. For this, I am grateful. The stairs from Sector Two are slippery and if not for the younger Guard behind me, I would have smacked my face on the dirty concrete more than once. Not to mention, it is dark and dank in the tunnels. Dirty water runs down the walls. It smells like rotting vegetation. I hold my handkerchief in front of my nose. The lavender scent blocks the other smells.

When I enter the room where Gavin waits in his clear glass cell, I am hesitant. I do not wish to see him. I must continue my cross-stitching after practicing my violin. There is much to prepare for—Mother has told me I will meet another Suitor tonight. One she has handpicked. If he is a good match, then we will be Coupled. This pleases me immensely.

The Guards let me in, and Gavin smiles when he sees me. I don't smile back. I don't even want to be here.

His smile falters. "Is something wrong?"

"My life is just about perfect." My voice is rough and scratchy like I accidentally drank seawater instead of fresh.

He knits his brow together. "O-kay, but that's not really what I meant."

"I am not your friend. I am here for answers," I say shortly, and begin to examine his shoulder. I don't know how I could ever think he was attractive. He's dirty and grungy. The hair starting to grow on his face gives him a wicked, shadowed look.

Maybe if he took a bath, I think.

He narrows his eyes and steps closer. I back up. I do not wish to stand so close to him. He does not smell good at all. I lift my handkerchief up to my nose.

He is not my friend. I am only here for answers.

"How are you?" He reaches a hand out, presumably to touch me.

I step away so his hand falls short. "Don't touch me."

"Why?"

I meet his eyes once before letting them flit away. "Why what, Mr. Hunter?"

"Mister? You were calling me Gavin last time."

My fingers pleat the skirt of my dress. "It was highly inappropriate. I apologize for my forwardness."

"Something is wrong." There is a hint of frustration and worry in his tone. "Did your mother threaten you?"

"Certainly not." I finally meet his eyes again and notice they are a beautiful gray. Almost silver in this light. What an unusual color. I didn't even know eyes could be that color. They remind me of the charm around my neck.

"Then what's going on?" he asks, pulling me out of my thoughts.

I force myself to focus on something else—anything that isn't his eyes. It is harder than I would have thought. "I am only here for answers."

Gavin shakes his head. "Not like this. Something's wrong with you."

I settle for hands. Hands aren't pretty. They're functional. *"My life is just about perfect."*

He paces the room. "Yes, yes, you just said . . ." He trails off and then spins toward me. "Wait. Why did you say that again?"

I raise an eyebrow. "Because it is the truth."

His eyes narrow and he comes back over, walking a circle around me. My eyes follow him. I'm not sure if it's to make sure he doesn't do anything, or for some other reason. "There's something not right here. Where did you go? Where have you been? It's been forever. The Guards have changed twice."

"That is none of your business," I snap. "Please remember with whom you are speaking."

His eyes flash. "I know exactly who I'm talking to. I'm talking to Evelyn. The girl who probably saved my life. For which I'm grateful."

I stare at the wall behind his head. It's damp and chipped in places. *He's only using me to get the answers he needs to find a way out of here.*

"Fine." Gavin sits back down on the floor. His expression

is . . . hard to read. "You want answers?" he asks. "So do I. We'll continue on with our earlier arrangement. One question, one answer."

I slowly lower myself to the floor and wrinkle my nose at the dirt. My pretty dress is going to get stained. The Maids will probably have to burn it, and it's brand new. Mother bought it not a week ago.

"I cannot promise to answer all your questions." I straighten my skirt over my knees, taking care to make sure they're completely covered.

He gives me a hard smile. "Then, neither can I."

I purse my lips. "That is an acceptable arrangement. I will go first."

His smile turns smug. "Fine."

I recall the list of questions Mother made me memorize before leaving her. "Do you know where the door you entered from is?"

He scrubs at a dirt spot on his knee, only succeeding in making it worse. "Yes."

I wait, but he does not volunteer any more information. "Where is it?" I ask.

He looks at me, amusement in his eyes. "Uh-uh. One question, one answer."

I close my eyes against the anger rolling under the surface. *Anger is a poison and will eat away at your beauty.* I take a deep, calming breath—*Calming lavender in. Green, poisonous anger out*—before opening my eyes. "Very well. What is your question?"

He doesn't even hesitate. His eyes are directly on mine, so intense I have to focus on not squirming. "Where did you go after you left here?"

"My Therapist. Where is the door?"

He furrows his brow and is silent for a minute. His voice is quiet when he finally speaks, as if he's talking to a petulant child. "I'm not sure how to get there, but it wasn't very far from your gardens. They're very pretty, by the way."

I don't know what that has to do with anything. "What are?"

His mouth spreads into a lazy grin and my stomach quivers. "Your gardens," he says. "I didn't see them for long, but they're very pretty. Did you design them?"

I smile at the visual of my gardens in my mind's eye. It relaxes me instantly. "Yes. Father let me choose the flowers and the arrangement."

He scoots closer, and this time I don't move away. I don't want to. It's like there's some magnet that's pulling us together.

"I liked them very much. You must spend a lot of time there."

"It is usually how I spend my day. Either attending to my flowers or cross-stitching or playing my violin."

"That must keep you busy."

I wave my hand in front of me. "Oh, I don't mind. *Idle hands lead to an idle mind.*"

Excitement lights in his eyes as if I've said something

important to him. "That's a very interesting thing to say." He studies me. "What else do you do for fun?"

"Fun?" I think about it. I've never been asked that question. "I read. Mother has an extensive library."

"Really?" He looks surprised. "I love to read."

I shift so I'm facing him and bend my legs underneath me. "Truly? All of my Suitors here are completely uninterested in reading."

He frowns. "Suitors?"

"Yes. The young men Mother has chosen as candidates for me to couple with. Which stories do you like? I wonder if we have the same books."

Still frowning, he names a few books I don't recognize, then asks, "Couple with?"

The memory of what Mother wanted me to ask disappears into the mists of my brain. "Besides being Daughter of the People, I have been chosen for a woman's highest honor. I have been selected to have a child."

"What?" he yelps, startling me. "You're still a child yourself."

Anger replaces my excitement and I cross my arms over my chest. "I am not. A woman is eligible to have a child at sixteen. I have been eligible for three months. *It is an honor to fulfill my duty and ensure only the best are born in Elysium.*"

He gives me a look that is half shock, half incredulity. "That is the most bizarre thing I have ever heard. What about family? Isn't that important here?"

A wistful feeling fills me. I don't remember my birth parents, which is what I assume he means. I run my fingers along my necklace chain. "Do you have a family?"

"Well, yeah," he says. I have a feeling he wanted to finish that sentence with, "Doesn't everybody?" but already knew the answer. Instead he says, "I have a younger brother and an older sister. My sister just got engaged so she and my mom are planning the wedding for the spring. She's twenty. We even have a dog."

"A dog? Really? Mother has shown them to me in books. They always look so sweet, but Mother says that's so we trust them." I look at him pointedly. "But they're Surface creatures—they'll attack without reason."

"Lucy? Attack without reason? Wow, your mom must have met some crazy dogs. Lucy wouldn't hurt anyone . . . unless they tried to hurt my family."

I move closer to him. "Can you tell me about them? Your family."

He touches a hand to my forehead as if to check if I have a fever. His skin is rough, but I like the feel of his skin against mine. It reminds me of . . . someone.

Timothy and I sit in our alcove, as far away from the Square as possible. No one comes here, because it's supposed to be where the Enforcers are, but Timothy figured out that it's just another lie. One of Mother's many.

No one comes here. Not even the Enforcers. It's too dark. You can barely see in front of your face, and most people want to congregate where the light is. Light equals life in this place. His fingers caress the bare skin of my arm. He feels rough in comparison to me, and his touch gives me tingles.

The thought causes me to jump to my feet as if shocked. "Skin-to-skin touching between unCoupled people is strictly forbidden," I gasp.

I touch the pendant around my neck, rubbing it between my thumb and forefinger. The memory fades back and the veil shrouding my brain lifts. I blink a few times, panting.

I glance around, furrowing my brow. I don't remember how I got here. I was just in Dr. Friar's office a second ago.

My heart is beating too fast. I need to calm down. Though I doubt they realize why I am agitated since they can't hear anything, the Guards have tensed outside the cell with their hands resting on their side arms. I sit back down so the Guards will relax again.

I stare at Gavin, unsure what to do, silent as I calm myself. I press a hand to my temple.

He raises his eyebrows. "Are you okay? You sounded really weird there for a bit."

I look down at the ground and into the shadows our bodies have made on the floor. *"My life is just about perfect."*

He sighs. "Yes, you keep saying that."

"I do?"

He watches me. "Yeah. You do."

"Oh," I say.

It happened again. I know it. The pain in my head is familiar. It hurts to think back; the same as it always feels when I get flashes of memories.

To take my mind off it, I look over at Gavin. His eyes are clear and his skin has lost that yellowish tinge it had. The tremors appear to be gone as well. "How are you feeling?"

"I'm much better because of you. Thank you." He reaches out a hand, then seems to think better of it and drops it to the floor. "You said you went to your Therapist. Why do you see one?"

"I said that?"

He nods.

I caress the charm, grateful for it as always. "I don't know. I assume it's because of my condition. I'm . . . forgetful." I pleat the hem of my skirt again, and then adjust it, so it's covering my knees.

He's watching my movements carefully, as if afraid I might have another relapse. "What do you do there?" he asks.

"We just talk. About my flowers, my books. Violin lessons. Things like that. *It's nice to have someone to talk with.*" I blink at the detached tone to my voice. It doesn't sound like me at all. "That sounded a little odd."

"Everything you've said since you got here has been weird."

"It has?" I glance around. The Guards are back to whatever game they're playing with little rectangles of cardboard.

"Yes," he says, drawing my attention back to him. "You've been trying to find out how I got in. Don't you remember?"

I hold a hand to my head as flashes come to me, but only vaguely. Like a dream. "No. Not really."

He scoots closer and bends down to peer into my eyes. "What else happens at these appointments? Do you remember?"

"Just what I said. He listens while I talk and we have a good conversation. *It's nice to have someone to talk with.*" I frown again at how different that last sentence sounded.

He adjusts his posture and there's excitement in it as he leans closer. He's mere inches from me, but I don't back away. "Do they give you anything while you're there? Do you drink anything? Eat anything?"

"No. We just . . ." I trail off when I remember the medicine Mother insists the Maids give me every morning. "Mother does sometimes."

He smirks. "I knew it," he whispers.

"Knew what?"

He leans forward so his mouth is almost next to my ear. His breath washes over my neck and I tremble. My body fights itself as half wants to pull away and the other strains to move closer.

"I think they're brainwashing you. It's the only explanation. Why you're constantly repeating things. Why you're a bit . . . strange."

I slide away slightly, so I can think properly. The only thing I can think about is how it's against the law to touch him, but how nice it feels when he touches me. "What's brainwashing?" I whisper, my pulse still skittering around my veins.

He pulls back and gives me a curious look. "It's a process that . . . persuades others to conform to the wishes of someone else."

"You mean Conditioning?" I ask. Conditioning isn't exactly that, but it sounds close. It's how we train the Enforcers. To get their bodies to learn the complicated maneuvers, to follow Mother's orders unequivocally, and to shut down their emotions so they won't interfere.

His eyes light up. "Yes. Exactly. That's what they called it during the War. Conditioning."

I shake my head. "They don't do that to me. Only Enforcers." However, my heart beats a little faster.

His eyes widen and his mouth works for a minute before he finally asks, "You Condition the Enforcers?"

"Certainly. How else would you train a three-year-old girl to be an Enforcer?" I ask.

Chapter Six

It is a privilege and an honor to serve as an Enforcer, Elysium's most prestigious designation . . . Conditioning is the ideal training method as it is safe, quick, and painless.

—EXCERPT FROM *SO YOUR DAUGHTER HAS BEEN CHOSEN TO BE AN ENFORCER. CONGRATULATIONS!* PAMPHLET

Gavin's jaw drops and his hands fall to his side. "That little girl was three when they started training her to kill people?"

"Yes. That's the age we all get our designations. And it's the perfect age to start Conditioning. The body is still adjusting itself to everything around it. The bones are still pliable and the muscles still developing. Mother tried other ages, but the candidates always failed."

"That's . . . that's awful." He reaches a hand out again, but glances at the Guards and lets it drop. "And you're sure they haven't done this to you?"

"Yes." My answer comes immediately, without question. As soon as it does, it feels wrong on my tongue. I rush to explain more, but I'm not sure if I'm trying to convince him or myself. "Anyway, none of the Enforcers remember anything from before the age of ten. It's part of the process. That's the age when they start their duties. Before that is inconsequential."

"But how do they remember their training?"

"That's part of the Conditioning," I say. "They remember . . . only what they need to remember." What they *let* them remember.

Perhaps it feels wrong because that has been one of my fears. That I was—am—Conditioned. It's truly the only thing that explains . . . everything. How Gavin claims I've said things that I don't remember saying. How I'm always forgetting things I know I did.

My fingers reach for the pendant again.

The concrete floor is almost unbearably uncomfortable and I adjust myself so I'm sitting on the floor with my legs crossed at the ankle in front of me. It's impossible to keep the fabric covering my knees, but comfort outweighs modesty at the moment.

Gavin watches the movement and follows the hem of my skirt up my legs before turning his attention to the laces in his shoes. "Do you remember everything?" From the way he asks, I know he knows I don't.

I look down at the ground. "No."

"But you still think they're not Conditioning you now?"

Hoped. Knew otherwise. Forgot.

I don't say any of these things.

"I'm the Daughter of the People."

He looks for a moment like he wants to ask more, but instead he asks, "How did you get to be Daughter of the People? Is Mother your real mom? Somehow I don't think so."

He is entirely too observant. I shake my head. "Mother . . . adopted me. She's been waiting for the perfect genetic candidate. So, she made me her daughter, and gave me everything I could possibly want. My only requirement is to be a Breeder—to couple," I say when I see the confusion on his face. "*And it is an honor to fulfill my duty and ensure only the best are born in Elysium*. We must continue my genetic legacy. There is no reason for mind control. I barely leave the Palace Wing, and when I do, the Guards are with me."

He's quiet for a few minutes. The room is silent, but it isn't uncomfortable. It's not like when I'm with Mother and the clock keeps ticking the time away.

"What about this coupling thing?" he says, and I jump. "Sorry." He chuckles.

"*It is an honor to fulfill my duty and ensure only the best are born in Elysium.*" I frown. Why does that sound so strange when I say it? It sounds right when I think it.

He smiles as if to prove my point. "And what about this? With me? I'm sure your mother wouldn't be happy you're not finding out anything about me."

I purse my lips, then say, "*I'm* not happy I'm not finding out anything about you." I look up to meet his eyes. "But that's for another reason altogether."

He grins. "Do you remember any of our conversation from earlier?"

No, I think. And that's the worst. That's *always* the worst. Not knowing what I've said. Or done. I chew on my lip before forcing myself to stop.

"Bits and pieces," I say finally.

But again he seems to know what I haven't said. "This has happened before, hasn't it? Isn't it always the same?"

I don't answer. It *is* the same. He continues to watch me and I finally understand what he's trying to tell me.

"I understand what you're saying." I know I shouldn't ask this, but I can't help it. I have to know. "And you think . . . it's a bad thing."

He looks astonished, the way his mouth hangs open. "Well, yeah. They're *erasing* your past! How can you even know who you are, if you can't remember who you've been?"

My own mouth drops open, but before I can say anything he's continuing. "And just a few minutes ago, you were so confused you didn't know where you were or what you've said. Do you really want to spend the rest of your life like that?"

I shake my head. "So . . . what would I do? To stop it?"

He taps his fingers on his knees. "How often do you go to the Therapist?"

"Only when Mother feels I should have someone to talk to. It's supposed to be every day but . . ." I touch the pendant again. "Lately, she hasn't been enforcing it."

"Why?"

"I-I don't know." I glance up at him. "I can't always remember being at his office or anything directly before or after, but it's been less and less lately."

"So, she only says you need to see the Therapist at certain times. Interesting. Probably has something to do with your behavior or something you do, then." His fingers stop tapping and he stares into space. "I'll bet it's whenever they see something they don't want to, and then they fix it." His eyes slash to mine. "Just don't let on that things are different. We can't let them Condition you anymore."

"Why do you care?"

He doesn't answer right away.

"You think it'll help you escape." It's not a question. I already know the answer.

He blinks and his eyes give away how surprised he is that I guessed the truth, before he stares at his legs.

I smile at him. "It's all right. I don't blame you for not trusting me. If I came from where you came from, I probably wouldn't trust anyone, either."

"What's that supposed to mean?" he asks.

"The Surface." I point up. "All that war, and fighting . . . I don't know how you could trust anyone."

"As opposed to here, you mean."

I nod.

"Oh, yeah, I've gotten a real warm welcome here."

"I admit you've gotten a bad first impression. The turret killing your friend, and being locked up here, but—"

He cuts me off. "What I find stranger than that is the fact that you *do* trust anyone living down here."

"You're lucky I do." I give him a sharp look.

"Oh?"

"Because what I *should* do is get all the information I can from you, then turn you over to the Enforcers."

He licks his lips, meeting my gaze even though I can tell he's nervous. "But you're not going to do that."

"No, I'm not."

"And why not?"

Now I'm the one who has to look away. I can't tell him that he makes me feel things I've never felt before. "Because I believe you when you say the Surface isn't everything I've been told, just as you don't really know what it's like in Elysium. And I believe you when you say you just want to go home to take care of your family. I understand duty. I may not trust my memory all the time, but I *do* trust my instincts. And my instincts tell me you need my help."

He flinches, just barely, but enough that I know he's still wary of me. "Nothing that's happened to me down here could be considered normal," he says, "but you might be the strangest thing of all."

"Strange?" I try to sound indignant, but I can't deny the shiver spilling down my back at the look in his eyes. He's not afraid anymore, not completely, but the same intensity is in those remarkable gray eyes.

"Fascinating," he says.

The shivers race to my fingertips, and I curl my hands into my skirt.

"So . . . you trust me?"

His eyes narrow a tiny bit. "Yes. I have nothing to lose, do I?"

"I suppose not."

"You do, though, don't you?"

I lift one shoulder. "Not if we do this carefully."

The corner of his mouth pulls up to a wry smile. "You are definitely fascinating, Evelyn."

Our eyes meet and something passes between us. Something I've never felt before, but it's familiar all the same. Then I blush and we look away from each other. My gaze meets the floor and it's quiet while both of us decide what to say next.

"So," he finally says, breaking the uncomfortable silence, "you aren't allowed to touch someone unless you're Coupled?"

I don't look away from the pitted floor. "Yes."

"Bummer."

I look up, questioning.

"I want to touch you, but I don't want you to freak out on me," he explains. "On the Surface, we'd usually do a handshake now."

My eyes widen, and I glance over my shoulder. The Guards aren't paying attention, but I'm unsure of the camera. Though, from its angle and my position to him, I'm fairly certain the space between us is not visible.

Carefully I slide my hand along the ground until it just touches his. He glances down and then back up. He moves his gaze to the camera, then the Guards before touching the tips of his fingers to mine.

It's barely a touch at all, but my heart skips a beat. I've never felt like this before. It's strange. Exciting. Terrifying. Fascinating. I have to fight to keep my hand where it is.

He grins. "So, Evelyn—"

"Evie," I say quickly. Breathlessly.

"I'm sorry?"

"Call me Evie. Please. Everyone else calls me Evelyn, but . . . I like Evie."

"Evie." He repeats it, emphasizing the short "e" sound, and runs his thumb over my fingertips. "I like Evie, too. It suits you."

I shiver at the tingles in my fingertips and we smile at each other, but then the doors open again. I panic, thinking Mother has seen him touching me and sent an Enforcer. I slide my hand away in a move I hope isn't noticeable and stand when I see a young Guard waiting for me.

"Miss Evelyn," he says, with a slight bow. "Mother has requested your presence. She has asked me to escort you."

My heart drops. She knows.

"Yes, of course." I turn to Gavin. "I probably won't be returning tonight. It would be in your best interests to think about cooperating with me and answering my questions."

At first he narrows his eyes, but I continue to stare at him, not even daring to blink, and hope he understands what I am telling him and acts like nothing has changed.

"I'll . . . consider it," he says after a moment.

I feel awful for leaving him here. Alone. It really is a dismal place and the Guards already don't like him. I hope he won't be any more damaged tomorrow.

If Mother lets me return tomorrow. Who knows what the camera has caught. Not to mention I can't remember anything from the beginning of our conversation.

To my surprise, *only* the young Guard escorts me from the Detainment Center. The rest of my Guards seem to have been dismissed. But given what Gavin just told me, and assuming he's right, it's probably not something I should question.

Lost in my thoughts, I walk ahead of the Guard. Up the slippery stairs, to my left and five hundred meters over the concrete floors, past the lonely Guard, then through the tube to the grand entrance to the Palace Wing, then straight to the golden elevators and up two levels, and finally down the marble halls, which lead to Mother's sitting room. She is working on her computer. The blue light from the holographic display shines on her face, but the sidewall of her alcove blocks the view of what she's working on.

She turns and smiles, then grimaces when she sees me. "Evelyn. You are a filthy mess. Kindly go to your rooms and prepare for the evening meal. Father and I wish to discuss something of great importance with you."

"Yes, Mother." I curtsey and turn to leave for my private quarters. The Guard stays behind with Mother at her request. Though that unnerves me, I'm grateful for a few minutes of solitude.

After washing, I change into one of my favorite dresses—a red taffeta dress with a fitted bodice, open back, and a semi-full skirt. Then I reapply my makeup: just a dash of rose dust on my cheeks, a candy red on my lips, and a darkening of my eyes.

The combination of the dress and makeup makes me feel pretty, but also powerful. A tiny bit rebellious. It shows a bit more skin than Mother will approve of, but not enough that she'll do anything about it.

The perfume bottles in front of me on the vanity call to me—all different colors and shapes of bottles. Some have intricate and delicate metal work, others are squat and somewhat ugly. I frown at them. Why do I have so many? I don't wear perfumes; my flowers coat me in my favorite fragrance.

Something tells me it is important.

I run my fingers over the pendant, and the image of a beautiful bottle floats into my mind's eye.

I open my eyes and find the bottle in the collection. Curious, I remove the stopper and lift it to my nose. The scent wafts up to me, and the memory of me sitting by the fountain in the Square filters into my mind.

I stared at the concrete floor, feeling a little lost. I didn't know what was going to happen, but I knew no one trusted me. I had no friends, and Mother thought I was a traitor. She'd forbidden any of the others to even look at me while she decided what to do with me.

I couldn't remember anything. Not even what happened to traitors. There was a niggling feeling that I should know, but no matter how hard I tried, I couldn't remember.

The man I now called Father sat next to me. He'd been one

of the top scientists. He'd been the one that developed the pressure nanos before he'd Coupled with Mother.

At first he said nothing, but finally, he said, "I convinced her," so quietly I almost didn't hear him.

I looked over at him. "I'm sorry?"

He smiled sadly down at me. "I convinced her you were special. She's making you ours . . . hers, really. But I'll always be here for you, too."

I blinked. I didn't understand.

He patted my hand. "You won't, Evie," he said as if he could read my mind. "But don't worry. You can trust me. Always." He glanced around while I tried to wrap my eleven-year-old mind around what he was trying to tell me.

Then he pulled open his sport coat and pulled a beautiful little perfume bottle out of the pocket. "Here," he said, "take this."

I took it and immediately lifted the stopper to my nose.

He smiled at me. "And now, you'll always remember what you need to." He touched my necklace and his smile was wistful. "The pendant to recover what is lost. The fragrances to fill the empty spaces. It's all we can give you now."

Pain throbs in my temples, my fingers gripping tightly on the bottle's cap. I remember. Father. I close my eyes and mentally thank him for giving me my memories. I guess I should be surprised, but I'm not.

I breathe deeply, the fragrance of the bottle overpowering my senses, filling me with the memory. It washes away the pain, and I look again at the bottles with a calculating eye. So many memories. So much lost.

So much to regain . . . again.

Unless they Condition me again. Take them all away. Like Gavin said.

My heart hardens. Not this time. Not. This. Time.

The door to my room opens and a Maid walks in.

"Miss, Mother is expecting you," the Maid says, politely averting her gaze to just over my shoulder.

I replace the stopper on the bottle and sweep past her, my shoes clicking on the floors as I make my way to the dining room. As in the rest of the Palace Wing, the floors and walls are made of marble, and the lighting comes from crystal sconces set every five or so meters along the wall.

I pause at the door. This *must* be important. They're using the good china. The silver sparkles in the light of the crystal chandelier hanging above the marble table. Father is already there. To my surprise, so is the young Guard. He sits next to Mother and she is smiling at something he is saying, but Father seems upset with something. His customary smile is replaced with a scowl.

Cold pours over me. It has to be about what happened in the cell. Why else would the Guard be here? I glance around the room in confusion. There are no other Guards or Enforcers.

What is going on?

Mother glances over. "Evelyn. You are late."

The Guard and Father stand as I make my way over to them. "I apologize, Mother. I wanted to take my time to look my best."

She purses her lips and Father chuckles. "No need to apologize, Evelyn. A woman is never late. Isn't that what you are always telling me, my dear?" he adds to Mother, a little sparkle in his eyes.

Mother nods and gestures for me to take the seat next to the Guard, who waits for me to sit before taking his. Father does the same and, the minute he does, the Servants are placing food and drinks all over the table, more than we could possibly eat. Caviar and crackers. Bean salad. Marinated tempeh with red peppers and broccoli. And other things that I can't name. I immediately think of Gavin practically starving in his cell, and try to formulate a plan on how to get him more food.

The Guard and Mother talk throughout dinner and don't seem to even notice I'm there. But every once in a while, the Guard includes me in the conversation. Father watches me for a while and I give him a brief smile and touch a finger to the pendant. He takes a deep breath and smiles back. I wonder if I should ask him for help with Gavin. But his smile falls when he looks at the Guard, which makes me uneasy. They have not told me the purpose of this formal dinner yet. It can't be anything good. But while the Guard has everyone distracted, I'm able to start secreting as much nonperishable food as I can into my handbag. When I've stuffed as much food as I can into it, I place it back by my feet and then sit up.

Everyone is staring at me.

Uh-oh. I pat a napkin to my face, though I haven't eaten anything. "Is there something on my face?"

Mother smiles at me. "No. I asked you how you felt."

"About what?"

Father lets out an exasperated huff of breath, but Mother only keeps smiling. There's a ferocity to it now. Like a cat playing with a mouse.

"Poor, ditzy girl," she says. "The conversation was too much for you, wasn't it?"

The Guard stiffens, but obviously knows better than to say anything. White, hot anger rushes through me in a bolt. Mother knows exactly why I can't concentrate. She makes sure of it, and still she lets everyone think I'm stupid. I wonder how many times has she said things like that that I can't even remember. My nails dig into my palms out of sight in my lap, but above the table, I only smile as if the insult has passed over my head. "Yes, Mother. I'm afraid I started to daydream about my gardens. They're so pretty at this time of year."

"Yes, they are." The Guard turns and offers me a smile. "Mother was kind enough to walk with me through them while you were getting ready."

"He will need to know them intimately if he wishes to protect you," Mother says.

I smile at him, ignoring her. "Oh. Are you one of my new Guards?"

Mother's smile seems frozen to her face. "No. That is what we were just discussing. He is one of your Suitors."

"Oh, I beg your pardon, sir," I say, shooting a glance toward Father. He only gives a slight shake of his head. "I was unaware." I turn back to smile at the young Guard, who blushes and smiles back.

Interesting. I don't remember him as my Suitor, but then again, they come and go so often it's hard to keep them straight in my head. Whenever Mother determines they are unsuitable, they stop coming.

I take the rest of dinner to study this new Guard. He's similar in build to Gavin, but with lighter hair and, of course, blue eyes. He's polite and makes an effort to include me in the conversation. He seems sweet.

After dinner, he bids Mother and Father farewell, then takes my hand and kisses the back of it. I stifle a gasp, shooting a quick look toward Mother, but she only smiles.

"Good night, Miss Evelyn. I look forward to our coupling," he says.

I gape after him, twisting the strap of my handbag in my fingers. Coupling? The *Guard* is the one chosen to couple with me? "Mother?"

She pats my shoulder. "You seemed to have trouble choosing. I was only trying to make it easier for you."

At this new betrayal, Gavin's advice to act normal flies out of my head. "I know, but . . . a *Guard*? Guards aren't exactly known for their brains. I don't want unintelligent children," I say carefully, remembering myself at the last second.

"This one is different. He shows . . . potential. You're three months past your sixteenth birthday. You need to choose."

"But I have plenty of time to find a more acceptable match." My heartbeat booms in my ears and I find it hard to swallow past the lump forming in my throat. It's supposed to be my choice who I couple with. Why is she doing this?

"Most girls your age have already found the man they want to couple with. They are already doing their duty and producing quality children. As Daughter of the People you have an even greater responsibility. You must set an example. You must do *your* duty." She presses her fingers to her temples and sighs. "It's my fault. I've spoiled you. Because of your condition, I've indulged you with your gardens. Your violin. Even your disturbing curiosity about the Surface. You've forgotten your duty and I need to correct that."

No. Please no. Don't do this.

"I've not forgotten," I say.

She goes on as if she hasn't even heard me. "It's my responsibility as Governess to ensure my daughter couples appropriately. I won't live forever, Evelyn, and neither will you. I need to make sure there is an acceptable heir."

"But, Mother—"

Her face hardens. "I will hear no more excuses on this matter. You've rejected every Suitor I've handpicked for you. Either choose a Suitor yourself or end up with the Guard, but you *will* do your duty for our people." She turns on her heel and walks out the door.

I turn toward Father, who has stood up from the table but is otherwise exactly where he was. "Father?" I ask.

He closes his eyes and sighs. When he opens them again, he won't meet my eyes and instead stares at the pendant. "I've done all I can to help you. It's worth more than my life if I help you anymore." He looks into my eyes for a moment, before he, too, walks out the door.

I stare after him. It isn't that I don't want to couple. I do. I've felt the pull as much as anyone. It's that I don't want to couple with the Guard. Or the other Suitors I can't even really remember. I want to find someone I'll be happy with. Someone I can talk to easily. Someone funny. Someone who makes me feel something.

Someone like Gavin, I have to admit as I turn and walk slowly to the stairs that lead to my gardens. Someone I can't have. All because he's not one of us.

CHAPTER SEVEN

Controlled coupling will ensure that only the best are born in Elysium. Mother bestows this gift only on the most deserving, and it is an honor and a privilege to fulfill those duties.

—BREEDER'S HANDBOOK

I wake with my face pressed against the cool glass of my garden walls. The sunlamps and exterior lights are on again, so I know it's daytime. Dazed, I stand and find my way back to my rooms. After eating the small breakfast the Maids have brought, I dress for the day.

I stare at my face in the mirror. I don't look altered, but I feel different. Completely different. How can one small revelation change everything? It's not like I didn't know I would have to couple with someone, and sooner rather than later. And it's not like I had much choice about who my couplemate would be. What frightens me now is wondering how many sessions with Dr. Friar it will take before I can't remember that I didn't like the Guard. Before I forget I'm being Conditioned at all. Before I can't remember that I ever met Gavin. Will there be a day when I look in the mirror and I can't remember anything except my own breakfast that morning?

A Maid knocks on the door. "Miss Evelyn, your Mother is requesting your presence in her sitting room."

Of course she is. "I will be along." Gavin's warning circulates in my mind. *Don't let on that things are different.*

I plaster on a smile and make sure it looks normal in the mirror before grabbing my handbag with the food in it and heading toward Mother.

She sits on her needlepoint-covered chair while a Beautician hovers over her, adjusting her hair and makeup. The way Mother watches the woman through her mirror reminds me of Cassiopeia, the mythological queen of Ethiopia who angered Poseidon by proclaiming she was more beautiful than his daughters.

She flutters her hand when she sees me and the Beautician leaves, but Mother continues to stare into her handheld mirror.

I go to stand next to her, my head bowed just a little and my hands clasped in front of me.

"How are you this morning?" she asks.

The answer is easy. I just have to let the programmed answer flow from my lips. *"My life is just about perfect."*

She glances over with a smile. "Very good. Were you able to get any information from the Surface Dweller yesterday?"

This answer is harder, but I say, "Not much to be helpful."

She purses her lips, then says, "You must try harder, Evelyn. We cannot afford to take our time."

"Yes, Mother."

Satisfied, she turns back to her mirror and touches a hand to her cheekbone. "Excellent. Now we can get on to more important matters. Tell me, what say you about the young Guard? Is he not the perfect match?"

I speak carefully, making sure my speech is impeccable. A wrong step could be fatal. "I do not know my feelings on this matter yet. I have much to learn about him."

She makes a *pssh* sound. "What is there to learn? He has good genetics. He is strong. And very striking, yes?"

"Yes, Mother. He's very handsome, but I know nothing of his personality." Not to mention I don't really want to couple with him. I don't want to couple with anyone, really. Well . . . not anyone from Elysium.

She waves this off as she turns back to me. "Nonsense. His personality is of no consequence in the bedroom, Evelyn." She brushes a strand of hair from my face. "I think you'll be very happy with him. He's different from the others and, genetically speaking, a perfect match. Won't you give him a chance?"

"Yes, Mother," I say, looking over her shoulder. Do I have any choice?

She pats my cheek. "Excellent. I knew you'd come around." She glances up when the door opens behind me. "Ah. Just in time."

I glance behind me and fake another smile when I see the young Guard. He blushes and smiles back.

Mother makes a shooing gesture. "Go. Spend time with your young man."

She certainly means the Guard, not Gavin, but I decide to take it the way I want. I bow my head and curtsey.

"Yes, Mother."

I exit the room and the Guard follows. He walks beside me, but doesn't say a word. While I know it isn't his fault, I do not wish to speak to him. I haven't decided what to do about him yet.

The Guard lets me in the cell, where Gavin paces like a tiger. Gavin looks up when the door opens and I gesture to the floor. We both sit, my body hiding the empty spot between us from the Guards before I push my bag toward Gavin.

"It's food. I saved it from yesterday's dinner. I made sure to grab stuff that wouldn't spoil so it should still be safe to eat."

He doesn't even bother looking at it. He has eyes only for me, and they're filled with worry. "Is everything okay? You seem . . . off."

Again, it's easier to let the programmed response flow. *"My life is just about perfect."*

He tilts his head and studies me carefully. "You gave me food, which means you don't hate me, which means they didn't give you anything . . . so this isn't your Conditioning. What's going on?"

Telling him won't change anything, so I ignore the question. "I am fine. You should eat while I'm here, so the Guards don't notice."

He sighs, but digs into the bag and takes a bite. "Oh my God. This is disgusting. What is this? Seaweed?"

Since he's shoveling more food into his mouth, I have to laugh. It must not be too bad. I stop laughing when it makes me question how long it's been since he's eaten. The state he was in when we caught him . . .

"How did you get all those injuries when I first saw you? It wasn't from the Guards," I ask.

He swallows. "A storm blew through while we were hunting. It was bad, so we ran to the closest place we could find. The rain was really thick, and I tripped. I took a header down a cliff, landing on a ledge halfway down. My partner followed me, but it was so slippery from the rain that he slid most of the way down. He couldn't climb back up with me, and he had to drag me to the cave. Inside we found a few things that belonged to our missing people. We decided to look for them farther in the cave, but then we got lost and I kept passing out. We wandered for days, I think, before we found this weird door. By that time, we were starving and I was feeling pretty shitty, so we opened the door and . . ." He looks down at his hands. "Well, you know the rest."

I don't know what a "header" is, but I get the general picture. It doesn't bother me he hadn't told me the complete truth in the beginning. He hadn't trusted me. I can't blame him.

We look at each other then, silent.

"One question, one answer?" he finally asks. It eases some of the tension in me to realize it's a question—a request. Not a demand. He's willing to answer my questions, even if I don't answer any of his.

I shrug. "What do you want to know?"

"Why do you look so sad? What happened?"

I glance behind me at the young Guard, who is watching me. He smiles, then blushes and turns back to the other Guards when one gives him what appears to be a playful punch on the arm.

Keeping my gaze on the Guard, I say, "Mother has chosen the Suitor I am supposed to be Coupled with."

The sound of Gavin's chewing slows, then stops. "I thought that was your choice."

"Apparently not. Time is running out."

"Time? You're barely sixteen. You have plenty of time."

"I guess not." A lump forms in my throat.

"What do you mean?"

I stare at the ground between us, now littered with crumbs and bits of leftover food. "Well, Mother is upset that I seem to have forgotten my duty. She's right."

"That's ridiculous." His fists clench and the cracker he is holding crumbles, spreading more crumbs onto the floor.

"I have an obligation to my people to make sure there is an appropriate heir."

He narrows his eyes. "Right this minute?"

"No, but soon."

"Why? No one is going anywhere."

I study the ground. "I think your showing up has made Mother anxious about me. She needs to make sure my genetics continue."

He doesn't say anything. I look up through my eyelashes. He's frowning. "So this is my fault?"

"Oh, Gavin, no." I shrug. "It's mine. Had I chosen a Suitor before now and become Coupled this would not even be an issue."

"How can you just take this so easily? It's like an arranged marriage or something."

"Yes, it is. And it's my duty." I shrug again. "It's fine."

He meets my eyes. "If that were true, you wouldn't be so upset."

When I don't say anything, he sighs. "Well, whoever it is, is going to be a lucky guy."

I give him a half smile. "Thank you." I gesture behind me. "If you really want to know, it's the young Guard."

Gavin shifts his gaze from my face to the Guard. If I wasn't watching him so carefully, I might miss the way his eyes narrow at the Guard before he lowers his gaze back to me. "He's not good enough," he says. "See how his shoulders are hunched and his arms swing in front like that?" I raise my eyebrows and he continues with a mischievous smile. "He looks like a gorilla."

I laugh and feel some of the tension from last night and this morning float away. We spend the rest of the day together talking about things that make us happy. His family.

My gardens. Books. Life on the Surface—including the animals, specifically apes. He seems to be taking special care not to talk about the whole coupling debacle.

I don't know what's changed from yesterday, but I learn a lot from him without even having to ask. I wonder if it's his way of showing me he trusts me, and hopes I'll trust him in return. That what he's said isn't a lie.

He's what's considered an Outlander on the Surface, which are people that live in settlements in the Outlands—most of what is left of North America. There are cities, but they are small, and few and far between. They're protected with gates and Guards, like my city. He and his family are not allowed anywhere near them.

Which, according to Gavin, is just fine with him. "I like my life. It's not perfect, but I can do whatever I want instead of following a bunch of silly rules, like curfews. . . ." He trails off when he realizes these silly rules are probably the same ones I'm forced to obey.

I only ask more questions about his world.

"Can I ask you something?" he asks, and I raise an eyebrow in answer. "I don't know if you'll know the answer, but where did all this come from?"

"Of course I know that. Mother is training me to take her place. It's my duty to know those kinds of things." I smile. "Mother built it to get away from the Surface."

"But *why?*"

I frown. "Because Surface Dwellers are bad. They destroyed

their own homes. Their people. Why would she stay?" I stop myself before I can say, "Why would anyone?"

"But that doesn't make much sense. I mean, why not a cave? Why *underwater*?"

I don't really know, so I say the first thing that comes to mind. "She wanted to be completely isolated from the Surface Dwellers."

He raises an eyebrow. "Okay, fine, but *someone* would have to go to the Surface for supplies. Right?"

"No," I say, pride filling me. "We are completely self-sufficient. All of our food is grown here, as is the cotton for clothes. We even have silkworms to make the finer things. Like my dress."

"But what about this glass? The metal? Where does the oxygen come from? Fresh water? Electricity?"

"We mine the metal—I'm not sure how, but there's a whole Sector devoted to it. The glass comes from the sand. Freshwater comes from the saltwater, we just remove the salt. Electricity is generated by the geothermal energy of the volcano. The oxygen comes from two things: There is an oxygen generator that takes the ocean water and, after the salt has been removed from it, splits the hydrogen from the oxygen. The oxygen is then stored and sent throughout the facility to mix with the oxygen from the trees and plants. The hydrogen is used to fuel the heavy machinery that's used for mining, et cetera."

He blinks a few times, then says, "Right. Sorry I asked. I think I'm more confused now than I was before."

I have to laugh and it isn't long before he joins me.

When it's time to leave, I struggle with it. I know I have to go, but I have the awful feeling I won't ever see him again. That somehow Mother knows exactly what's going on in this cell.

My new Suitor walks me back. And I have to stifle more than one giggle on the way back when I realize Gavin was right and the Guard does walk with his arms swinging in front of his body. It's rude of me to keep thinking of him as just "the Guard," but I refuse to learn his name. If I wasn't expected to couple with him, I would just continue to call him by his designation. His name would be inconsequential. Therefore, knowing his name would be to accept what Mother is doing, and I don't. I'm going to figure a way out of this coupling if it kills me. Which, I have to admit, it very well might.

Mother is waiting for me when I get back to the Palace Wing. She smiles at the Guard, then dismisses him. She gestures to the chair in front of her and I sit, making sure my ankles are crossed and the hem of my dress covers my knees.

"Anything from our guest?" she asks with her eyes fixed on mine.

"No. He refuses to give me any information." My gaze wobbles. I so badly want to look away. But if I do, she'll know I'm lying. Then again, maybe she already does.

She taps her fingers against her marble end table. "That's too bad."

I look down at my hands. "I am sorry, Mother. I will try again tomorrow."

"No," she says, and my head jerks up to look at her. She meets my eyes without wavering. "I doubt anyone followed him. The alarms would have been triggered by now. It was a miracle he was able to get here in the first place."

Unable to stop my curiosity, I take a chance, and ask, "How *did* he get in?"

She stares at me with narrowed eyes, while I fight the urge to fidget. I'm sure she'll ignore me, but she surprises me when she smoothes out her face and says, "I am not entirely sure. That is why I wanted you to get answers from him." She smiles at me. "It is not your fault, Evelyn. You did the best you could. But his time for cooperating is up. I have no wish to waste any more time on this. He'll be executed."

Panic blows through me, tickling my nerve endings and causing my heart rate to accelerate. This is an entirely new sensation. And I don't care for it.

"No, Mother. You can't do that!" I say without thinking.

She raises an eyebrow. "Why not?"

I wrack my brain for an answer, but the only one that comes out is "I wish to couple with him." Oh, Mother. Where did *that* come from? A flush creeps across me then, thinking about it. I must have only been thinking it because of the situation with the Guard. Surely she will kill him now. Just to spite me. Just to remind me who's in charge, and that it isn't me.

But she only tilts her head and narrows her eyes. "Why?"

I can't back down now, and since she seems willing to at least pretend to listen, I give her the one reason I'm hoping she'll understand. "Because I'm sure his genetics are superior to those eligible here."

That gives her pause. "What makes you say that?"

"You've seen him. He's strong. He's tall and smart. Uh . . . hardworking. He won't be a burden to us."

She nods her head as if in understanding. "Those *are* wonderful qualities. For someone born here. But he's a Surface Dweller, and anyway he's flawed. His eyes are gray. And his skin is a few shades too dark."

Thinking fast, I try to find every plausible excuse. "His skin color is from the sun. A few months with us will remove any color from the skin. And I don't think that particular gray is a flaw. He says his whole family has them." I have no idea if that's true or not, but it'll help the excuse I just came up with. "You and I were talking the other day about finding something to set us apart from the Citizens. Instead of something that can be copied by anyone with art sense, why don't we do it genetically? The gray eyes could be that thing. Obviously it wouldn't work with you or me, but my children and their children . . ." I clasp my hands together in my lap to keep myself from going on. I've already shown how much I want this. She might kill him now just because she sees how much I want to save him.

"Gray eyes to set us apart?" She purses her lips and taps a nail to them. The silvery striations in her own eyes are already the envy of most of the women. I've never been happier her eyes aren't pure blue. "What was his designation on the Surface?"

I can't remember if I'd told her before or not, but it won't hurt for her to know. It would probably help, actually. "A hunter."

"How interesting." Her eyes sparkle and she nods. "I like it. We will have to make sure his genetics are appropriate. We don't want any flaws in your children." Her eyes turn hard. "If he is not a genetic match, he will die. Are you willing to sacrifice him?"

If I don't do anything, he'll die anyway. It's not like he, or I, have a choice. I just have to hope he's as genetically superior as his looks promise. "Yes, Mother."

She arches an eyebrow. "If he is flawed, you will lose *all* ability to choose. I will choose for you, and I won't change my mind this time. Do you understand?"

"Yes, Mother," I say, even though I know Gavin can't stay here. *Won't* stay here. He's got a family and a life that doesn't involve me, and it's not right to keep him. But part of me hopes he will. That he'll decide to stay here. With me.

She smiles, but there's a look in her eyes that makes me nervous. "Very well. Let's inform our guest of his choice, shall we?"

"Choice?"

She gives me a smug look. "Well, he has to approve of you as you do him, Evelyn. It's only fair. But if he does, he will have to choose to conform to our rules. And if he doesn't . . . well." She lifts a shoulder, then pats my hand as if to console me.

CHAPTER EIGHT

. . . Sweeter than the honey from a bee,
Softer than the petals of a rose,
Deeper than the bottom of the sea,
Stronger than the mightiest of foes,
Perfect is the love of Mother for me . . .
—FOUNDER'S DAY CHILDREN'S SONG

Twisting my hands together, I lead the way to Gavin's cell. Each of my footsteps echo along the hallways, mocking me. Teasing me. I don't know what to think of Mother's easy agreement, especially since she insisted on coming with me, instead of just using her hologram. If she's willing to risk the turrets, there has got to be a catch to this.

Gavin is sitting in that same corner he seems to favor when we arrive. He smiles when he sees me, but it falters when he notices Mother behind me.

The Guards straighten to attention. They don't say a word as they let us into the cell and shut the door behind Mother. One stays at the control panel for the doors, his hand only inches from the release button. The difference between their behavior with Mother and their behavior with me does not go unnoticed.

Gavin's eyes travel back and forth between Mother and me. He unfolds his long legs, and stands slowly. Standing, he dwarfs both Mother and me, and makes the entire cell seem smaller than it was. His posture is cautious but relaxed.

Mother smiles at him. "You're a very lucky young man."

His eyebrows jump up. "I am?"

She walks a circle around him, her eyes traveling over every inch of him. "It appears you've had a positive effect on Evelyn."

His eyes move to mine and I see the question in them, but I don't respond. I can't. His eyes fill with a tinge of suspicion before they turn back to Mother.

"I'm not sure I understand what you're trying to tell me," he says, a bit tense now.

"No. You're just a foolish Surface Dweller, but not as simpleminded as I had first thought. You were able to get Evelyn wrapped around your finger in only two days. I have to admit I'm impressed." She gives him another smile when he doesn't say anything. "Impressed enough that I have decided to honor her request and grant you the privilege of making a decision."

His eyes cut to mine again and I meet them without hesitation. I hope he realizes I'm not betraying him. The suspicion is still there, but he doesn't say anything to me.

"What decision?" he finally asks.

"We're offering you the chance to get out of this cell. Permanently."

His eyes bore into mine. "And what is the cost?"

She laughs, but her eyes are considering. "Very smart," she says. "I think Evelyn may have made a good choice." She pauses. "The cost is you will have to couple with her."

His jaw drops. "Excuse me?"

I try very hard not to laugh. It was probably the last thing he expected her to say.

Mother, on the other hand, doesn't bother to conceal her chuckle. "Evelyn has decided you are superior to her choices here and wants to be Coupled with you." She walks around him again, studying him as if he's a test subject, while he keeps his eyes glued to mine. "I think she may be right," she says. "Of course, we will have to do a full genetic workup to be sure. But before that can happen, we need you to make a decision. Will you couple with her?"

I hate that she hasn't given him the full choice. That if he says no, he'll die. But I fight the urge to plead with him using my eyes. He needs to make this decision on his own. There's no way to tell him the consequences should he refuse.

To my surprise, he doesn't even hesitate before he answers, "Yes."

"Smarter than I thought," she mutters. "Very good. We'll run the genetic testing to make sure you are the perfect match Evelyn thinks you are. I'll let Evelyn handle that since you seem to trust her." She walks to the door, pausing when she's next to me. "You have made a very wise choice."

She gestures for the Guards to open the door. As she leaves, she says, "Get Evelyn a genetic testing kit."

Out of the corner of my eye, I see the Guards exchange a look, but one rushes off to do her bidding. The door shuts with an ominous click, which echoes throughout the room despite the soundproofing.

Gavin hasn't taken his eyes off mine. "Would you care to explain what the hell just happened?" There's no inflection to his voice. For some reason that bothers me more than if he was angry.

I turn around and face the opposite wall, twisting my hands together before I force myself to let them fall to my side.

"Mother questioned me when I got back. She was not happy you haven't answered questions." I pause to give him time to realize I haven't shared the information he gave me. "She was going to execute you. The only thing I could think of to buy us time was coupling. I just blurted it out. To my surprise, she agreed and now we're here."

He still doesn't say anything and my nerves stretch to breaking. When I can't take it anymore, I turn around and see him staring at me. His eyes are blank.

The silence actually feels heavy. As if each tick of the second hand piles another brick over my head and I'm just waiting for them to fall on top of me.

"Please say something," I whisper.

"What did you trade for this?" His voice is soft, but there's an edge of steel underneath.

Of course that would have to be the first question he asks. "Nothing important." No matter how hard I try, I can't meet his eyes.

"Evelyn. What. Did. You. Trade. For. This?"

I close my eyes and say in a voice barely loud enough for me to hear, "My ability to choose my coupling partner if your genetics aren't good enough."

He's silent again, so long I'm forced to open my eyes to try and see what he's thinking.

His eyebrows are knit together. "I thought you'd already lost it."

"No, she gave me a time limit before. I had to choose on my own and quickly, or she would choose for me. But now I will have to go with whomever she chooses, which will probably be the young Guard. She seems to have a fondness for him."

Just then the doors open and the Guard in question hands me a testing kit. He leans down to whisper in my ear. "What are you *doing*? He's beneath you."

I narrow my eyes, straighten my shoulders and stare him down. "I am aware of this. However, Mother and I have plans that you are not privy to and are none of your concern. Also, I do not like to be questioned in such a manner, sir. You will leave at once or I will tell Mother of your impropriety."

Without waiting for an answer, I spin on my heel and go to Gavin, who is smiling at me.

"What?" I ask when the Guard shuts the door.

"That was really hot," he says, and winks at me.

I kneel to the floor and remove the materials I will need. "What was?"

He joins me and bumps his knee against mine. "The way you told him off like that. Most of the time you seem like this little docile creature, and then you do something like that. It's pretty hot."

"Actually I was going for cold. Hot would imply I haven't—"

His laugh cuts me off. "No. I thought it was sexy. Hot equals sexy in my world." His fingers graze lightly against my fingertips as a slight blush heats my cheeks. Then he clears his throat. "So, um, what's up with all this stuff? Isn't it just a blood test?"

I let out a breath and pull out a cheek swab. It looks like a bristled cleaning brush except smaller. "No. In order to make sure we get a good sample and make certain it's done right, I'm going to grab everything. Hair, saliva, skin, blood. And then I'll take it to the lab myself. After his outburst earlier, I don't trust the Guard to make sure the samples get there. Open your mouth."

He obliges and I swab the inside of his mouth with three swabs, then get a scraping of his skin, a sample of his hair, and draw some blood. When I finish I pack everything as neatly as possible back in the kit and stand to leave. "I can't come back until the tests are done, but I'll let you know the results if I can."

He nods, and I gesture for the Guards to let me out. The

young Guard appears immediately at my side and walks with me as I go to the lab. The labs are near the Residential Sector, on the complete opposite side of the complex from the Palace Wing. To get to them we have to pass through the Square.

As we pass through the Square, it seems like it's taking a hundred times longer than it should and I feel the Citizens watching me. Not in the normal way, but because the truth of what I'm doing feels like it's written all over my face. And I'm sure that one of them is going to see it and go running off to Mother, but they all just smile and nod in greeting.

When we pass one of the alleys, I feel a flash of déjà vu and have to stop. I don't know why, but I'm drawn to the end of it.

At the end of it, I press my hand to the brick wall. An image of a smaller version of the Square flashes through my mind so strongly that it has to be a memory. I stumble backward and knock right into the Guard, who can't quite catch me before I fall onto the ground.

Immediately, he helps me up and asks if I'm okay, but I'm still staring at the wall. What was that? I press my hand against the bricks again, but nothing happens this time.

"Miss Evelyn," the Guard asks, drawing my attention back to him, and the rest of the memory fades as if it was never there. "Are you okay?"

"Y-yes. I just—" I stop myself from blurting it out. I shouldn't tell anybody until I know for sure what I've seen.

"I just wanted to touch the bricks. I like the roughness," I tell him, turning around and leading the way out of the alley, making sure to trail my fingers over the bricks as we leave.

He doesn't say anything, but I know he doesn't believe me.

When we finally get to the DNA lab, I poke my head in and immediately spot my best friend, Macie, sitting at one of the microscopes. The lab hasn't changed in the six years since I first remember seeing it. The walls are all white, as is the floor and the ceiling. There is no view of the ocean, and it always makes me wonder how Macie survives working in such a claustrophobic environment.

There are three long rows of white lab tables with a dozen microscopes per row. Lining the walls are more white lab tables with all sorts of strange unidentifiable things placed over their surfaces.

Macie hasn't changed all that much, either. Her hair is shorter and no longer in the twin braids she wore when we were ten, and the glasses she used to wear were recycled after the surgery she had last year, but other than that she looks the same.

I don't remember how we met, but I know she is the one person I consider a true friend. I trust her almost as much as I trust myself. I hope that she feels the same way about me, because I need her help.

"Macie!"

She looks over and smiles at me, showing off her burgundy

lips. "Well, look what the catfish dragged in. Been a long time." She gets off her stool and gives me a hug. She's taller than me, but only by a few centimeters.

I return the hug. "I know. I'm sorry. Time seems to slip by sometimes and I don't know where it's gone."

She laughs. "Isn't that always the case? I was just talking to Nick about that the other day. I get so wrapped up in this stuff I forget about our dates."

"So, you're still seeing him?"

"Yes." Her blue eyes sparkle when she says, "We passed our genetic matching. We've been approved for coupling."

"Really? That is so great! I'm happy for you." I give her another hug.

She returns the hug. "Thanks. Though I think this is all going too fast for him. He's been humming some children's song the past few days."

I chuckle. "Probably just imagining those pretty babies you're going to make."

She pulls back and I notice sadness in her eyes. "I'm sorry."

"For what?" I ask. She couldn't possibly know what's happening. I doubt even the Guards really know, and besides Mother—who won't say a word—they're the only ones who could.

She gives me a strange look. "I heard Timothy disappeared. I know you were really close to him."

"Who?" I furrow my brow. That name is familiar to me and my knees feel a little weak at the mention.

Macie's eyes narrow and then she lets out a disgusted breath. "She did it again. I knew she wouldn't leave you be."

So, Gavin *was* right. Mother is Conditioning me. And apparently everyone knows it but me. My hands tighten into tight little balls, my nails biting into my skin. But I can't let on that I'm aware of what's going on, so I just say, "I'm sorry?" and force my fingers to relax.

She shakes her head. "Never mind." She gestures to the kit in my hand. "If that's about Three, take it to Tony. He's handling all that. Won't let anyone near it but him." She rolls her eyes.

My heart somersaults at the mention of Three, but I frown. "It's not about Three. What's wrong with Three?"

She shrugs. "The *master* won't share, but I heard some Guards complaining about leaks the other day. Anyway, how can I help you?"

A leak? How can there be a leak? I was just touring the mining operation yesterday . . . or was it longer than that? I press a hand to my aching head. I can't remember.

I hand Macie the kit with all the samples. "I need you to run this."

"Another Suitor?" She shrugs and looks back into the microscope. "Fine. Just put it on the corner. I'll get to it in a minute."

I hang on to it and glance at the cameras around the room. They're all off. They won't turn on unless there's a security breach. I just have to hope Macie won't consider what *I'm* doing a security breach . . . but we've been friends for so long, and she's never liked Mother. I don't see her turning down the chance to do something behind Mother's back, especially something as simple as making sure the results are what I want. The only problem will be the other Technicians around the lab. The closest is on the far side of the room, but I still have to be careful.

When I don't put the kit on the table, she looks over with a frown. "What's wrong?"

I step closer and lower my voice. "This is the DNA from the Surface Dweller."

Her eyebrows jump up. "What?" she says loudly.

I glance around quickly, but no one seems to have noticed her outburst. "Shh. Please. I need your help."

She glances around and leans toward me. "Of course. Anything. You want me to say he's inferior?"

"No. Just the opposite. Whatever the result, I need you to get his DNA into the computer."

She wrinkles her nose. "A Surface Dweller?"

"He's not like what Mother makes them out to be. He's really . . . nice." I bite my inner cheek to keep from making the same mistake I made with Mother.

She smiles and her eyes sparkle like they had when she talked about Nick. "What's his name?"

"Gavin."

"You like him," she says, her voice soft and knowing.

My heart leaps into my throat. "I suppose. He's pleasant enough."

"I mean you *like* him."

I frown. Is it that obvious? "What in Mother's name would make you say that?"

"Because like recognizes like."

"What?"

"Never mind. Don't worry about it. Just tell me what you're going to do." She leans closer, the huge smile still on her face.

"I don't want you to get in trouble, so I'm not going to tell you. But, please, it's important." I grip her hands tightly in mine. "Mother has to think that Gavin is a perfect match. I need his DNA in the computer. Will you do that for me?"

"Sure. Of course." She nods and can't hide a smile. "I knew you'd come back to us and that witch wouldn't keep you under her thumb for long." She grabs the kit from me. "I'll get started on this right away, Miss Evelyn." She raises her voice and winks at me. "Tell Mother she can expect the results within the hour."

I mouth *thank you* to her. "Very well. We appreciate your assistance in this matter."

The Guard is still waiting for me when I leave the lab. The whole walk back he steals glances at me. I'm concerned he eavesdropped, but I doubt he'd have heard anything. Although I'm sure he'll report back to Mother that I'd spent entirely too much time talking with Macie.

"It's nice seeing her again," I say, keeping my eyes forward.

"I beg pardon, Miss Evelyn." He glances at me.

"I said, it's nice seeing Macie again. It's been entirely too long. We had a lot to catch up on. I apologize for making you wait so long."

He grins at me. "It's not a problem. A woman should never have to rush."

I smile, grateful for the manners classes Mother insists all children take. *Good manners are the mark of a civilized people.*

An hour. That's all I have to wait. Just an hour. I can handle that, as long as Mother keeps her end of the bargain.

CHAPTER NINE

An Enforcer must be ready to act at a moment's notice. Even a second's delay can mean the difference between life and death.

—ENFORCER STATUTE 105B.4

Mother comes for me herself in exactly one hour and fifteen minutes. She seems pleased, which worries me.

"Good news," she says, and actually claps her hands. "The lab tells me Gavin is indeed a perfect match for you."

Relief washes over me, but I only say, "That *is* good news."

"However," she continues, and my stomach clenches. "You have a habit of changing your mind. So, since I do not wish to waste any more time on this, the coupling will happen tonight."

I frown and feign reluctance while my insides jump around like rubber balls. "But it takes three days for the paperwork to be processed."

She smiles wider. "I am the one who approves the paperwork, and I've already approved it."

I sigh as if I'm not happy with the situation. "Very well, Mother. I will prepare for tonight." I turn and start to my rooms.

"No," she says, and I stop in midstride. "You will inform Gavin of the plans. I'm not going down to that filthy place again. Once is quite enough for me."

"Yes, Mother. As you wish." I silently cheer, smiling to myself.

I will indeed inform him of the plans.

Back in the cell, Gavin and I sit on the floor in the corner. I'm not sure if it's necessary anymore, but I block the camera again and wonder if she's ever even watched us. I can't imagine her not using that against me.

Or she's playing me like a drum and watching every move we make, waiting to see what I do and pouncing when the moment's right.

The thought doesn't exactly fill me with confidence.

"So?" Gavin asks.

He's acting like he doesn't have a care in the world. As if his life and my freedom aren't waiting on this information and the plan trying to form in my head as we sit here. His legs are stretched out in front of him and crossed at the ankle. His arms rest loosely at his sides, but he might as well have them crossed behind his head, as calm and collected as he appears. Not even his eyes give anything away.

It's a little unsettling, actually. Only Enforcers can cover their emotions so well. It makes me wonder if he's as good at faking them as he is at covering them.

I push the thought away. Now's not the time. "So, you're a perfect match," I say with a smile.

"Seriously? Wow." He goes a little pale, but he smiles and there is a little sparkle in his eyes. Just that little bit of emotion makes me feel so much better.

"Well, I don't know for sure," I say, drawing symbols in the dirt on the floor. "I have a friend in the lab. She could have faked the results. But for our purposes, you are perfect."

"Oh, okay."

He looks disappointed, so I say, "Your blood is also in the computer, which means you won't be targeted by the cams or turrets. You'll essentially have free rein of the facility once they let you out of here."

He chuckles, but the sound is off, as if he's laughing more at himself than me. "So, that's what your plan was. Not coupling, but to get me into the computer."

"Yes. But . . ." And now on to the news I've been dreading sharing. I'm not sure how he's going to take it. I stare at the symbols I've written on the floor, trying not to see him out of my peripheral vision. "It appears we'll have to go through with it anyway."

He pauses. "What do you mean?"

"Mother has stipulated we couple tonight. She doesn't want me changing my mind again. I have a feeling it's to test how serious I am about this." I finally look up, unable to stop myself. "And you."

He looks into space for a while. Then he clears his throat and shrugs. "I suppose considering all you've sacrificed for me, I can make one of my own." He turns to me and winks, his eyes flashing with amusement.

Relief blows through me and I relax for the first time since I sat down. "Yes, it must be terrible for you."

He smirks, but then his face sobers and he reaches out to brush a strand of hair from my face, letting his hand linger along my cheek before he jerks his arm back.

I can only assume he remembered he can't touch me.

Grateful the Guards can't see my face, I blush. The burn of it travels from the tips of my toes to the roots of my hair. We stare at each other and it feels like there's a magnet in his eyes, drawing me ever closer. Even if I wanted to, I can't tear my gaze from his. My fingers itch to touch his again. Just a light brush of skin against skin. I crave the rush it gives me. The mix of emotions it stirs in me. The instant of pure panic, quickly covered by wonder and joy. I wonder if he feels the same when he touches me, if that's why he's constantly reaching out. My mouth is suddenly dry, and even though I want to speak, I can't.

Instead, we both look away from each other.

"So—" we say together.

"Go ahead," I say.

He shakes his head and gestures for me to continue. "No. Please. You first."

For some reason, though I've been planning this event for years, I'm nervous. I shouldn't be. I've been taught everything I need to know to please him . . . but he's a Surface Dweller. Things are different up there.

I glance over and he's staring again. It makes my skin warm and my blood hum. There's just something about him that makes me realize it doesn't matter. No matter what I did, it wouldn't be wrong.

"Are you sure about this?" he asks. "I mean, this is a big step. Kids and everything."

"It's the only way to save you," I say, "but we don't have to have a child. I can secure . . . things that will prevent a pregnancy."

He blinks. "You can? But why do you? I mean, what's the point? I thought only people who are approved to have kids have kids, so why do you have stuff to prevent pregnancy?"

"Breeding can only be authorized by Mother, and only for Coupled Citizens," I explain. "But the physical act strengthens pair-bonding, which in turn strengthens society. We simply ensure no unauthorized breeding with contraception."

He glances at the camera and then leans in close. His breath tickles my neck. "But . . . won't they be watching?"

"No. Not in my private quarters." At least I don't think so. I've never had a reason to check.

"Then why are we doing it at all? We could just fake it."

I jerk back as if he's slapped me. "You don't want to?" I keep my voice steady, trying not to betray the hurt that comes over me at the thought.

"No, that's not it. It's just . . ." He breaks off and seems to be intently studying the drawings I made in the dirt. "Never mind."

I sigh. Of course he doesn't really want to couple with me. He said earlier that I'm just a kid. "We have to because they will check."

His eyes slice to mine, filled with confusion. "Check? How do they do that?"

I simply stare at him and he blushes again. "Never mind," he mutters.

As neither of us has a choice, I might as well relieve some of his fear. "Don't worry," I say. "I am well versed in this. I won't disappoint you."

Now he seems even more confused. His whole face is scrunched up. "Well versed? You mean they teach you how to . . . ?"

"Of course. Pleasure ensures coupling, and coupling ensures the continuation of our people. We learn everything we need to know," I reassure him.

"Great," he mutters. "That's more than *I* needed to know."

His tone is wrong. I can't decipher it.

"What's wrong?" I ask. "You won't have to worry about showing me what to do. Isn't that good?"

"No," he says bluntly, almost angry.

"Why not?"

"Because now I have to worry *I* won't know what to do."

I furrow my brow. Oh. "Do you want me to teach you?" I ask quietly.

He jumps up and away from me, his whole expression horrified. "No. No. *God* no."

I clasp my hands together in my lap and stare at them. "I'm sorry. I didn't mean to offend you."

"Oh, geez." He sits back down, but doesn't move to touch me. "You didn't. I'm just nervous. Just . . . let me. Okay?"

"If that's what pleases you."

He closes his eyes and leans back against the wall. "Close enough."

Before I can say anything else, the young Guard opens the door. I twist my body to see him. "Mother wonders if you've explained tonight's plans to the Surface Dweller." He refuses to meet my eyes, but there's a hardness about him that wasn't there before.

It worries me, but I pretend nothing is wrong. I stand. "I have."

"Then she says you are to prepare for tonight. I am to escort you back."

"Very well." Stifling a sigh, I turn to Gavin, who is watching the Guard with narrowed eyes. If I didn't know better, I'd say he's jealous. "I will see you in a few hours."

Then I turn and follow the Guard out the door and to my rooms.

Mother is waiting for me. She's had the Maids clean my room and apply clean sheets to my bed. The scent of lavender from the sheets and bleach from the chemicals they used to wipe down my bathroom swirls in the air. The clothes I am to wear are already laid out for me. I had planned on stopping by the lab again to speak with Macie, but I don't think Mother has any intention of letting me out of her sight.

And she doesn't. The whole time the Maids are pulling and primping my hair, applying tinted liquids, creams, and powders to my face, then buffing and filing my nails, Mother stands by, watching me closely, while I look out my window into the ocean, trying to calm myself with counting the fish in the school that's right outside.

She helps me into the outfit I will wear for the coupling. It looks more like an under-thing than an actual dress as it's not exactly appropriate for a dinner engagement, but it is perfect for a seduction. It's all black. And just what he'll expect, Mother assures me.

I stare at myself in the mirror. A hurricane of emotions storms through me, and it's difficult to differentiate one from the rest. But I think embarrassment is the strongest.

Mother ties the laces of the strange outfit so tightly it hurts to breathe, but it gives me the appearance of actually having hips. Despite the fact that I am technically a Breeder, my body is built more like an Enforcer. All muscle, no curves. The skirt stops high on my thighs. I'm sure one wrong move will reveal absolutely everything.

It surprises me that I'm nervous to be wearing something so revealing. With the makeup and tousled hair, I look magnificent. Sexy. The dark temptress. Just what Mother says will appeal to a Surface Dweller. But just the same I can't help but think how glad I am that no one but him will see it.

Just as we finish, there's a knock on my door.

"What? I said no interruptions," Mother calls out.

A Maid cautiously pokes her head into the room. "Ma'am. There's trouble in Three."

A little thrill goes through me at the mention of Three, but I don't know why and I don't let Mother see it.

Mother scowls as she turns back to me to adjust something on my outfit. "Have Veronica handle it. That's her job."

This time it's a shudder that goes through me. I hate Enforcers and Veronica especially gives me the creeps. She watches me entirely too closely and most of the time I have a feeling she's smirking at me behind my back.

The Maid nods and leaves, shutting the door behind her, but before she can say anything to me, there's another knock on the door.

This time it's Mother's personal Maid who steps into the room and whispers something to Mother before walking back out the door without even glancing in my direction. Mother immediately stands and tells me I can have awhile to myself to prepare mentally for my coupling.

At first, I breathe a sigh of relief when I'm left to my own devices, but then my instincts start humming. Why did Mother leave me alone now? Especially when she was so concerned I'd change my mind. Surely she'd want to be here in case I started to get cold feet, so she could convince me otherwise, right?

Whatever made her leave has something to do with me. I know it. I just have to find her and figure out what it is.

I slip out the door and down the hallway, hoping to find Mother quickly and quietly. It doesn't take long. I pause next to the library when I hear Mother's voice say my name. I creep closer to the door to listen in on what she's saying, being careful to step lightly so my heels don't make a noise.

"Evelyn has chosen, and I made a deal. I'm sorry you were not chosen," Mother says.

"I don't think it was her choice, though, milady." This from a man, a man that sounds remarkably like the young Guard.

"Why would you think that?"

"Why would she choose a Surface Dweller? He must be using her so he can escape."

Although I am unable to see what Mother is doing, I'm sure she's pursing her lips, considering what he's saying carefully and deciding how to respond.

"Yes, I am aware of what he's doing," she says.

I press closer to the doorway. So Mother knows that this is all a ruse. Nothing less than I expected, but I wonder what she plans to do about it.

"While I do not presume to question you, I do not understand why you are letting them couple," the Guard says.

"My reasons are not your concern. Rest assured, he has not fooled me. He will still die tonight." I suck a breath in through my teeth, but otherwise do not make a noise. Every muscle in my body tenses.

"Yes, milady." The Guard sounds pleased, and it surprises me how much I want to smash the smile off his face. There's a red haze on either side of my vision, which, aside from that, has become extremely clear.

The sounds inside come to me as if I'm in the room. The incessant ticking of Mother's favorite clock, the whispers of linen against leather, their breathing, even their heartbeats. Slow and calm from Mother. Irregular and quick from the Guard.

The scent of his cologne and Mother's perfume makes my nose itch and burn, but I don't dare move. I don't want to miss a thing. Every bit of information I can collect now will be to my advantage later.

"Excellent," Mother says. "For your service, I will keep my promise to you and you will have Evelyn." It's not an easy task to fight back the urge to burst into the room and declare I'm not property. That I'm not the wage to be paid for killing a Surface Dweller. *My* Surface Dweller.

"Thank you, milady," he says, and from the sounds, I know he has taken Mother's hand in his and kissed it, as is expected of him.

The chairs creak as they stand and I hurry as quickly and quietly as I can back to my room. Looks like I have yet another change of plans. The escape will have to take place tonight, whether I'm ready or not.

CHAPTER TEN

Festival! The one time each year to let our hair down and celebrate what Mother has done for us. Because we know no one wants to miss all the fun and excitement, attendance is compulsory.

—FESTIVAL FLYER

Tearing through my room, and ignoring the sudden headache that screams through my head, I grab absolutely anything I think might be useful and shove it into the evac pack Mother put together for me ages ago. Since she filled it herself, it has all sorts of things that will come in handy. It's only to be used in emergencies, like a Surface Dweller invasion or a leak—something that means we have to escape quickly. I can't think of any greater emergency than this.

I yank a dress over my outfit and shove a complete change of clothes in the bag. If we run into trouble, I won't be much good in stiletto boots. I pull them off now so I can sneak out, and hitch the pack onto my back.

When I pass the library, Mother is still talking to the

Guard. I block their voices from my head. I don't have time to chance hearing something that will stop me from going through with my plan. The headache disappears as quickly as it appeared, but I don't question it. I just keep moving. I hurry down the halls, sticking to the shadows, and rely on my instincts to get to the Detainment Center, hoping I won't run into any Enforcers along the way.

When I reach the turrets that are just outside the entrance to the Detainment Center, I hide my backpack behind it in the alcove, then take a second to catch my breath and remove the dress, pull my boots back on, and adjust the lingerie Mother tied me into in an appropriately seductive way before sauntering into the room. The less time the Guards spend thinking with their brains the better. They exchange a look when they see the little black outfit I'm wearing.

"Miss Evelyn," one says, and tries to avert his eyes. If nothing else, I have to give him credit for that. "We weren't expecting you."

"Mother has asked me to retrieve Gavin for the coupling."

They look at each other again, and I worry that Mother has already told them Gavin is to be executed.

I raise a brow. "Is there a problem?"

"No, Miss." This from the thinner one who is still being careful to avoid looking at me. "I'll open the door right now."

Gavin is waiting for me when the door opens. I hope Mother wasn't right about him trying to bolt now. To my relief, he doesn't. He only gives me a strange look. "Nice outfit."

I smile. "Yes. I agree. It's time for our coupling. If you'll follow me?"

He trails me out the door and the Guards move to escort us. I turn and stake them with my eyes. "I have this covered, gentlemen. I don't think Mr. Hunter has any intention of running. Do you?"

"No. I'm looking forward to this," Gavin says. He seems to realize something's up and manages a pretty good leer at me before turning his lazy grin to the Guards, who glare at him.

"Mother has requested you remain here until told otherwise," I continue. "Mr. Hunter may be joining you again this evening after we're . . . finished."

The Guards exchange another look, then shrug. "Better than transporting Citizens from Three," the thicker one says.

What is it about Three that always makes my stomach flip?

"Any word on when they're going to get that leak fixed, Miss Evelyn?" he continues.

So there *is* a leak. Interesting. I wonder why I haven't been told.

"Soon" is all I say, mentally filing it away to deal with later. I saunter out the door, leaving Gavin to follow or not, only pausing when I get to the turrets. "Do you trust me?" I ask without turning around. I wiggle back into my waiting dress.

"Yes, of course," he says.

"Stick your hand here." I indicate the glass eye of the turret, which is just a few inches above the ground and just below the barrel. It will scan his DNA. Even if he sets it off, it shouldn't hurt him, I hope. If Macie hasn't done her job, everything I've planned past this point will not matter.

He does as I request, but the turret doesn't make a sound. Not even a hiss of the steam that powers it. I smile. Excellent.

I shoulder my bag. "Follow me. Just do as I do. Okay?"

He falls into line next to me. "Why do I have a feeling something went wrong and we're not doing the coupling thing?"

"Mother decided you were just manipulating me and she was going to kill you anyway. I'm making sure that doesn't happen."

Gavin is silent for a minute. The only sounds are the clicking of my boots echoing along the corridor.

"That's not what you think, is it?" he asks.

"That you're manipulating me?" I glance over at him. His face is a careful blank mask when he nods. "No. But I don't really care. I'm helping you escape, even if you are."

He frowns. "What about you?"

"What about me?"

"Aren't you coming?"

"Of course not. Why would I leave? This is my home. I'm just going to make sure you get back to the door that leads to the Surface. You're all healed, so you should have no problems getting out okay after that."

"But what about the Enforcers? Won't they kill you for helping me?"

A chill tickles my spine and I suppress a shudder, but I

say, "I'm the Daughter of the People. Mother will never believe it was me who helped you."

He doesn't look convinced. "I'd feel better if you came with me," he says.

"If you're really concerned about me, you won't argue with me. The clock is running and the sooner you get out, the less chance they'll figure it out."

"But the Guards saw you."

"Who will Mother believe? The Guards? Or her own daughter? Now *come on*!"

"Fine, but this conversation isn't over," he says, and I fight the urge to roll my eyes. "So, we're on the run now, right?"

"Yes."

"Great." He grabs my arm and spins me around, and then pushes me back with his body so I bump into the wall. Before I can say anything he leans down so his mouth captures mine.

At first I freeze, afraid of the punishment that's surely coming. I start to struggle to get away from him, but then, as my mind fogs from his scent and taste, I melt in his arms. If not for his hands holding me steady at my hips, I would be a puddle on the ground. His lips are sweet and soft, but insistent. The kiss makes my head spin. As far as first kisses go, I can't imagine a better one.

Without warning, another memory slides in: a different dark corridor. A different pair of lips on mine. The scent of Gavin mingles with the memory of the other person's and, for a moment, I'm confused. Terrified. Something bad is going to happen. Or maybe it already has.

Before I can try to think, Gavin changes the angle of the kiss and his touch quickly overpowers the other memory, making me forget everything but him. For once I'm grateful for not being able to remember.

Then, just when I make the conscious decision to take more, he's pulling away, but only enough so our lips aren't touching.

"I would have been ready," he whispers.

I can only nod when he backs away. My head is still swimming as I hitch my backpack farther up on my back. I don't have time to think about this. I blindly turn around and walk headlong into the wall.

Whoa! I shake my head, trying to clear it.

Gavin chuckles and turns me around so I face down the corridor. "I think we go this way," he says.

A little spurt of anger from the embarrassment of it all clears my head. "I'm fine." I march in the direction of the Palace Wing. "If I take you back toward my gardens, can you remember the way to the door you came in from?"

The smile slides off his face. He's all business now. "Yes."

I try not to think about the kiss, but it doesn't help that my mind keeps replaying the scene over and over in my head, distracting me. I touch my fingers to my lips. They feel tender and swollen. My lipstick is all gone and I slide my eyes to the side to sneak a peek at Gavin. His lips carry a tint of the red that had been on mine.

My stomach flutters at the same time that I lift a foot to climb the slick stairs, and I slip. Before I can crash face-first into the stairs, Gavin grabs me around the waist. Then, in one move, I'm being spun around to face him and he's only centimeters from me.

His pulse flutters in his neck. I see what's in his eyes and my body responds in kind. But before anything happens, he's righting me so I stand, somewhat shakily, on my feet.

"Oops." His voice is light, despite his rapid breathing. "Don't want you to get hurt before we figure out a way out of here."

Still staring at him, I nod before straightening my dress and turning to walk up the stairs. What is this? What's wrong with me? I'm not entirely sure what Gavin was doing—or what game he's playing at—but this time I'm careful to watch where I'm stepping.

I stick carefully to the shadows. It's of the upmost importance that no one sees Gavin. Sector Two is filled with people, and although he's been allowed to wash, Gavin's not as clean as the people of the city. It's not a stretch to see he's the Surface Dweller.

I turn around to make sure he's still with me, only to panic when I see he's drifted away from the safety of the shadows and is instead staring at the glass ceiling and heading toward the glass walls.

Glancing quickly to make sure no one's seen him, I rush over to him and grab his arm and firmly but gently guide him back to the shadows.

"Don't do that! Pay attention," I say. "Do you *want* to get caught?"

He shakes his head and we start back to the Palace Wing, but it isn't long before Gavin starts drifting off again. While amusing and kind of sweet, it's annoying to have to keep pushing him forward whenever he pauses.

Just before we reach the marble arch that frames the tube entrance to the Palace Wing, I pull Gavin into the shadows. A Guard waits at the gates and an Enforcer should be somewhere nearby. I rely on the hope that Mother hasn't anticipated me rescuing him and hasn't alerted anyone here to be on guard.

"Just follow my lead, all right?" I say. "Don't say anything, and look a little scared."

He places a hand on my arm. "Why?"

I slide my arm out from under his. "We have to get by that Guard. If he senses something is wrong, he'll alert Mother. I have a plan, but you have to trust me."

"I do," he says, keeping his eyes directly on mine.

I straighten my shoulders and saunter up to the Guard with my hips swinging. The Guard's eyes darken and he smiles when I stop to talk to him.

"Good evening. All is well?" I ask.

"Fine, Miss Evelyn." He glances over and narrows his eyes at Gavin. "Are you aware this man is the Surface Dweller?"

I laugh. "Yes. Mother has chosen him to couple with me. Apparently he has perfect genes and will help foster the growth of the perfect heir."

The Guard's eyes widen. "Him?"

"Yes. Ridiculous, isn't it? But Mother is quite insistent." I sigh heavily. "Well, we've got to go, Mother has us on a schedule."

The Guard, still in shock, waves us on. Gavin stops in the middle of the tube and looks around, his eyes wide. "It's gorgeous," he says. "No wonder you don't want to leave."

I smile, looking around as well. The lights outside are fully lit and make the water appear to be a beautiful sapphire blue. Different schools of fish swim around. Their colors stand out in beautiful jewel tones of blue, yellow, and orange. I press a hand to the glass and one of the little blue ones swims closer, as if he's trying to touch my fingertips.

"Yes, it is, isn't it? It's easy to take it for granted sometimes."

With a sigh, I pull my gaze from the water and continue forward. He follows, still gazing at the water. We have to take the stairs because the elevators are loud, not to mention there shouldn't be anyone using them. It is only for family, not for the Guards, Enforcers, or Servants, and I'm supposed to be safely shut in my room right now. Taking the stairs is faster anyway.

It's times like these that I wish my gardens weren't on the very top of the three-story building, but there isn't anything for me to do about it now. If all goes well, there will be no reason for me to do anything about it at all.

We finally get to the door that leads to the gardens, and it's almost time to let Gavin take over, but I pause and signal for him to wait for me. We'll pass right by the entrance to the family wing, and I don't want anyone to hear me.

I stoop to slide the zipper down the boot and slither the

leather down my leg before doing the same with the other. When I stand up, Gavin is watching me with a strange expression.

"What's wrong?"

He curses under his breath and shakes his head. "Nothing." He strides away and I frown as I chase after him.

About two hundred meters from the entrance to my gardens there is an alcove that's about five meters by five meters. It houses a camera and a turret, both mounted to the ceiling and facing not toward the hallways, but the utility closet that houses the electronics for both of them.

"That's it," he says, nodding his head toward the utility closet door. His stance is wary, and he keeps casting glances all around. He must not trust me, despite what he said earlier.

"Are you sure? It's just a utility closet." I've seen dozens just like it.

He points to what appears to be a bloodstain on the wall and floor. "I'm sure," he says.

I stare at the stain for a long time. Why is that still here? Mother should have had the Servants clean that up a long time ago. It also dawns on me that Mother obviously already knew where he'd come from. So why all the secrecy? Why all the questions?

Only one reason: She was waiting to see why I was so interested in him. Something shiny grabs my attention, and I see a little silver loop. It looks like an earring. I grab it and show it to Gavin, who stares at it, sadness pooling in his eyes.

"It's Con's," he says, taking it from me.

"Your friend?"

"Yes."

I raise my brow. "He wears jewelry?"

He smiles, but it's still sad as he pockets the small loop. "Yes."

"I see," I say, but I don't really. Why would a man wear jewelry? Only women do here.

But that doesn't matter now. I place my hand on the glass plate next to the door. A red light emits and traces over every inch of my hand. Then the door unlocks with a click and I pull it open.

Gavin is right. It's definitely not a utility closet, but it won't do us any good, either. There's a wall of dirt and rocks blocking the entrance. Apparently Mother knew what I was planning. She's blocked the entrance—and the only means of escape he has.

Chapter Eleven

Differences are the root of all evil. Accordingly,
all differences will be eradicated. At any cost.
—Mother's journal, page 176

Of course she has. She knew the whole time. She was just playing games with me, trying to figure out why I had taken to him. I should have known. How could I be so stupid?

"Damn it!" I punch the rock wall, causing the now somewhat fragile rock to crack and splitting my knuckles. Little bits of rock and dust fall to the floor in a cascade.

Gavin jumps forward, taking my hand gently between his. "Hey, hey. Don't do that. You're going to hurt yourself. It's not that big of a deal. If there's one, there's more. She wouldn't block off y'all's only escape."

Blood trickles from the wounds in my hand. I don't think I've ever punched anything in my life. It hurts like hell, but I don't care. I yank my hand from his grasp. *Why* does he keep persisting in touching me when he *knows* it's forbidden?

"That's not it. She was expecting this. She was playing us the whole time and I fell for it. Damn it." I kick the door shut, then hiss when pain zips up my toes. I quickly shove my feet back into the boots to avoid jamming my toes into anything else.

He narrows his eyes. "If she was expecting us, where are they? Shouldn't they be trying to stop us?"

He has a point. I glance around and listen. Not a sound. Not even a peep. The slamming of the door should have brought *someone.*

"You're right. Something is wrong." I press my fingers to my eyes, smearing blood on my face. "Okay. This is what we're going to do. We need to get out of the Palace Wing. It definitely isn't safe here. Then we'll need to come up with another plan. Follow me."

It's obvious Mother already knows what we were planning, or at least was sure Gavin would try something. But I need to get us out of here and to a place they won't be able to find us—and it's very much an *us* situation now. But finding a place they won't find us is much easier said than done, especially with Gavin looking like the Surface Dweller he is.

I remember there's supposed to be a waterproof map in my evac bag. Extremely mindful of the time we've been standing there, I pull out the map and study it quickly.

"What is that?" Gavin asks.

"A map. It lists all the designated evacuation areas in case of facility failure or Surface Dweller attack. If we stand any chance of escaping, one of those will be it."

He lifts an eyebrow. "A map? Can we trust it?"

I don't even spare him a glance. "Of course we can. It's supposed to be used for emergency evacuations. Mother doesn't want her Citizens to die and she especially wouldn't want me to die."

He doesn't look convinced, but doesn't say anything.

"All right," I say after a minute. "It looks like there's an evacuation area in the Square of Sector Two. Let's head over there."

I fold up the map, but keep it in my hand, so I can reference it quickly if I have to change course and pinpoint the exact location.

We slip by the Guard, who is too busy reading something on his holoscreen to notice us—not that he would be looking anyway. His duty is to prevent people from getting in, not from getting out.

This time we hurry to the Square, still keeping to the shadows and avoiding the large crowds of Citizens. It's more crowded than usual today because of Festival. With all the Couples dressed in their colorful carnival clothes, we probably won't stick out as much as I thought we would, but I'm still the Daughter of the People and highly recognizable, and so is Gavin with his torn and dirty clothes. The only problem is, the farther into Sector Two the thicker the crowds. Even in the shadows it's difficult to push our way through so no one will notice.

Making it worse, Gavin gawks at everything. It makes him stick out like a sore thumb, but he keeps up so I don't say anything. I need to focus on getting us through here. My nerves are stretched to breaking and my heart is in my throat because I've spotted three Enforcers. They don't appear to have noticed us and from their relaxed postures I know they aren't on alert, but I also know that doesn't really mean anything. If I can see them, they can see me. We must tread very carefully.

Six Guards are straight ahead, but they appear too busy flirting with the group of young women surrounding them to be paying attention. Since it's either them or the Enforcers, I lead Gavin in their direction, double checking our position against the map and the location of the evacuation area. It looks like the evac area is in the middle of the Square, which doesn't make sense, but maybe there's something there I don't know about.

When we reach the designated spot on the map, I frown. This can't be right. This is a supper club. Only Coupled Citizens and their families are allowed in here. But, I've been here a few times with Mother to catch a show with our dinner and I think I remember there being some kind of back room. Maybe that's the evac area.

Being mindful of the Enforcers and the Guards, I rush into it, with Gavin nipping at my heels. While music is playing, something from the entertainment for the night, I'm sure there's no one in here yet. It must still be too early for the dinner crowd, but I don't stop. My heart is thumping so hard I can feel it in my head. I pretend like I'm supposed to be here and keep walking until I find what I'm looking for—a drapery-covered wall. I push it aside and see a door. I open it to reveal a set of stairs, leading up into darkness.

Gavin shuts the door behind us and the sound from the club becomes muffled, with only the *thump, thump* of the bass audible. At the top of the stairs the sound of music gets louder again and I can see lights peeking through a tiny gap in the wall. Curious, I go to it and find it's another curtain. I'm actually peering out from behind the bronze metal latticework behind the bar. I release the curtain and continue forward, my foot kicking something that hits the wall with a metallic clink.

I lift it up and study it in the light dripping in from the gap in the curtain. When I see what I'm holding, my blood turns cold. It's a casing to a bullet. I'm sure this is where the Enforcers hide to watch over the Citizens. I glance up at the wall, just to verify, and sure enough there's a plaque with one of Mother's Enforcer statutes on it. The one about an Enforcer having to act at a moment's notice. I'm sure if I looked farther I'd find another.

"We have to get out of here," I say.

"You brought us here," Gavin replies with a tight laugh.

"I know." I guide the way to two doors. The one ahead of me leads to another set of stairs. It seems familiar to me, so I'm hopeful it leads to the evacuation area.

At the bottom of the stairs, a quick study reveals a large room and a second exit. That must be the evacuation area. I lead the way over to it. A group of large boxes blocks the door and when I try to push one, I know it must weigh at least fifty kilograms. I'm not sure if I can even lift it, but before I can try, Gavin picks it up and moves it out of the way. Impressed, I can only stare as he moves the rest of them. Before long he's cleared us a path and I'm opening the door.

The hinges make a squealing sound as I push the door open, and the breath I didn't know I was holding releases in a hiss when I see not a tunnel like I was expecting, but the back side of the supper club with an unimpeded view of the other half of the Square.

Gavin peers over my shoulder. "Um . . . I may be wrong, but that doesn't look like an evacuation tunnel."

I only turn to glare at him and slowly close the door, hoping the squeal of the hinges doesn't alert anyone to our presence.

"Now what?" I mumble, and take a closer study of the room.

There's a broken light in the far corner and it appears no one has come into this area in a long time. There's a thick layer of dust on the boxes and on the floor. We leave footprints in it as we make our way to the shadowed area. My prints are quite small compared to Gavin's. Then again, he's tall. Even in my boots, he's at least fifteen centimeters taller than me.

For lack of a better plan, I sit on the floor and start going through my backpack, hoping for a better plan to come to me. I'm not sure why Mother's map was wrong, but I have a bad feeling that Gavin was right about everything and I don't really want to think about that right now.

I'm pretty sure there's a first-aid kit in there, unless Mother's messed with that as well, and my hand is beginning to really hurt. Besides, there's a lot of blood, and if it drips, they might be able to follow us.

Gavin sits and watches silently as I try to fumble open the kit. He finally takes it from me. "Here, let me help you."

After opening the kit, he uses the antiseptic wipes to cleanse the wounds and sucks in a breath when he sees the large gash across the top of my hand.

His touch is gentle as he says, "You have to be more careful. Your hands are too pretty to be smashing into walls like that."

"I'll keep that in mind," I say, handing him the healing wand. "Just press the red button and hold it over the gash. It'll do the rest."

He studies it for a few seconds. "This is that thing you used on me, right?"

"Yes."

"How does it work?"

I watch his fingers as they hold the wand. They're long, like a musician's hand. "Do you play an instrument?" I ask.

He gives me a strange look. "No. Why?"

"Your fingers. They're long, and I thought . . ." I trail off and blush when he grins. "Never mind. We use the wand instead of sutures, which really only make things worse and invite infection. It super accelerates the body's own healing processes. It only works on small to moderate wounds, though. Anything severe would just retear, which is . . . not ideal."

He considers this, nods, then does as I ask. His face lights up as he watches the wound knit itself back together. "There. Good as new." Before he releases my hand, he presses a kiss to where the wound was, keeping his eyes on mine.

Tingles zip up my arm and I can only stare at him as he takes the antiseptic towel and gently wipes it across my face, cleaning the dirt and blood from it.

His eyes are sad, and cold air fills the space he vacates when he pulls away. It makes me shiver, so he pulls me closer again, chafing my arms with his hands. "It's really cold down here." I don't have anything to say to that, so I don't say anything; I just let him continue to rub my arms, enjoying the warmth of his skin on mine. He clears his throat a minute later. "Feel better?" he asks.

I nod. "Thanks," I say, and although I find now that I don't want to, I pull away. Our time here is short. It won't be long before Mother comes looking for us.

I dump out the contents of my bag and reorganize it, while taking an inventory.

There are two first-aid kits. The stupid map that didn't help at all. Some small, waterproof case that clinks when I move it. My extra set of clothes, which I set off to the side so I can change. And a few rations of food, which won't last very long, especially not with two of us eating it now.

Gavin stops me and gestures to the case. "What is that?"

"I don't know." I pull it out and flip open the flap, then pour the contents into my palm. It's a series of vials, each with different caps: a smaller version of the DNA testing kit and an envelope made from some kind of slick material.

Frowning, I tear open the envelope.

CONGRATULATIONS!
YOU'VE BEEN SELECTED AS MOTHER'S SPECIAL FEW.

Since you're reading this, chances are you're facing an emergency of a fairly large scale that you are unlikely to escape from alive. But, good news! You've been hand-selected by Mother to preserve your genetic makeup for a special new program that will allow Mother to use your DNA to repopulate Elysium in just this type of event.

Before you report to your assigned evacuation location, please follow all instructions as carefully as possible. Maintaining a quality sample is crucial, so don't rush! When you've collected all required samples, seal them in the waterproof container provided.

If you are currently undergoing a Surface Dweller attack, please make sure to place the sample in one of the safe, but accessible places noted on your map. In case of flooding, or other facility failure, place your sealed container as close as possible to one of the exterior walls of the facility and activate the flotation device at the top of the container. The device is only sufficient to bring your samples to the Surface, so please don't attempt to use it as a personal flotation device.

No matter what cataclysmic event you're facing, please be sure to double-check the seals on all of your samples and the tamper-proof container before reporting to your designated evacuation area. Thank you for your generosity. Long live Elysium!

I can only stare at the letter with my jaw hanging open. I have no idea whether to laugh or cry.

"Evie? What does it say?" Gavin asks and, wordlessly, I hand him the letter.

At first, he looks confused, then he starts laughing, and he looks over at me. "Is this serious?" he asks, but even I can tell he's being sarcastic. "She actually wants you to stop running for your life and take the time to not only fill these vials with God knows what, but then hide them safely? No wonder that map led us down here. She has no intention of letting you—or anyone—escape. And you want to stay here? Unbelievable."

I blink, looking again at the kit in my hands. In some small way, I almost admire Mother's efficiency. But that feeling is overwhelmed by shock and . . . revulsion. How could anyone be so calculating?

"Evie?" Gavin asks when I haven't moved for some time. I slowly raise my eyes to meet his. He seems angry as he takes the vials from my hands. "Want to know what you can do with these?"

"What?"

"This." He drops them onto the floor, then smashes them under the heel of his shoe. He smiles at me. "That. Now, is there anything in that pack that can actually help us?"

I shake my head. "Maybe the first-aid kits?"

He grimaces. "Let's hope we don't need those. So . . . what now?"

I don't know. The first order of business is to change in case we have to move quickly. Running in heels is not ideal. I've almost twisted my ankle twice in these things. Gavin is in a pair of jeans, but he's still wearing his dirty, torn T-shirt.

"Put this on." I toss him the extra shirt I'd grabbed for him. It will probably be too tight for him, but it's too large for me—I sometimes use it as a nightshirt—and I hope it'll be big enough to do for now. "We need to disappear, and the dirt and blood on your white shirt is like a beacon."

He removes his other shirt and pulls on the one I handed him. It's a little tight, but it looks really good on him, showing off the lines of his muscles. Somehow, it's almost more alluring than seeing his bare chest.

To distract myself, I start to change my own clothes. That's when I realize I need to strip in front of him. "Turn around," I say.

He spins in a circle, his arms at the ready to defend himself. "What? Why?" He frowns at me.

"I need to change. I can't keep running around in this silly dress and stiletto boots."

He laughs and covers his eyes with his hand, making a

show out of peering through the crack between his fingers. "It's not like you haven't already shown me almost everything in that cheap excuse for a dress already, you know."

"Keyword is almost." I wag my finger in a circle, and wait until he turns around with a sigh and a muttered "Harsh."

I wiggle out of the dress, then ball it up and toss it in the bag. Never know when it might come in handy. Then I pull on the black skirt and shirt. They're loose enough to be comfortable, yet tight enough not to be a hindrance if I need to fight. I pause in the middle of straightening my shirt.

Fight? And just what exactly do I think I could do in a fight? Garden them to death?

When I glance up to tell Gavin he can turn around, I see the mirror on the far wall. His eyes stare into mine perfectly. He has a grin on his face.

Who the hell puts a *mirror* in a supper club cellar?

"You could have told me there was a mirror there," I say, fighting my blush.

"What's the fun in that?" He turns to face me. "Besides, I didn't see anything. I closed my eyes. For most of it." He grins at me again.

I roll my eyes, but sit back on the floor, then pat the floor next to me. "We need to figure out our next move. We can't just stay here. Someone will come down eventually and then we're finished." I pause, because it looks like something is bothering him.

"What's up with the lighting here?" he asks.

"I'm sorry?"

"The lighting. Everywhere you've taken me is all dark and dingy. The only places with normal lights are the Palace Wing, the prison place, and the Square. It's like I'm in a creepy horror movie." He shudders.

I want to be angry he considers my home creepy, but I can't, because I'm terrified of his world, too, even if I am sort of curious. It's supposed to be hell on Earth, with demons running around killing one another. Huge animals that kill you in your sleep. Insects that burrow into your skin and use you as a host until they control your mind.

I push those thoughts aside. Gavin isn't the animal skin–wearing savage I'd expected of a Surface Dweller, and when he talked about his home in the cell, he made it sound not so bad. And it seems Mother has lied about more important things. It wouldn't surprise me if she'd lied about the Surface as well. What better way to make sure people didn't want to leave the relative safety of Elysium?

"Citizens tended to congregate where there's more light, and after the Enforcers . . . became necessary, the shadows served another purpose. Now Mother keeps the places where she doesn't really want people to gather the darkest, while the places where she wants people are the brightest."

"That, sadly, makes a lot of sense," he says, but then frowns. "Okay, so, Mother is the Governess? How'd that happen?"

"It's kind of a long story, but Mother had this city built during the War. She wanted to have a safe place away from all the bombings and fighting that happened on the Surface. She hired a few top scientists, and then recruited other people to live down here. But they had to fit the image of the ideal person."

"There is no such thing as the perfect person," he interrupts, then gives me his lopsided grin. "But you're pretty damned close."

I place my hands on my hips and let a small smile form. "According to Mother's scientific data, I *am* the perfect person." I tug on my hair. "Blond hair, blue eyes. Pale skin. The people she recruited even had to pass an intelligence and psychological test. She started the city with only fifty people. And we grew from there."

"You said *Mother* started this place?"

I nod.

"That's not possible," he says. "There is no way your mother started this facility." He crunches his face up in concentration.

"Sure it is. Why not?"

"The War was over fifty years ago, Evie. Your Mother doesn't look any older than thirty."

"Fifty years ago? That's not possible. I was one of the first children born here. The city is only *maybe* twenty years old. And Mother started this when she was in her early twenties. So, she's in her forties, at least."

"No, Evie, it can't be. There's no freakin' way. If she started this during the War, then it's over fifty years old. So, either she's lying about *when* she started it, or she's lying about *who* started it."

The silence drags out while I consider this information. If

he's telling the truth, then Mother's been lying to everyone for a long time. But how did she fool the people that have been here from the beginning?

Suddenly a speaker over our heads crackles to life and Mother's voice flows into the room, causing us both to tense as if our muscles are made of violin strings and someone is turning the pegs.

"Attention, Citizens of Elysium," she says. "We have an emergency."

Gavin and I exchange a look as a chill fills my body. She knows we're gone. I'd been hoping to have a course of action before this happened.

"The Surface Dweller has escaped our Detainment Center, and it appears that he has kidnapped the Daughter of the People. For your safety, and that of my daughter, please report any sightings to the nearest Guard or Enforcer, but do not approach them. I repeat, do not approach them. The Surface Dweller is possibly armed and definitely dangerous. Your cooperation is appreciated and will be rewarded."

She follows the announcement with a description of Gavin—paying special attention to mention his gray eyes and darker skin—and then repeats the announcement.

The blood freezes in my veins. There's no way we're going to be able to get around now without being seen. I'm too noticeable and so is Gavin. We won't last a minute out there.

Chapter Twelve

*Mother's word is law. Everyone must follow the law. If you do
not, then you are a traitor and will be treated as such.*
—Citizen's Social Code, Volume III

What do we do now?" Gavin asks. He's already standing. He's tensed as if to run, but I can only tell because the ropes of muscle stand out against his shirt. His eyes are calm and direct as they watch me.

I don't know, I want to scream, but only say, "We're going to have to find another escape tunnel. And we're going to need to get away from the Enforcers and the Guards."

"How long do we have here? It doesn't look like anyone's been down here in ages." He runs his finger along the box and holds it up to me, showing me the dust on the tip. "I doubt they'll come anytime soon."

"Mother gave me that map. She's going to know I used it. This is the first place they'll look. Maybe not here specifically, but one of the 'safe zones' marked on the map. We need to find somewhere safe where there aren't people and not on the escape map. The Residential Sector is probably our best bet. There are vacant quarters. We can find one and that'll give us at least a little while to plan."

He thinks for a minute, his eyes staring at the ceiling. He huffs out a breath and crosses his arms over his chest. "It'll have to do."

I kneel to draw in the dust along the floor. "Here, pay attention. In case we get separated, you need to know how to get there. I don't know how much of what Mother said she thinks is true, but on the off chance she honestly believes you kidnapped me . . . if we're caught, you'll be safer if I go back to them willingly." He watches my hand as it draws on the ground, but now his eyes jerk up to mine. He opens his mouth to object, but I keep going, pretending I don't see it. "You need to make sure to run as fast as you can into the shadows and to here." I mark an X where the entrance to the Sector is. "I'll meet you there when I can."

It's quiet while I draw the rest of the map of the Square. I can't trust the accuracy of the map Mother gave me, so I have to take the time to draw this one.

"It's important to stick to the shadows. Your eyes and skin will give you away. No matter what happens, you have to make sure to get to *here*. Do you understand?"

He doesn't say anything, and from the fact that his jaw is clenched and he won't look at me, I know he's angry with me. Hesitantly, and fighting the urge that wants me to not do it, I cup his cheek in my palm to try to get him to look at me. "Please. Promise me." I let my hand drop to my side. "Please. No matter what. If you get caught, we'll never get another chance to do this."

He sighs and then nods. "Fine," he says shortly. "But how long do I wait if you don't come?"

"Twenty-four hours. If I don't come for you, that means I'm physically unable to. Whether I've been confined, or Conditioned, or—"

"Killed."

My heart jumps into my throat, but my voice is devoid of emotion when I say, "Or she kills me for defying her. Yes. That's why it's important to memorize this map of the city. If for some reason we get separated and I don't meet you at the rendezvous point in twenty-four hours, you'll need to find another escape tunnel by yourself."

It's quiet again while he takes a few more minutes to memorize the layout of the city.

"I don't think that'll happen," I say when I'm sure he has the route locked in his memory, "but *an ounce of prevention is better than a pound of cure.*" I swipe a hand through the dust, erasing the map.

I gather my pack and sling it over my shoulder, then head to the side door. I hold my breath when I open the door and don't release it until I see there's no one around to hear the door's squeal. I gesture for Gavin to follow, then make a dash for the deep shadows along the wall.

If we can stay there, and as long as we can move silently,

we should be able to avoid detection. Unless we run into an Enforcer, which I pray we don't. When I feel a hand on my shoulder, I glance behind me and smile—Gavin hadn't made a noise.

Must be his hunter training. I have to admit I'm impressed.

We creep along the edge of the building slowly. Each step seems to take forever, but rushing headlong into anything without looking could be disastrous.

If I could have had time to plan this all out appropriately, I'm sure Gavin would be on his way home by now. But because I've had to wing it, we're stuck slinking in shadows and hoping for a miracle.

I'm so lost in my thoughts, I almost scream when Gavin squeezes hard on my shoulder. I turn to scowl at him, but he places a finger over my lips and tilts his head to our left. That's when I hear it: running footsteps. I halt, pushing myself as far against the wall as I can. He does the same and we both hold our breath as a group of Guards rush past. I hope the shadows are dark enough that we won't be seen. Or that the Guards will avoid looking too deeply into the shadows, which they should. No one wants to run into an Enforcer.

"A woman says she spotted them over by the fountain," one Guard is saying. "It's probably not them. If he managed to kidnap the Daughter right under Mother's nose, I don't think he's dumb enough to be out in the open after that announcement."

Gavin raises his eyebrows at me, while I stifle a laugh with my hand. When they pass, we move even quicker toward the Residential Sector.

Several times along the way we have to pause and wait for more Guards to pass by, but I don't notice a single Enforcer. Where are they? Mother wouldn't entrust something this important to the Guards alone.

Then, without warning, we lose the ability to use the shadows. We have to cross an alleyway that is brightly lit and there are dozens of Citizens around. If we take the chance and run for it, we'll be spotted. But the longer we wait, the more likely someone—probably an Enforcer—will find us. The thought causes a shiver to sputter up my spine.

I glance back at Gavin, who is studying the street as closely as I am. He looks down and a slow smile crosses his face. He quickly squats down and wiggles a loose brick from the wall. Then he wings it behind us and across the street into a store front, completely shattering the glass.

He pushes me forward, but my feet are already moving in a mad dash across the street and back into the shadows. Even though I hear shouting voices and running feet, I don't bother turning to look. I just keep going until we get to the corner we need to be at, an even darker alcove.

More Guards pass by our little street.

"Good thinking," I whisper to him, then I turn back to face the dead end.

I recognize it from where I stopped earlier on my way to

see Macie. That feeling of déjà vu hits me again, as does the elusive memory of an area that looks like an exact duplicate of Sector Two. Except the windows to the shops and restaurants are boarded up and the entire area has an abandoned feeling.

As the memory takes shape, I begin to understand. *"Oh,"* I say.

"What?" Gavin asks.

"I think . . . I think I might have a plan after all. There's something here. Behind this wall."

He looks at the wall with a skeptical expression. "You sure?"

"No, but I think so."

"We don't exactly have time to try this out just because you have a vague idea."

"We don't have time to *not* check this out. It's worth the risk. Trust me. Please." I look over my shoulder at him.

After a second, he nods. "I trust you."

Grateful for it, I furrow my brow as I try to remember and my thoughts get muddier and muddier. It's a place I knew of before going to the Palace, I'm sure of it. Somewhere I wasn't supposed to be. But I only get a headache for my trouble, a sharp, stabbing pain in my temple that causes me to gasp and clasp a hand to it.

"You okay?" Gavin touches a hand to my temple.

"Yeah. Fine." I run my fingers over every brick and groove while Gavin keeps watch. I don't know how he plans to protect me from the Guards or Enforcers without any weapons, but considering his strength, it wouldn't surprise me if he took them on barehanded . . . and won.

There has to be a way in. Some kind of latch. Mother wouldn't want to use something that had a key that could get lost, and a hand plate or key code would be too conspicuous.

If there's even anything there.

Finally my fingers catch on a little button that is barely visible. I press it, then there's a click and the wall moves, pouring out a cloud of dust through the tiny crack. The dust chokes me and I stifle the urge to cough and tug harder on the door. It swings completely open with a loud squeal.

Suddenly, I hear running feet coming toward us.

I quickly scoot through the opening and Gavin crawls in behind me before shutting the wall with a click.

The close call makes me giddy and I start giggling. Gavin gives me a strange look, but he, too, is laughing.

"That was close, huh?" he asks, his eyes already scanning our surroundings. He's frowning, but his eyes are alight with excitement.

"Yes." I glance around. The area is just as I remembered, very similar to what we just left. In fact, it's almost as if we've stepped through a mirror and come out in a reflection of our own world. It's an abandoned Sector. A thick coat of dust covers everything and is making breathing difficult, but otherwise it looks like the Square does every morning before anyone is awake.

"Wow. This place has got to be more than twenty years old, right? I mean it just feels old. Way old. Like it's been empty and abandoned for ages." Gavin does a quick whole-body shake, then pushes the hair that fell into his face back. "It's kinda eerie."

The strangest part is the lights are fully functional. It's lit up like a beacon. There are no shadows anywhere.

I rub my arms briskly. "I know. Okay, let's try to find an escape route. Let's look for a utility closet." I step forward, ready to walk the perimeter for a door, but he holds up a hand to stop me.

"Okay, I could be wrong, but this was a working Sector at some point, right?" he asks.

"Yes, it seems like it."

"Well, I'm thinking from the fact she gave you and probably everyone a fake escape map, and that letter made it sound like she didn't really care if people escaped or not, she probably wouldn't just have the escape door in plain sight, right? She'd probably have it hidden. Like this entire Sector."

I have to admit that he's probably right. "So, what then?"

He seems a little surprised I've asked him for advice, but says, "We should search the perimeter of this Sector for another of those catches like we used to get in here."

"Okay, good idea." I smile at him and he smiles back.

I lead the way to the perimeter. "It would be faster if we split up, but I don't think it's a good idea. We have no way of communicating with each other and you don't know the city. You could get lost or hurt and I'd never know it."

He puts a hand on my shoulder and squeezes. "We'll be fine," he says. "You just keep looking for that door and I'll cover your back."

For over an hour we go over the perimeter before I find a section of the wall that looks slightly different from the rest of it. I trail my fingers over the bricks looking for the catch.

"I found something," I breathe when my fingers find a smooth spot on the rough bricks.

When I press it, a section of the wall moves, but only slightly. Just enough for me to grab a corner and pull, but I can't budge it.

Gavin kneels next to me and places his hands over mine. Together we tug until a small section of the wall reveals a space only large enough to crawl through. I peer through and see what looks like a lab of some sort. Only tiny. It can't be any larger than five meters by five meters. And along one wall is a stockpile of weapons and ammunition.

I back out quickly. "That's definitely not our exit," I tell him.

Just then another ear-splitting screech sounds from the far side of the city, drowning out whatever it is he says.

The wall! I share a glance with Gavin.

Someone is coming.

I take a minute to study our surroundings. The only place to safely hide is this hidden room.

"We'll hide in here, but we left quite a large trail in the dust," I say. "We'll need to destroy part of it."

Gavin narrows his eyes. "Or create a false one."

Or two. "Take your shirt and drag it along the ground. Run as fast and quietly as you can to the corner and around it. Find a door or shop or something to lead the trail to, then run back here as quickly and quietly as you can."

He nods and takes off at a sprint, dragging his shirt behind him and destroying the footsteps he makes in the dust almost as soon as they appear. I take my pack and do the same in the opposite direction, going toward the entrance. Then I make an abrupt turn at one of the boarded-up restaurants and drag my bag inside and through the door. It won't trick them for long, but I hope it's long enough to buy us time. I run back through my cleared path and back to the small door.

It's only about two hundred meters around that corner, but my heart races as I run back, worrying Gavin won't have enough time to get there and back. He's quicker than I think, though, and he's already back when I get to the door. I crawl in beside him while he shuts the door behind me.

We both huddle by the door in order to hear the Guards. We try to monitor our breathing, but between the dash we made, and the nerves from waiting to see if our ruse worked, it's hard not to pant.

His hand trembles on my back. I shoot him a concerned look, but he shakes his head and holds a finger to his lips, warning me not to say anything yet.

We don't have to wait long for the Guards' voices to come to us. They're muffled and I have to strain to hear what they're saying.

"I didn't know this existed, did you?" a deeper voice asks.

"I think Mother said something about using this for the refugees from Three. . . . There's two trails."

Even though my heart trips again at the mention of Three, I'm able to count two heartbeats during the silence and I swallow hard. Gavin's hand clenches on my back. It sounds like they've stopped right in front of the door.

Please let them fall for the trick. Please. Please. Please.

"You go that way. I'll keep following this one."

"Sure, boss."

I wait until the sound of their footfalls trail off before taking the chance and leaning back against the wall.

Gavin leans forward to whisper in my ear. "Where did you go? I was worried they had found you."

"I created that second trail. It would seem kind of strange that a much thicker trail started right at the door, wouldn't it?"

"Smart thinking. Next time, warn me, okay?"

"Of course. Where did you lead them?"

"I found another service door, like the one I came in from. I thought it might be another exit, but it's just a closet."

I hear the Guards' footsteps returning and signal for Gavin to stop talking.

The Guards pause a few meters from where we are, probably where the trail splits.

"Didn't find them either?"

"No, the trail stops in a restaurant's cellar. You?"

"Ended at a storage closet. Nothing in there but service supplies."

"Mother can't be serious about moving the refugees here. It would take weeks to get this place cleaned up enough to be livable."

Their voices trail off as they walk back the way they came. Gavin stands and holds his hand out to me. "Now what?"

"Now we wait and see if it's a trap," I say, letting him pull me to my feet as I take a closer look at the room we're in.

"What did they mean about refugees?"

"Oh. Sector Three"—there's that stupid flutter again—"has a leak or something. They're probably just taking precautions in case it gets worse."

He wanders around the small room while I go to the one and only lab table. I trail my hand over the dusty microscope.

"Why are there so many weapons here?"

"I don't know. Only Guards and Enforcers are supposed to have weapons."

"Is this where Mother keeps them, maybe?"

I look at the stack again. They're piled neatly by type, but they're all dusty and don't look like they've been handled in years.

"I don't think so. Mother has a strict policy on keeping weapons in top condition. I doubt she'd ever let them get this dirty."

He goes over and kneels in front of the stacks, while I go

to the desk to see if there's anything there that might suggest an escape route. I don't think I'll find anything, but it never hurts to look.

The top is empty, but the rest of the drawers are filled with old-fashioned writing utensils. There's even some kind of book in the top right drawer. "Eli" is engraved on the gold plate located on the cover. The leather binding creaks as I open it, the paper quietly crinkling with each page turn. "Look what I found."

"What is it?" Gavin says, coming to stand behind me.

I flip through the book and scan the pages for relevant information. "It looks like a journal of some sort."

Gavin quietly reads over my shoulder, but I'm reading so fast he can't keep up and just rests his chin on me instead. His breath warms my neck, which makes my own breath catch. At first I'm not sure if it's from the fact that he shouldn't be touching me, but then I realize I'm enjoying it, even though I shouldn't be.

It's distracting, but I don't want him to move, so I make myself concentrate on the letters in front of me and not on the tingles running from my shoulder, where his chin rests, to my heart.

At first it's just a bunch of entries about the inventions the writer—Eli?—came up with and how. Then there are a few entries about the epidemic that killed half the Citizens. I remember that from my classes about the importance of hygiene and making my monthly medical appointments.

Then there are a few entries about how he was trying to

convince someone named Abby—Mother?—to hire someone from the Surface to develop a device to prevent another outbreak.

02.08.30–1000

It seems that Abby has taken my advice and hired an expert from the Surface named Ms. Lenore Allen. She is to arrive this evening. I know Abby isn't happy about it with her distrust of all Surface Dwellers—but even she can see the logic of it after that epidemic. We need something to protect what's left of our population. Abby may be young, but she's smart. Her father's daughter.

02.08.30–2345

I've met with the engineer from the Surface. Lenore's qualifications are beyond reproach and I dare say perfect for this task. Lenore's ideas are simply fantastic. Turning the Surface military tech into something to save people instead of harm them? Brilliant, I say! Abby has asked that I work with Lenore myself (and to keep an eye on her—she still doesn't trust Lenore), and it's my privilege to do so. I'm certain we will work well together and I find myself excited to be working alongside such a brilliant woman.

There are a few more entries here about how wonderful this Lenore—or Nora, as he began to call her—is and how well they're working together. Then there's more entries detailing their plans for the Surface technology. I don't understand most of it, to be honest. There is a complete log of the sub-jects they used for testing—the control groups, as well as those infected with viruses or bacteria. I can't believe they'd injected innocent people with viruses that could very well have been a death sentence.

But then there's a breakthrough apparently.

12.15.31–1837

We've done it! Nora and I have done it! The nanobots are working perfectly. All infected subjects' blood work shows an immunity to previously deadly strains of bacteria and virus. There also appears to be no ill effect, aside from the initial reaction to the injection of the nanobots. It is noth-ing short of miraculous. Abby is still suspicious of the tech-nology, since it derives from Surface technologies, but I'm convinced that they're ready for full deployment to the pop-ulation. And, to prove I'm in earnest, I've allowed Nora to inject me with the bots, and I've injected Nora. Now I'm off for a celebratory dinner with the lovely Nora.

I wonder if she likes roses.

The next entries explain exactly *how* Eli and Nora cele-brated. For the sake of their privacy, I skim over the details, only making note that they got caught by this Abby person and how she then instituted a new law that made Eli and Nora want to leave.

But then an entry catches my attention and I slow down to read it carefully.

Abby has officially leaped off the deep end. I can't believe I didn't see her madness before now. Of course, in hindsight, it all makes sense. How foolish I was! At least now Nora is safe. I forced her back to the Surface. But I came back. Seeing how Abby used our nanobots against me, I have no doubts she wouldn't hesitate to use them against the Citizens. I could never live with myself if I left them helpless. A few trusted friends and I have developed a plan to wrest control of the city from Abby. My God, she's demanding everyone call her Mother now. She's drunk with power.

Our first step is to start making weapons, because I know she won't go without a fight, but in order to make them without Abby knowing, we'll have to split the manufacture of the weapons between several people. On top of that, there should be several teams, so if one team is discovered we still have others for backup. And each team will not know anything of the others. Location, team members, etc. Even I won't know the details. In the meantime, I'll start looking for a way to deactivate the nanos, so they can't be used against us.

There are more detailed entries about what weapons he himself was making and how he'd discovered some kind of electromagnetic field or EMF around the submarine bay and how he was worried what it would do to the nanos. Because of this, he started researching possible ways to counteract any of the effects it might have and leaving more and

more of the revolution planning to his closest friend . . .
Dr. Friar.

5.12.32–2256
All is lost. There is a traitor in our midst and we've already lost two of our teams. The members—all of them—have simply disappeared, but I have no doubts that they've met their final resting place at the bottom of the sea. I will lose no more lives over this and have given the order to abort the plan and to commence the immediate evacuation of the teams and anyone else who wants to leave. I have a feeling I know who betrayed us and I can only be grateful that at this point none of the remaining teams know the evacuation plans of the others. And that I know nothing of the others' plans, because I have no doubt that Abby knows of my plans and will stop at nothing to prevent my escape. In the case that none of us make it, I'm leaving this journal in my secret office in the hopes that someday someone will see it and learn what's really going on here. Even my betrayer doesn't know about my office here. And maybe someone will succeed where I have failed.

"Well," I say finally, "apparently there was a rebellion gone wrong and the Citizens in this Sector had to abort rather quickly and escape the city."

"That's why there are so many weapons here."

I nod. "That's what it appears to be."

"So, what did they use to escape?"

"It's not very clear. Actually, everyone had a different escape plan and no one knew what the other was, but he used the submarines. They're in Sector Three." My heart does a little somersault and I press a hand to it, unsure why the thought of going there makes me giddy. "Mother keeps them hidden away." But I spin the journal around to show Gavin what I've just found: a map. Another present from Eli to whomever finds the journal. I tap my hand on the book. "And we're going to go find them and get you on one."

Chapter Thirteen

Failure to attend bi-yearly health exams can result in acciden-
tal erasure from the system, which could cause the cameras and
turrets to mistake you for a Surface Dweller.

—SIGN IN THE MEDICAL SECTOR WAITING AREA

Subs? Are you serious? That's great. So, what's the plan?"
He looks as happy as a child with spare credits in the candy
store. It surprises me that he isn't bopping up and down on
his toes and clapping his hands. Then he stops and his eyes
meet mine. "You said *I'm* going to use one. You're still not
planning on leaving with me." It's not a question.

"No. My life is here, Gavin."

"Do you still really believe she thinks you have nothing
to do with this? She's not stupid, Evie, and neither are you.
She knows you're behind this and she's never going to let
you get away with it. Do you really want to lose all your
memories? Again?"

I look down at the ground. He's right, and I know it. But

if he's gone, is there any reason to remember this? Better question: if he's gone, will I *want* to remember this? "We'll figure it out when we get there," I say after a moment. I can't tell him what I'm thinking; there's no way he'd understand.

I can feel his gaze on me, but don't look at him. "Yes, I suppose we will." He sounds tense, but he drops it.

I look down at the map again. "Well, we have to get to the other side of the city. It's in Sector Three. Looks like we're going to have to take the Tube after all. It's the only way to get there. That's going to be fun." I roll my eyes, feeling a little proud of myself for the unladylike gesture. Not to mention the sarcasm. "I'm not even sure how we're going to get *to* it, let alone get into it and to Sector Three without someone noticing us."

"The Tube?"

"It's like a"—what do they call them?—"a subway? Train? Anyway, it goes through a tube from here to Sector Three."

He nods his head and points back at the book still in my lap. "Maybe there's something in the journal. How was he going to do it?"

I read quickly through the entries again, but the only thing I can get out of it is he was in such a hurry, he was just hoping no one—including Mother—would notice a whole Sector fleeing at the same time, but didn't hold out much hope for that.

I have to wonder if his plan worked, though. Maybe they did get away with leaving all at once—it's not like anyone really looks different. It's not as if *we* really look different. I'll fit in easily enough, especially if I dress exactly like the others. It's just a matter of finding a change of clothes.

The problem will be Gavin. His hair is an almost perfect match, even if it's a bit dark and dirty. His eyes and skin are the catch.

"We're in trouble. Your skin is too dark and your eyes are all wrong. There's nothing we can do to hide them," I say, my voice thick with frustration.

He shrugs, and I fight the urge to kick him. He's not taking this seriously.

"My eyes are gray. It's not that easy to tell blue from gray from a distance in sunlight, let alone the shadows in this place. It'll be all right."

I tilt my head to the side as I stare at him. Actually, he's got a point. If he keeps his eyes averted, we cover most of his skin and we don't get too close to people, we should be fine.

Now I just have to get better fitting clothes for him. Preferably something not all ripped and dirty.

He looks down at himself the more I continue to stare. "What's wrong?"

"We need to get you cleaned up and dressed."

"How are we going to do that?"

"This is a duplicate of Sector Two, which means there should be apartments on the other side of the Square. Since the lights work, let's try to get into one and find out if the water works, too."

He turns toward the weapons. "We should probably take

some of these, too. I'm pretty sure I don't want to take the chance of running into an Enforcer without something to defend myself."

"Good idea."

I bend down over the pile of weapons and look closely at them. While they're covered in dust, they appear to be in working order and fully intact. I pull out two of each weapon and lay them across the ground at our feet, checking them for damage as I go.

"These will have to do. Take one of each." I gesture to the four guns.

"What are they?" he asks, and lifts one of the rifles, studying it closely. He holds it gently, cradling it in his arms. Not in fear, but in love. It's strange, but Mother did say Surface Dweller men were fond of their weapons. I guess she was right.

"That's an M50 Reising. It's a submachine gun, but it was actually designed as a compact semi-automatic carbine that is also capable of fully automatic fire. It has an automatic fire rate of four hundred fifty to six hundred rounds per minute." He gapes at me. I hand him a small handgun. "That last one is a bit old-fashioned. You'll probably get more use out of this. It's a plasma pistol. It heats up the air to a comfy eight-hundred-and-fifteen degrees Celsius, creating a ball of plasma, which it shoots in any direction you want, effectively ending the life of almost anything it comes into contact with."

He stares at it. "I guess I shouldn't put this in my pants then."

I can't help but laugh at his expression. It's a cross between horror and fascination.

"Relax. It will only go off if you press the trigger and the safety in the back here. It's not even loaded right now. You need the silver canisters to charge it. Don't worry," I say. "You'll have more problems with the Reising going off accidentally than you will the pistol."

He doesn't seem so sure, but he carefully places it in his pocket. Then he pulls the strap of the Reising over his shoulder, obviously a lot more comfortable with that than the pistol. I load the two backpacks I found in the metal cabinet with ammo, grenades, and mines.

I split them evenly, and then heft the first bag and sling it over my other bag.

Gavin does the same, grunting a little. He turns to me. "These are heavy. How the hell did you lift them?"

"This is nothing. Can't weigh more than a few kilos, I'm sure. I saw you move those boxes; you should have no problems lifting it."

"How do you know all this?" he asks, gesturing to his Reising. "The guns?

"I—" I stare at him, then the gun in his hands. "I don't know. I guess it's another thing I have to figure out what it means." Not again. I rub my fingers over the pendant, hoping for even just a spark of a memory.

"Why are you doing that?" he asks, staring at my pendant.

"I don't remember where I got this," I say softly. From my

memory with the perfume, I have an idea. But the actual memory itself, right now, is lost. I run my fingers over it, then take it back and curl my hand around it, letting the chain dangle from between my fingers. "But sometimes, when I realize I'm forgetting things, I can start getting some of the memories back, if I concentrate on this long enough. Certain scents are the same way. Not all memories. Maybe not even most. But I have to hope it'll be enough and one day, I'll remember everything."

I straighten my shoulders and lift my chin, waiting for the look, but instead he wraps his hands around mine over the pendant. "And I'll do whatever I can to help you remember who you are."

A few minutes later, we walk into the Residential area of this abandoned Sector. The elevator still works, so we close the gate and push the button for the topmost floor. At first it does nothing, but then with a jerk it rushes up. At the top floor we let ourselves into one of the apartments farthest from the elevators. None of the doors are locked and again I wonder if it's because Mother plans on filling this place with people from Three.

These apartments are exactly like the ones that are in Sector Two. It amazes me how well they've held up over the years. The only damage is a blanket of dust and a few spider webs. The couch is in perfect shape, as is the wood on the end tables and the flat screen television in the corner. It looks so strange sitting where the holo-projector should be. I want to turn it on, to see if it's one of those 3-D ones that were so popular before the holos, but there's no time.

I show Gavin to the bathroom, which is all gray granite, and cross my fingers when I twist the handle of the shower. After a few long seconds where nothing happens, water rushes out and pounds against the granite of the shower stall. There isn't any soap or shampoo, and the water is barely above freezing, but he'll be able to rinse off all the dirt at least.

I hear Gavin's cursing as he steps under the spray and can't help but laugh.

While he showers, I go through the wardrobe in the sleeping quarters to find suitable clothes for him and myself. Looking like me isn't going to help me anymore. Neither is looking like the Daughter of the People.

I'm in luck. It looks like a family lived here. Or at least a Couple. There is a full selection of clothes that should fit Gavin. I pull out a pair of slate gray slacks, a white button-up shirt, and a tie that matches the slacks. They should cover his skin nicely.

Then I slip into a summer dress. It's a little short, but other than that it fits like it was made for me. It's also made from cotton, so I won't stick out as much as if I were wearing my silk dress.

I find a pair of black leather sandal wedges that I can run in if I need to, then I gather up Gavin's clothes and step into the bathroom to set them on the counter for him.

In a classic case of worst possible timing, he steps out of

the shower just as I look up from the clothes. My jaw drops and I have to force myself to shut it. I can't help it—my eyes travel the whole lovely way from his muscled shoulders to his stomach and back up again. Water slides gloriously over every muscle, causing them to glisten in the lights.

I'm barely aware that I'm staring until he says, "Enjoying the view?"

Heat rushes into me and I blush from the tips of my toes to the roots of my hair. I quickly avert my gaze to the wall behind him. "I'm so sorry. I just meant to drop off your clothes for you. I, uh, I'll see you . . . out there . . . when you're finished."

I rush out the door on shaky legs. The minute I hit the living room, I lower myself to the couch and stare off into space.

Oh, Mother. My mind keeps replaying what I just saw. Wavy, golden hair. Thick muscular chest, hard, toned abs. Bronzed skin. And . . . I shake my head. *That* is not something I should be thinking about.

I fan a hand in front of my face. It feels hot, like someone has raised the temperature a good twenty degrees.

I pick up the journal to try to read it while I wait, but I can't concentrate. The only thing I can think of is Gavin.

He steps into the doorway between the living room and bedroom. I stand up quickly, embarrassed to be caught thinking about him, and the journal drops to the floor with a thud.

He gives me a look, then holds out the tie. "I'm not wearing this," he says, as if daring me to argue.

He looks even better wearing the clothes I gave him. I can't help myself. I find my legs carrying me across the floor to him.

I'm not even sure what I'm doing. *Why* I'm doing it. But I *want* to, *need* to.

I push myself up onto my tiptoes and press my lips against his. Caught off guard, he stumbles backward, but he recovers quickly.

I wind my arms around his neck and he places his hands on my hips and pulls me closer. My heart pounds so hard all I can hear is the whoosh of blood in my ears and the gasping of our breaths colliding.

The hallway was so dark, I couldn't even see Timothy, but I knew he was there. I heard the uneven gasps of his breath and felt them against my face. His hands were still on my cheeks.

"Are you going to tell her?" he asked.

"First thing in the morning," I replied, feeling the familiar tickle in my stomach.

"You won't forget?" he teased. Then before I could reply he kissed me again, pressing me against the wall behind me. The concrete was cold against my skin, and I pressed harder into the warmth of his body.

I closed my eyes. Cold air rushed in between us and I opened them only to see we were in Mother's parlor. Timothy stood in front, between two Guards. His eyes blackened and blood running from his broken nose.

Two bullets ripped into his chest, hitting both lungs. He collapsed to his knees as the Enforcer that shot him stepped back into the darkness. But just before she did, she looked up at me and I found myself staring into my own face.

I yank away and clap my hands over my mouth trying to shove my heart back where it belongs. It wasn't real. I don't know anyone named Timothy, and I didn't kill him.

Gavin steps away, gasping. "I-I'm sorry. Are you all right?"

I back away and turn around, so he can't see the tears trying to force their way to the surface. I swallow them and hug myself until I'm sure my chattering teeth won't come back.

"Evie?" He places a hand on my shoulder.

I yank away and stride to the door. "The tie is unnecessary. You can leave it."

He looks at me a moment, then finishes dressing.

Minutes later we're cautiously pulling the door to the rest of the city open again.

The "memory" replays in my head, but I force it away. I can't try to remember it now. I need to focus on not getting us killed.

The store with the window Gavin broke is blocked off and Guards linger around it. We stick to the shadows, but they don't even glance in our direction. The crowd thickens the closer we get to the Square, but we're able to move through the Bazaar and across the Square with minimal fuss since no one likes looking in the shadows and we aren't running into Enforcers.

The only problem is Gavin is gawking again. I can't blame him for gaping at the people spinning around wearing their colorful costumes. Mother wanted it to be like some huge party the Surface Dwellers had before the War. Mardi Gras, I think she called it. And it's very pretty and colorful.

As we near the Tube station that will take us to Sector Three, I notice the crowd has thinned again. Everyone is at Festival. No one is using the trains and I thank whoever is looking out for me, because I don't have to worry about tipping someone off when we step out of the shadows to cross to the Tube.

I sigh a breath of relief, then pause. I hear a hissing sound and the grinding of gears.

I look around, trying to figure out why I recognize the sound and why it makes my blood run cold. Suddenly my right shoulder is on fire. I slap a hand to it, feeling something wet, warm, and sticky. I glance over and see my hand covered in blood, and more is pouring over my fingers. When I pull my hand away, there's a hole in my dress, right in the center of the bloodstain. A hole that can mean only one thing.

I've been shot.

Chapter Fourteen

Due to her perfect genetics, Evelyn Winters has been chosen as my daughter. However, Evelyn is not just my daughter: She is everyone's daughter. The Daughter of the People. She loves you as I do and you are to love her in return. Anything less will not be tolerated.

—Mother, from Evelyn's debut speech

Screams fill the air as the turret claims victim after victim. I fall to the ground, pulling Gavin with me. His eyes are as round as saucers when he sees the blood soaking my dress.

He stands, trying to remove the backpack, but I yank him back down to the ground.

"Stay down," I hiss. "Do you *want* the turret to see you?"

"See me?" he whispers back, but at least he's lying on the ground. Then he blinks. "A *turret* hit you?"

"Yes. What do you think hit me?"

He lifts his eyes toward the ceiling before he closes them. "Well, what do we do? We can't just lie on the ground until the Guards come."

"No, we can't. But they won't come until the turret stops. Then they'll collect the bodies and move on. So we'll just have to move quickly when it stops." I press a hand to the wound, wincing when the pressure brings tears to my eyes. That can't be a good thing.

"How long will that be?" He's staring at my blood-covered hand now and his voice wavers slightly. "You'll bleed to death if we wait too long."

"Stop it!" My voice is rougher than I intend from the effort it's taking to stop my teeth from chattering. Being shot hurts a lot more than I thought it would. Like liquid fire covering my shoulder. "It's just a small wound. Probably a through-and-through. It didn't hit any major arteries or I'd be bleeding a lot more." I glance around and notice the turret has claimed only four people. Three are moving around and moaning. One isn't. Everyone else has disappeared. The turret pulls back into the ceiling with a hiss, its job done. "Move! Now! Get in the shadows."

To his credit, Gavin bolts to the shadows without question. I follow closely at his heels. "We have to keep moving. The Guards will come with Enforcers soon," I say, and push him in the direction of the Tube station, which is just a few meters away and completely empty. We'll have to wait to use it until the Guards and Enforcers leave, but we should be safe. It'll give me time to assess the wound and bandage it properly.

Unfortunately when I fell, I got all turned around and we

ran to the wrong side of the terminal. In order to get to the train, we'll have to cross back over to the other side.

I listen for a second and then, when I don't hear anything, tug on Gavin's arm and dash across the terminal. He follows without hesitation. But the turret must still be malfunctioning, because the minute it senses us, it drops from the ceiling again and starts shooting. We both drop to the ground immediately.

"What the hell is going on?" Gavin demands.

"I think it's malfunctioning. That happens sometimes. That's why there aren't any in the Palace Wing except in that one alcove."

"Malfunctioning? And you just accept it?"

"I don't really have much of a choice," I spit out. "What do you want me to do? Go up there and fix it? Do you have a wrench on you? Because I don't."

"That's not what I meant," he mumbles.

The turret disappears again and I make another try for the wall, but since we're the only ones in the area, it drops down again and so do I, hitting my shoulder against the concrete. I cry out and Gavin reaches out for me.

"We'll have to crawl to the other side," I say, gasping for breath and trying to see past the stars swimming in front of my eyes.

He nods, but his eyes are on my shoulder. "Can you do that?"

"Of course. It's nothing."

He doesn't look convinced, but doesn't say anything and slithers forward, pulling with his arms and pushing with his legs.

I have no idea if my arm can do anything other than lay there, but I refuse to be a hindrance to him. I will make it to the other side by myself.

My arm, though, has other plans and refuses to cooperate. The slap of footsteps echoing off the walls warns me the Guards are on their way and close. We have to hurry. Finally, with a glance at the turret, Gavin slides his arms around me, then quickly stands, pulling me with him. The turret drops again, but he's dashing into the shadows next to the abandoned ticket booth before it can do more than hiss. With a quick glance into the booth, Gavin carries me into it and under the control desk.

It's the perfect hiding place. The Enforcers and Guards won't come in here because there are no bullet holes in the glass, therefore a waste of time to search for victims beyond a cursory look through the windows, and the attendants won't return until the Guards give the all clear.

I probe the wound to see if there's a bullet still lodged there, but it only makes me dizzy and nauseated.

Gavin pulls a first-aid kit from the bag, but I shake my head. "No," I gasp out. "Get the one on the wall there. We don't want to use our supplies unless we have no choice." I whisper more from pain than necessity.

He nods, then quickly and quietly removes the one from

the wall. He settles himself next to me and pulls things from it. "I-I'm not sure if I remember how to use that wand thing."

"I'll talk you through it, but first you need to check to see if the bullet is still there."

He raises startled eyes to mine. "What?"

"Please. If it's still there, we'll need to remove it." He swallows and he looks a little pale, even in the dark. "What's the matter? Afraid of a little bullet? Does someone else have to clean up for you after you kill an animal?"

"That's different," he says, not looking at me.

"Not really," I say with a shrug, and then hiss when the movement causes pain to scream through my shoulder.

Gavin's eyes meet mine and there's something undecipherable in them. "I don't want to hurt you."

My stomach twists. "Well, that's too bad," I say. "It's going to hurt. There's nothing either of us can do about it, so I need you to just do it." He only sits there, watching me. Knowing what I have to do to convince him, I lift my hand to his cheek. "Please," I say.

He sets his jaw, then presses me against the wall and uses the antiseptic wipes to clean his fingers. "I'll apologize ahead of time." Then his fingers are probing the wound and I grit my teeth to prevent myself from crying out.

My other hand claws at the concrete floor in an attempt to curb the dizziness from the black-and-red spots flashing in my eyes. Even my toes curl in my shoes. Anything to keep myself from making this harder on him than it is already. Several times, I have to fight the urge to beg him to stop. I asked him to do this. He needs to do it.

"Tell me about you," I say through gritted teeth.

"Huh?"

"Please. I need to take my mind off this. Tell me about yourself."

"Um, okay. Well, like I said, I'm the middle child, which sucks, let me tell you."

"Sucks?" I ask.

Gavin lets out a strained chuckle. "I don't like it."

"Why?"

"Well, you're always getting blamed for everything. And you're never old enough for some things, and old enough to know better for other things. It's the paradox of all middle children."

I wince and he starts talking really fast. He likes to play something called baseball. He also likes to surf, which apparently requires obscene amounts of time floating over the waves on wood. His father taught him to fish, and his grandfather taught him to hunt, but they both died when he was young. And he still misses them. He never met his grandmother; she died a few months after his mom was born.

His mother taught him to cook and he makes a "mean" steak. Whatever that means. He swears it'll make even my vegetarian tongue tremble in delight.

He talks about how annoying his sister is now that she's getting married, constantly vacillating between tears and screaming. And that his brother is a pain to take hunting, because he's still really young—not even ten—and never shuts up, which is why he'd been hunting with the friend the turret killed. Because he'd wanted to have some peace and quiet and Con, the boy, was the quietest in their village.

We're both quiet when we realize how close he could've been to losing his brother, instead of some boy he'd barely known.

He pushes me gently forward and probes the wound in the back, before letting me rest against the wall again. "There isn't a bullet. Or any fragments. It went through, like you said."

I swallow the lump in my throat. "Good. Then it just needs to be cleaned and bandaged. The wand won't work. It's too deep a wound."

"Are you sure? We don't want it to keep bleeding. Isn't it better to at least try to close it and hope for the best?"

"No. Not unless we absolutely have to. Otherwise I'll just end up tearing it and making things worse. The chemical hemostat will have to do." I gesture to a small square silver package in the kit. "Just push a sponge into both sides of the wound. It'll stop the flow of blood and prevent infection."

Gavin tears open the package and carefully pushes a sponge into the wounds. Tears sting my eyes, and I can't control the wobble when my head spins again.

"Are you all right?" he asks.

"Yes. The chemical burns. It'll pass." I lean against the back wall and pray for that to happen soon.

"Are you sure? You look like you're going to faint."

"Just clean the wound and bandage it. We need to be able

to move quickly if we have to and I don't want to be in the middle of you fixing me." I know I'm not being very nice and I hate that, but apparently manners don't come easily to me when my skin is melting off my shoulder.

He opens his mouth and I think he's going to say something about my attitude, but then he closes his mouth and firms it into a straight line. He carefully cleans the wound and then covers it with a special bandage that won't stick to the wound and wraps my entire shoulder in gauze.

So much for not sticking out, I think. Though I appreciate that I don't have to explain how to clean and dress wounds. Must be his hunter training. I suppose accidents happen and he'd have to know the basics.

"There's a pressure syringe in there and a purple vial. Just attach the vial to the syringe and press it against my skin."

"What is it?" he asks, but does as I ask.

"It's a mild pain reliever. Nothing that will impair me, don't worry. It will be enough to take the edge off." I hope.

Gavin injects me, then packs everything nicely back into the kit. "Thank you," I say, realizing I haven't said it yet. I've only bossed him around.

He smiles and, after a short hesitation, presses a gentle kiss to my lips. I hold my breath, panic pinching my throat closed. I mentally shake my head when he settles next to my left side. What's wrong with me? I'm trying to help a Surface Dweller escape Mother. That's worse than a kiss.

"It's not a problem," he says, pulling me out of my thoughts. "It would kinda suck if my girlfriend died before I could introduce her to my mom, you know." He watches me out of the corner of his eye.

I blush, and tingles of pleasure bloom all over as I duck my head, hiding my face from view with my hair. I like the sound of that. Even if it was only meant in jest. "My girlfriend." It has a nice ring to it.

While I wait for the medication to kick in, I debate for a minute or two with myself, then nestle in next to Gavin. He winds his arm around my waist and pulls me closer when I start shivering. At first I stiffen at his touch, but then I relax into him. Just having him hold me makes me feel a little better.

My body is going into shock, but the injection should take care of that. Unfortunately, it can take up to twenty minutes, but at least there will be some kind of relief coming.

"So, how about explaining about that turret thing while we're waiting? How do you know it was malfunctioning?" He takes my head and pushes it down so it's resting on his shoulder.

I adjust so I'm a tiny bit more comfortable, but keep my head on his shoulder. It feels too good to move. "I don't. Not for sure. But it happens often enough there's a good chance that's the problem. For some reason, the turrets' sensors malfunction. No one is sure why or what causes it. Mother has them taken offline until they're fixed, but it's almost impossible to anticipate the malfunction."

"Don't they get maintenance?"

"Yes. Once a month, and a thorough tune-up twice a year,

but it doesn't seem to matter. That's why Mother had them removed from the Palace Wing. She didn't want one going off accidentally and killing us."

"That's really kind of her." His voice drips with sarcasm.

"I asked her about removing the turrets from the rest of the facility and she did remove some, but not all of them. They are there to protect the Citizens from Surface Dwellers."

"Like me?" Gavin asks, moving his gaze back to me.

"Yes, but you're in the system. Macie helped me get you in there. That's why I used the coupling excuse. So I could get your DNA and have it entered into the system."

He runs his fingers down my arm and then interlaces them with mine. "Why did it leave us alone when we dropped to the ground?"

I stare at our conjoined hands. I have to force myself not to pull away. His skin is golden next to the paleness of mine. I half expect him to start glowing. "It works by motion," I say. "So it doesn't waste bullets on a dead body. The minute the targets drop to the ground, it's supposed to stop firing. Since most people panic and flee when they're fired on, it works well."

Gavin's grip tightens around my hand, grinding the bones against one another. I hiss and he lets up. "Sorry," he mumbles. "So, because you knew it would stop shooting at us when we dropped to the ground, we were able to beat it?"

"Exactly. And now all we have to do is wait out the Guards' investigation, then the turret will be taken offline, and Citizens will start returning to this area. Then we can be on our way. Simple."

He caresses the side of my hand with his thumb. It feels nice, but I have a feeling he doesn't even realize he's doing it; while it's all I can focus on.

"How do we know that another turret won't malfunction?"

And now we get to the crux of our situation.

"We don't. We'll just have to make sure we're careful and aware of our surroundings at all times. We'll watch for more malfunctions."

"How do we do that?"

"The turrets in the common areas are in the ceilings. You can tell where they are by their sensors, which hang down slightly from the ceiling on black posts. We'll just make sure to watch them carefully. Not to mention you should be able to hear a hissing sound."

"And if we see or hear a turret, we drop to the ground."

"Or we get out of sensor range, which will allow us to keep moving."

Gavin's silent, and I start to get drowsy as the minutes drag on.

He startles me when he finally speaks. "What's up with that sign on the other side of this booth? Also? Why is there a booth? It's not like you need tickets or something. Do you?"

I laugh. "No. It prevents unauthorized travel between Sectors Two and Three." I pause, trying to remember what sign he's talking about. "The 'Caution: Stay clear of tracks. Strong magnetic fields in use, which may affect the operation of your nanobots' sign?" When he nods, I say, "All Citizens have nanobots—little microscopic robots—in our bodies to prevent pressure sickness." At least, that's what I thought they were they for, but now the journal has me questioning even that.

"Pressure sickness?" he asks.

"There's so much pressure at this depth, gases would eventually build up in our blood," I explain. "The nanobots make sure to clean out the excess so we don't get sick. They actually accelerate healing, too. They're pretty amazing. You'd get them, too, if you stayed."

"So how come I'm not getting sick down here?" he asks.

"It takes a long time, and you're more at risk if you go back to lower pressures quickly."

"The bends," he says.

"Yes."

The Guards' voices grow closer, which means they're nearly finished. The turret has been taken offline if they're creeping into sensor range. They'll just make sure there aren't any more dead bodies over here, and will soon move on.

I place my finger over my lips and gesture to the windows. Gavin nods and we both make sure we're in the shadows of the desk and not visible from the windows.

"All clear over here," a Guard calls. It sounds like his voice is just on the other side of the glass.

A young female voice from slightly farther away calls, "No sign of the renegades?"

"No, sir," the first Guard responds, confirming my thought that the girl is an Enforcer.

"Very well. Go back and attend to the wounded."

The station is quiet. I wonder if it's okay to take a peek and see if everyone is gone. However, before I can, I hear Mother's voice. "Did you locate my daughter?"

At first I start, because I think she must have joined them, but the voice is tinny and I realize it's just her holo. I let out the breath I was holding.

"No, milady," the Enforcer states. "The turret malfunctioned."

Mother makes a noise of disgust. "This wasn't a malfunction, you idiot."

Gavin and I exchange a wide-eyed look.

"Milady?"

"I removed their DNA from the computer. The camera caught them in the Square. If this turret went off, it was because it didn't register their DNA."

Chapter Fifteen

*Conditioning is an important part of your daughter's training.
But there is no need to fear. All the Conditioning takes place
while she's asleep. She will feel nothing other than a quick sting
of the needle filled with "happy juice" that will ensure the perfect atmosphere for Conditioning.*

—EXCERPT FROM *So Your Daughter Has Been Chosen
TO Be an Enforcer. Congratulations!* PAMPHLET

Of course it wasn't a failure. Were they ever? Probably not.
The computer was programmed to locate by DNA. All they
had to do was delete the person from the computer, so it
would think they were Surface Dwellers and open fire.

That was exactly why Mother wasn't afraid to go down
to the Detainment Center to speak with Gavin. She *knew*
they wouldn't go off.

Gavin and I wait for them to finish their conversation,
hoping Mother will drop something else important, but she
doesn't, and I have to wonder if she knows I'm nearby and

wanted me to hear that I'd been removed from the computer. I pray they don't get smart and decide to check the booth. They'll find us in a heartbeat.

They don't, and I hope it's because they think we ran with the crowd to blend in, even if I'm especially grateful we didn't do that. How many more lives would we be responsible for if we had?

"I know what you're thinking, and it's not your fault," Gavin says. He runs his hand down my arm and interlaces our fingers again.

I shake his hand away, not in the mood for his coddling. "Yes it is. I was stupid enough that I didn't think Mother would pull our DNA from the computer. She used my own plan against me."

"What else could we have done? How else would we get here?"

"I don't know." I clench my fist so hard my nails dig into my palm, breaking the skin. "Something. Anything would have been better than getting innocent people killed because of me."

He takes my hand and straightens out my fingers. There are four little half-moon shaped marks in the heel of my palm. "Let's put that off to the side for now. We need to get to the subs." He pauses as he stares at me.

I shake my head, but he cuts off my refusal. "She's going to kill you, Evie. The turret was planned to go after *both* of us. Not just me. I'm not leaving you here. You're coming with me." His tone becomes more forceful with each word and I'm pretty sure he's close to demanding that I listen to him this time.

Even though I can't imagine leaving my home, I don't see a choice. If I stay, I'll die. Mother will see to that. The wound in my shoulder is proof.

Slowly, I nod. "Okay."

"No, you don't— What?" He looks dumbstruck at my agreement and I have to laugh.

"I said, okay. I'll go with you. You're right. She'll kill me if I stay."

He closes his eyes and lets out a long breath. His features visibly relax before he opens his eyes again. "Great. How are we going to do it now if our disguises aren't going to work?"

"I don't know. Every time I plan something she's one step ahead of me." I rub my hands across my eyes. Voices are coming our way, along with the scraping of shoes against concrete. "We have to leave this room. The Guards have opened the station again. The booth worker will be back soon."

He glances around until his eyes focus on the dark area to the right side of the booth. "The sensors didn't seem to pick us up in the shadows. Let's hide there for now, until we can think of something."

I nod and we hide in the shadows just as a worker enters the booth from the other door.

It's a woman; I can see her clearly through the window. If she looks closely she'll see us, too. But she's too busy fiddling with buttons on the control panel in front of her. Exactly above where we were hiding.

"Didn't think I'd ever thank a Surface Dweller for anything, but he picked a good night to try to escape. Now that they've shut down the Tube, I'll get to go to Festival and not have to keep coming up with excuses to keep people from going back to Three," she says.

"But what about Miss Evelyn?" another female voice asks. I can't see her, but it sounds like she's on the other side of the booth, closer to the concrete wall.

The first woman turns around, confirming the other woman's position for me. "I do feel sorry for her. Poor thing is so daft she probably doesn't even know what's going on."

Narrowing my eyes, I fight the urge to tell her exactly what I think about her.

Gavin squeezes my hand and, when I glance over, he shakes his head.

I return the squeeze to reassure him I'm not going anywhere and go back to listening to the women's conversation.

I freeze when I see how close she is. I dare not breathe in case she hears me, but she's studying something on the wall. Not me.

"Ugh, the Guards took our first-aid kit. Now I'll have to fill out a requisition before I leave," she says.

"Would you like me to do it? I don't mind. I didn't really want to go to Festival anyway," the other woman says.

"Would you? I'll just fill it out for you, if you'll take it to Supply."

"Certainly. My pleasure."

Waiting for the women to finally leave, I have to listen to their chattering about the men in their lives and clothes. And they called me daft.

When they finally leave, we sneak back into the booth and Gavin bursts into laughter. I stare at him in shock.

"You should have seen your face after they called you daft. I thought you were going to strangle them," he says, practically doubled over with laughter.

"I wanted to," I say with clenched teeth.

"Apparently they don't know you too well."

With a tilt to my head, I ask, "Why is that?"

"If they did, they would know you're far from daft. In fact, I'm pretty sure you're the smartest woman I know."

"I don't know. I guess I'm not so smart after all."

He squeezes my good shoulder. "Hey, you've gotten us this far and we're not dead yet. That's saying something. They don't even know where we are exactly. We just need a way to get our DNA back in the system, right?"

I stare at him in disbelief. He's absolutely right. Why hadn't I thought of that?

"Um, Evie? Am I wrong?"

"No. That's brilliant. Especially for a Surface Dweller." I grin when he scowls at me. "And I know what our next step is."

"Oh, great. What is it?"

"We have to find Macie. She'll get our DNA back into

the computer. And she can probably check while we're there to see if there's a *real* evacuation map. The scientist said that the others had different evacuation plans. That *must* mean there are other ways out of here. Maybe there's something close and we won't have to go to Three. The only problem is getting to her lab. Hopefully she's there and not at Festival." Plus, I'd like to find out how to bypass that EMF. The scientist never did say whether or not he found a way around that.

He doesn't look as relieved as I feel. "Can you trust her?"

"I would trust her with my life," I say.

He crosses his arm over his chest. "Oh. That's good, because that's exactly what you're doing, you know. And, not to be selfish or anything, I'm also worried about *my* life."

He's right. Again. I know I can trust her with my life, but what about Gavin's? Will she help me help him? Or will she turn him in?

She did help us once, when she thought I liked him. Would she do it again now that everyone thinks he kidnapped me?

Like everything else lately, it's not like I have much of a choice. I have to try. I have to trust her. She's our only hope. Our only chance. If we have any chance at all.

Now I have to figure out how to get from here to there. There has to be a way to get to Macie without being detected. I study the area around the turret, trying to figure out how to turn it off without Mother noticing. Then I narrow my eyes.

How do they get it up there? Where do the wires run? How do they replace the ammo? Perform maintenance?

A small grin grows slowly on my face as it dawns on me. It's so obvious I can't believe it didn't occur to me before.

"The maintenance tunnels," I say.

"Huh?" Gavin asks.

I turn back to him. I'm so excited about this plan, I'm practically bouncing on my toes. "The maintenance tunnels. That's how we're going to get to Macie. Follow me."

"Wait. If we're going to use maintenance tunnels to get to Macie, how come we can't just take them to Sector Three?" Gavin asks.

"Because the tunnels don't reach from here to Three. The *only* way to get there is via the Tube."

"That seems kinda stupid. What happens if the Tube breaks?"

"Then we wait until it's fixed."

"And if there's an emergency . . . Oh, right, never mind."

I laugh and pat his arm before turning to find the tunnel entrance.

Along the bottom of the wall that the booth is attached to is a small metal door. It's gray, almost the same color as the concrete, and barely visible. If I hadn't known it was there, I'd never have seen it. Actually. . . . how *did* I know it was there?

The hole is small, but large enough for a grown man to crawl through. Even someone Gavin's size. There's a code box instead of handprint verification next to the door and using the same instinct that guided me to the abandoned Sector, I pull off the face of it and reconnect some wires. The door lock opens with a *clunk* and I pull the door open and crawl in. I'm expecting it to be pitch dark, but while it is darker than the Tube station, there are small red lights set every few meters so it's bright enough to see. It dead-ends immediately, but a ladder leads up to another larger tunnel toward the top.

Taking a deep breath to relax my nerves, I start up the ladder. It's hard work since my right arm doesn't want to co-operate very well, but at least the medication Gavin gave me earlier has dulled the pain and I'm able to slowly make my way up. Gavin follows, making sure the door shuts behind him. It locks again with another clunk that echoes. I wince and hope no one is in the tunnels.

We're halfway up the ladder when Gavin curses under his breath.

"What's wrong?" I ask, pausing.

"Just keep going," he says, his voice tense.

"Do you see someone?" I ask, and pick up the pace. I don't think they'd have found us already. The wires weren't snipped for long enough. The whole thing had taken less than fifteen seconds.

"No. Just keep going."

I close my eyes briefly in relief, but keep moving. "Then what's wrong?"

It's quiet for so long I chance a peek down at him. He's keeping his eyes fixed on the wall behind the ladder and reaching blindly for the next rung.

"Gavin?"

"I can see up your dress, okay? It's . . . distracting."

I blush and speed up my pace again. When I finally make it to the tunnel, I sit and call down to him that I'm up.

He glances up and I smile at him. He doesn't smile back, but hurries up after me. The tunnel isn't large enough for us to go side-by-side, so I have to follow behind him. The whole time I'm listening for sounds of other people in the tunnels. A few times, I have to pause and listen past the thudding of my heart in my ears, because it's so loud and I don't want to miss anything.

When we get to a split, Gavin gestures for me to go ahead and lead the way. I squeeze by him, but I have no idea where I am. However, some nice soul has marked the floor of the tunnels. Left is toward the Palace Wing. And to the right are the Residential, Medical, and Science Sectors.

I go right, hoping Macie didn't go to Festival. I have no clue what is waiting for us at the other end or where exactly we'll end up; I just hope it's not anywhere near a turret.

"So, this friend of yours," he says after we've been crawling for a few minutes, "you really think she'll help us?"

Without pausing, I glance over my shoulder. "She did before."

"What do you mean?"

"She's the one who put your DNA in the computer in the first place."

"Really? Why did she do it?"

Without thinking, I say, "She thought I was falling for you."

He grabs my ankle, stopping me. "Why did she think that?"

Realizing my mistake instantly I wince, but look at him over my shoulder. "She said, 'like recognizes like.'" I turn back around. "We have to keep going. I'm not sure how long we'll have before a maintenance worker comes through. These probably aren't used very often, but . . ."

He doesn't let go when I try to move forward. "What did she mean by that?"

I sigh and look back over my shoulder. "I don't know. I assume she meant because she's in love with her chosen mate that means she can see it in other people."

"Was she right?" His eyes search my face, but it's hard to tell exactly what he's thinking. I don't know exactly what I feel for him, but I'm pretty sure I wouldn't be risking my life for someone I only liked. I don't have time to think about it, either. I need to focus on getting us out of here alive.

I turn back around so he can't see my face when I say, "Come on. We need to hurry."

There's a moment of hesitation before he lets go and I continue through the way I was going.

There are more branches along the way—some tunnels that angle up, while others angle down—and more directions, getting more specific with each one. Finally we reach another ladder that is marked as between labs one and two. Since Macie's lab is number two, I go down it and push open the little door.

Poking my head out, I scan quickly for turrets and cameras.

I don't see any and there's no one in this particular hallway, so I squirm out the door and impatiently wait for Gavin to do the same. Then I'm pulling him to the lab, taking a quick peek through the door to make sure there aren't turrets.

The camera is in the corner, but if we stay by the wall, it shouldn't register us. I step into the room and put my back to the wall. Macie raises her eyebrows, but doesn't move from her seat.

It's not exactly the welcome I'm expecting. Little warning bells go off in my head.

"Where have you been?" She narrows her eyes when she sees the bandage on my arm. "What happened?"

I resist the urge to run over to her. "Mother. She set the turrets and cams on us. That's why we're here. Can you put us back into the computer again?"

She doesn't move. "Us?"

I gesture for Gavin to come closer. "Gavin and me. We're both running."

There's a shadow of surprise on her face, but then she finally slides off her stool. I take a step forward, relieved, but it's short-lived.

"No," she says, glaring in his direction and crossing her arms over her chest. "He's a Surface Dweller. A lying, manipulative, and dangerous Surface Dweller. He means nothing to me. And neither do you."

She spins on her heel and marches out the door before I can stop her.

Chapter Sixteen

Failure will not be tolerated.
The only result of failure is death.
—Enforcer Statute 104a.3

It takes me a minute to realize what's happening.

"Macie! Please, stop." I chase after her, grabbing her shoulder.

She stops, but doesn't turn around. "Why should I?" She spits it out, as if even the thought of talking to me makes her sick.

I have no idea why she's acting like this, therefore I don't really have a reason to make her change her mind, but I do know one thing. "Because if I were in your shoes, I'd help you."

"But you're not, are you?" Even though there is a slight quiver, her voice is filled with venom. I pull my hand back when she shrugs it off. "You've *never* been in my shoes. And you never will. You sit in your gardens, clipping your flowers and dreaming your little daydreams, while everyone else caters to your every whim. You want crème brûlée at three in the morning? By Mother, the Maids are going to get it to you. A little thirsty? The Guards will drop everything and bring you a soy latte. You say the water outside your walls is purple, they'd change the curriculum to state the water is purple."

She spins around. Her eyes are swirling with anger. She glares at me as she hisses out the rest of her rant through clenched teeth.

"Mother and Father adore you. You can do no wrong in their eyes. And that includes not listening to your Guards. Ever. *You don't care about anyone but yourself.* When you sneak off and disappear for hours, do you get in trouble? No. Your Guards do. *And now when the Governess is willing to give you a Surface Dweller to couple with, because you wanted it*"—she says *it* like Gavin is a disgusting bug instead of a person—"*instead of one of your own kind,* you run away? And now you have the audacity to ask me for help. Again. When you don't care about anyone but yourself. You had me fooled. I thought you cared about me. I thought we were friends. *But now this Surface Dweller comes and you show what you really are. A selfish, flighty, and foolish little girl.*"

Shocked, I open my mouth to speak, but no words form. Her words stab at my heart. I know other people think I'm a spoiled little girl, but Macie is my closest friend. I never expected to hear that from her. Why is she saying that when just yesterday she'd bad-mouthed Mother for Conditioning me again?

I don't realize I'm shaking until Gavin slides his hand into mine and squeezes, before releasing it and standing next to me. Standing *with* me, even when my heart is being crushed under the heel of my best friend's stylish shoes.

"I-I don't know what you're talking about," I finally manage. "You're my friend, Macie. My *best* friend."

"Sure." She waves her hand as if motioning me on, then turns around. "Just take your Surface Dweller and go. You're not welcome here."

"Macie? Please—" I reach over to her again.

"I said get out of here!"

I'm not exactly sure what I'm intending to do. Tears sting the backs of my eyes, which is stupid—I know better. *Tears solve nothing. Emotions are worthless. They only show weakness.*

I blink them away and try to speak again, but Gavin touches my arm. "She's not going to help, Evie. Leave it be."

I turn to face him. His eyes look like the storm clouds I've seen in books as he glares at Macie.

"Besides, anyone who thinks you're selfish, flighty, and foolish doesn't know you at all. We'll figure something out." He frowns down at my shoulder and I look over to see the bandage is now stained rusty with my blood. "We'll need to fix you up first, though." He turns cold, hard eyes to Macie. "Will you let me take care of this before you kick us out, or will you have your friend bleed to death?"

Her eyes are round as saucers as they watch the bandage grow darker. She seems rooted to the floor.

"We don't have all day. Will you let us stay or not?" His

tone is harsh, which seems to snap her out of whatever it is she is thinking.

"Y-yes, of course. She can sit in my seat. I'll get a first-aid kit."

She rushes to the wall while Gavin tries to help me onto the stool.

"I can get on it myself," I say. Macie's words are still playing over and over in my head. I refuse to prove her right by letting Gavin answer to my beck and call.

He ignores me and lifts me to place me on the chair, being careful not to jostle my arm. He then slowly and carefully removes the dressing, which causes the clotted blood that had formed over the wound to tear loose. I hiss at the pain. Blood drips down my arm in tiny rivulets. I watch as each drop falls to the floor in a steady drip, drip, drip. They slowly form a little pool next to the stool's silver leg.

That's a lot of blood, I think. More than it should be. I know I should be alarmed at how much I'm losing, but I just continue to watch the pool expand, my mind growing fuzzy.

When Macie returns, she opens the kit. To my surprise, she doesn't say a word. In fact, she digs into the kit and starts handing items to Gavin, who takes them without sparing her a single glance.

Every once in awhile he glances up at me, worry forming lines around his eyes. Otherwise his face is a blank mask, those gorgeous eyes staring into mine. The loss of blood seems to have dimmed the panic I feel when I touch him. I lift a hand to his face. It amazes me to know how much he's come to mean to me in just a few short hours.

I open my mouth to tell him, but Macie interrupts me. She goggles at the wound. "A turret did that?"

Shaking off the dizziness, I'm relieved I didn't say anything. Gavin doesn't need me spouting my feelings in a fit of delirium. "Yes. It went off down at the Tube station," I say. "Apparently Mother isn't playing around. She wants me back. Dead or alive."

Macie gasps and stares over at the camera. I follow her gaze. The red light is off. Thank Mother.

Her hands clench at her side. "Bitch!" she proclaims, and I lift an eyebrow, but don't say anything.

Gavin glances over, the shadow of a smile on his face. "I can only agree with that," he says. He cleans the wound and redresses it, murmuring something softly under his breath. I can't hear what he says because my head is spinning again, and there's a buzzing in my ear, like hundreds of little bees are next to my head. The pain is horrendous. Worse than when I was initially shot. I wonder if that's because the adrenaline and medication are wearing off and with it the numbness they provided. When are the nanos going to start working?

Whatever it is he's saying, Macie is watching him with her eyes wide open in surprise. I move my gaze back to Gavin and try to focus on his mouth. I hope to be able to read his lips, but it's no use. The harder I try to force the dizziness away, the worse it gets. So I just stare at him instead.

When he finishes, he leans forward, keeping his eyes on mine, and I wonder if he's going to kiss me again, but he sighs and steps back instead.

The dizziness slowly ebbs and dies away. I smile at him and cup my hand along the side of his face, enjoying the roughness of the stubble on his jaw against my palm. "Thank you."

He clears his throat and steps away. "We'd better get going." He shoots another glare at Macie. "Before she turns us in."

"I'm not going to turn you in," she says softly. "But yes, you better get going. The Guards will be here any moment to make sure everyone is at Festival."

I slide off the stool, but sway when a wave of dizziness washes over me. Gavin grabs my good arm to steady me, while Macie grabs the other. I cry out, the red flash of pain making me even dizzier.

Gavin pulls me away and steps between us. "Leave her alone! Are you trying to kill her?"

I gape at him. I've never heard him raise his voice before.

Macie's eyes flash. "Of course not. I was trying to help her."

"Yeah, right. You just said you wouldn't help her. Because of me. And if that's the kind of help you're offering, we're better without it. Now get out of the way." He pushes past her, gently pulling me with him.

"It wasn't because of you," she says. "But she's right. No matter what she's done to me, she's still my best friend and I can't just watch her die."

I stop, and even though Gavin tugs on my hand to keep going, I turn to face her. "What do you mean? What did I do to you?"

She frowns and her eyes harden again. "Mother revoked the coupling."

"What? Why?" I ask, but I fear I already know the answer.

She tilts her head. "She knew I'd helped you before. I don't know how, especially since I didn't *have* to fudge the results. He *does* have the perfect genetics. But I had all my privileges revoked. That includes my Coupling License."

"Oh, Macie, I'm so sorry. I didn't know. I didn't think—" I take a step toward her to give her a hug and try to fix what I've done, but she backs away.

"No, you didn't," she says, her tone harsh. Gavin makes a sound in his throat, but she doesn't let him speak. "But that doesn't give me the excuse to just let you die. Come on. Both of you. You can stay with me until we come up with a better plan."

She brushes past the both of us and stops just this side of the door, looking back when she notices we haven't moved.

"No. We just need your computer access credentials. We need to put ourselves back into the computer. Find a *real* map of the facility. And—" I stop myself from talking, because I don't know how much I should tell her. I still trust her, but I've gotten her into enough trouble. I really don't want her to get into more. Finally, I say, "Then we'll be on our way." There's no way I'm going to let her get in more trouble because of me.

She shakes her head. "I can't help you."

Gavin and I exchange a look. "Why not?" he asks. He crosses his arms over his chest. It's not hard to see he doesn't trust a word she says.

She glares at him. "Mother took my privileges away, Surface Dweller. Remember? That includes my computer access. I can't even work."

"Then what are you doing here?" I look over her workspace. For the first time I notice her desk is completely bare. Not even the microscope is there. Underneath the desk is a box filled to the brim with her possessions. I recognize the statuette of a cat I gave her for Christmas last year. Even though it's on the top and protected by clear plastic bubble wrap, I can see the pink ears sticking out the top.

"Cleaning out my desk," she says. "I've been fired. Once I return to my quarters, I'm on house arrest while I await my new designation."

Gavin turns toward me. It's clear he has no clue what she's talking about. "What does that mean?"

I ignore him. "What about your coworkers? Can you get into their computer profiles? Surely you can't be the only one with the same credentials."

She lets out a loud sigh, but goes to another station. She plugs a series of numbers and letters into the terminal and a screen pops up. For the next few minutes, she swipes, taps, and types into different programs and screens. Finally, she turns around with a frown. "I can't access Mother's computer from this terminal. She's implanted new security protocols.

I'll try another terminal that should be able to access her files no matter what."

I nod and wait, impatiently tapping my fingers on one of the lab benches. When we're on the final terminal and after several attempts, the computer buzzes again. She drags a hand through her hair and turns to me.

"I'm sorry, but it seems that Mother's got her computer locked up tighter than a clam with lockjaw. There's no way I can access anything you want from here."

Gavin turns to me. "What does that mean?"

I sigh, feeling a weight as heavy as bricks weigh down on me. "It means that I'm going to have to go back to the Palace Wing and hack into Mother's computer manually in order to gain access to the files we need."

Chapter Seventeen

Greed has poisoned men's souls. Surface Dwellers have destroyed what was once beautiful and turned it into a ghostly illusion of what they call peace. But down here, we have real peace. There will be no fear, or sickness, hunger, hate, or greed. We have created our Utopia. And it is magnificent.

—Mother, from Founding Speech

Gavin gapes at me. "We have to go back to the Palace Wing?"

"No." He sighs in relief, but I keep going. "*I* have to go back to the Palace Wing."

"Not without me you're not. We're a team. You need me."

"You don't know the area. You'll only be a hindrance." He jerks like I've hit him and pain fills his eyes. I pause, thinking I know the reason he's worried. "I'm not going to leave you. I'll come back for you once I fix things."

He shakes his head. "That's not what I'm worried about. I know you'll come back. *If* you're alive. But it's the alive part I'm worried about. You're already wounded. It's only going to get worse. You need my help."

I open my mouth to argue, but Macie cuts me off. "We don't have time for this. The Guards are going to come by any minute. If they catch us here, we're going to be in trouble. We have to figure out a way to get by those turrets and cams, though."

I shrug. "That's the easy part. We'll just go the way we came to get here. Through the maintenance tunnels."

Her face lights up. "Yes. That's perfect! Go on. I'll meet you at my quarters."

She guards us while we climb back into the maintenance tunnels and then shuts the grate behind us.

I really hate these tunnels. They're worse than the Detainment Center.

Even though Gavin can see straight up my dress, I take point. He wants to be behind me in case I get dizzy and fall. I'm not sure how that would be much better, since I'd just end up causing us both to fall, but there's no shaking him. He's nothing if not persistent. And I can't help but wonder if his refusal to let me go last has something to do with him not wanting me to go to the Palace Wing by myself. Is he worried that I'll run while he's climbing the ladder?

I have to admit it's a good idea, but it's too late now. I'm already halfway up and he's close behind. I reach for another rung but my bad arm, which already feels like I'm ripping it apart, gives out on me. I slip and only catch myself from falling into Gavin by centimeters. When my body weight jerks my good arm out of socket, I bite back a scream.

A red wave of pain causes my head to spin and my stomach

to roll. Fearing I'm not going to make it up into the tunnel before I get sick, I grit my teeth against the excruciating pain and pull myself up with my bad arm ladder rung by torturous rung.

Through the buzzing in my head I hear Gavin, but I can't make out what he's saying. It doesn't matter, though, because I finally make it to the top. Belly crawling over the top of the ladder, I use my legs to propel me forward, then squirm on my hand and knees until I can't move any farther. My stomach heaves and I gag, trying not to vomit. This isn't the place. But pain is still bursting throughout my shoulders. I finally give up and lay facedown on the concrete of the tunnel. The surface is blissfully cool against my skin.

After a few seconds the buzzing in my ears stop, but the world hasn't stopped spinning.

Gavin carefully wriggles over me and kneels next to my head. He brushes the hair away from my face. "Evie, what happened?"

I'm afraid to open my mouth. My stomach is still topsy-turvy. Squeezing my eyes shut, I gasp out, "Arm gave out. Slipped. Caught myself. Other arm out of socket."

Gavin sucks in air through his teeth, then gently rolls me over onto my back. The movement causes both my arms to explode with fresh pain, and I bite back a scream.

"Oh, sweetheart, I'm sorry. I know it hurts," Gavin says, "but I have to look at it." When I signal for him to continue, he prods around one shoulder and then the other, while I continue to grit my teeth and try not to scream. I don't know who's in the tunnels and I really don't want to draw attention to us.

"You're bleeding again," Gavin says, his tone sounding oddly flat. "And your other arm is out of joint. I can put it back in, but it's going to hurt like hell."

Oh, how the roles have changed, I think, remembering how only days ago I'd said almost the same to him.

I open my eyes and stare into his. "Do it."

He swallows, then grabs my arm, and yanks as hard as he can, pushing with his legs on one wall and using the other wall against his back as leverage. There's a white-hot flash of pain and my head swims again, before darkness leaks in.

It's a blur for a while, but I fight the unconsciousness while he wraps more bandages around the arm that was shot. The next thing I know, I'm being asked if I think I can keep moving.

"I think so. But it'll be slow going."

"It's okay," Gavin says. "We're not in any hurry. Just go as fast as you can. I'll be right behind you."

It's a painstakingly slow journey to the ladder to Macie's quarters, but we finally make it.

I stare down into the reddish light and darkness of the ladder well. "I don't think I can go down on my own."

There's silence behind me and I glance over my shoulder to see Gavin watching me with a considering look on his face.

After a few seconds he nods to himself. "Right. Well, you'll just have to ride piggyback."

"What?" I ask.

"I'll carry you. Just hang on to me."

It worries me that he may not be able to handle both our weights on the ladder, but I don't have a choice. He scoots by me and takes a few steps down before I carefully crawl onto his back. I grip him around the waist with my legs, using my thigh muscles to carry most of my weight.

He slowly lowers us to the ground. When we reach the floor, my legs wobble, and I crash onto the floor.

Gavin sits next to me. "Are you okay?" I nod and he's silent for another minute before he asks, "Are you sure we can trust her?"

"You asked me that before," I say. "My answer hasn't changed." I try to stand, but he stops me.

"But she already said she wouldn't help us."

"Because the last time she did, she got punished. But she didn't run to tell the Guards or Mother. We can trust her." I push him away and this time he doesn't stop me.

"It could be a trap to get you back into the Palace."

"It's not."

"But—"

"It's not, Gavin. I know her as well as I know myself. It's not a trap."

He meets my eyes and his are swirling with so many emotions, I can't distinguish one from the next. "How well do you know yourself, though? Really?"

He has a point, and it stings, but we don't have a choice, just like he didn't have any other choice but to trust me.

"You may be right," I say slowly, "but it's better to move forward at this point than to sit around and wait for Mother to find us. It's only a matter of time and, at this moment, we have the power of surprise on our side. She has no idea what we know. Or what we're doing."

Gavin looks at me, considering. "Why is it so important to get into Mother's computer again?"

"I have to get to Mother's computer because it can put us back into the system so the turrets and cams don't take notice of us. And because she probably has the only true map of the facility, which while not strictly mandatory since we have the journal telling us how to get to the submarines, there might be something in *this* area we can use instead. The quicker we get out of here the better, and even if there isn't any other emergency exit, then knowing what the scientist was talking about regarding EMFs would be extremely beneficial to me, since I know EMFs can damage my nanos. So if there is one, I need to know how to deal with it. Mother, I'm sure, has detailed instructions on the things. For her own safety, if nothing else." And, of course, to find out what Mother was planning for me since I know the truth about almost everything else now. But I don't tell him that, I just say instead, "And since no matter whose credentials we used, we couldn't access her system, I have to go and get on to it manually."

"You're set on going to the Palace Wing, then?"

"Yes."

"Then I'm going with you," he says.

"No. You're not."

"I am. You can't stop me. You couldn't even make it up the ladder by yourself. You *need* me."

I don't say anything. I know he thinks I've given up and will let him go, but I've already made up my mind and no amount of arguing is going to change it. I will go to the Palace Wing by myself. I'll just have to find a way to keep him from following me, which will be easier said than done.

Despite the fact I'd told Gavin the truth—I trust Macie completely—my heart beats a little faster. It is also completely possible I don't know her as well as I think I do.

People do things that are completely out of character for them in the name of love. And there is no doubt in my mind how much Macie loves Nick.

But we'd been friends for so long. Would her disappointment over Nick be enough for her to betray me?

Turns out I have no reason to worry because Macie is alone and waiting for us next to the grate, and she quickly ushers us into her quarters before anyone can see us. She narrows her eyes when she sees there's more bandaging on me, but doesn't ask.

I can't decide if that's a good thing or a bad thing.

The apartment is the same as every other apartment in the Residential Sector. But it's smaller than the one we broke into in the abandoned Sector, since she's sixteen and living on her own. If she and Nick became Coupled, they'd get a larger "family apartment."

I sit on the couch and drink the water she offers, but

Gavin is far less trusting—not that I blame him—and stops me from drinking the water until he's had a chance to scrutinize it. He gives it back to me with a huff. Then he searches her quarters for anyone that shouldn't be there.

Macie doesn't stop him or go with him, and in fact appears amused when he finally settles himself next to me and reluctantly takes his own glass, studying it carefully as well.

"Don't trust me, Surface Dweller?" she asks.

"No," he says flatly.

"Good," she says. "That makes two of us. I don't trust you, either. I'm positive you're using her and I will prove it, but for now we have to get along." She glances at me. "For her sake, if nothing else."

The two nod at each other and, while there is still a heavy feel to the room, the tension decreases.

When my stomach rumbles, Macie smiles at me. "Hungry?"

I nod and she lifts an eyebrow at Gavin, who sighs, but also nods. When she gets up, I realize this may be the only opportunity I have. Gavin will be upset, but there's no other option. If I stand any chance of getting to the computer and back alive, he can't be with me.

I stand, grateful I'm not dizzy. "I'll help you get everything together," I say to Macie.

She nods and leads the way to her kitchen.

Gavin stands, but I gesture for him to sit. "Please. Let me have a few minutes alone with her. I need to try and fix this. I don't want to leave it like this."

He sits back down. "I'll be waiting right here."

Feeling grateful that he trusts me and guilty that I'm using it against him, I go into the kitchen. Macie is looking into the refrigerator, pulling out ingredients for sandwiches.

The minute the door closes behind me, I say, "Where's the maintenance entry?"

Macie turns, her face scrunched up in confusion, holding two jars in her hands. "I'm sorry?"

"Your maintenance entry. Where is it?"

She slowly places the jars on the counter. "Why?"

I fight the urge to yell at her. "Because in order to get our DNA back in the computer, I need to use the tunnels," I say.

She stares at the door to the living room as if she can see through it. "What about him? He doesn't trust me. He's going to think I sent you to your death or something." The smile she's wearing slips off her face and she pales. "I could very well be sending you off to your death."

"I know the Palace Wing like the back of my hand. There's no one more qualified for this than me."

"*If* you can remember your way around," she says.

I only stare at her.

She eyes my shoulder. "That's not healed. It's going to slow you down."

I shrug, trying not to wince at the sharp pain that zigzags across my shoulders. "Not as much as you think."

She opens her mouth to argue, but Gavin's voice sounds from the living room.

"Everything okay in there? Do you need any help?"

Giving Macie a look, I call back through the door. "We're fine. Just getting some hors d'ouevres put together. Macie likes to throw a party when guests come to visit."

She forces a laugh. "I can't help it. Guests are a rare thing for me lately."

Gavin doesn't respond, and I hope he hasn't caught the strain in her voice. Either way, I need to hurry. "Macie. Please. Where's your maintenance entrance?"

She sighs, then gestures for me to follow. She leads me back toward the bedroom and then points to a section of the wall. She presses her hand to the side near the corner and there's a soft click. The wall swings toward us without a sound.

"Thanks," I say as I slip through the opening.

"Wait! What do I do about your boy?" she asks with a smirk. "I can't stay in the kitchen forever."

I glance back at the door. "Tell him the truth. That I went to fix our problem. Just don't show him how to get to the tunnels."

"What if you don't come back?"

I meet her eyes. "Then I'm asking for another favor. Please figure out a way to get him out of here. Alive." Then I pull the door shut. And while the click is practically silent, it echoes in my head like the hammer on a gun.

Chapter Eighteen

There is a need for something special. To make the Citizens better than they are. But it must be kept secret. I fear the critics will not understand if it's revealed too soon. Meet me in your lab at 1800 to discuss it.

—Mother, in a note to her most trusted scientist

These tunnels are different than the ones I used before, brighter and not as musty smelling. There are no red lights in these. Water drips off the mess of pipes and wires running along the ceiling. And this passageway is large enough that I can stand easily. It's so tall, I'm sure even Gavin could stand easily. At the thought of Gavin, guilt tugs at me, but I ignore it. I'm doing this for both of us. I just have to hope he'll understand.

The other difference is that these tunnels are used regularly, while the others are only used in case of a problem. Mother found the sight of dirty, grungy workers unpleasant, so she created these to keep them out of view. In essence, they are the city's servants' tunnels.

I tread as quietly as I can, which isn't easy. The ground is gritty and the soles of my shoes make crunchy, scratchy noises with every step. Although I'm sure it's not all that loud, probably no louder than a soft whisper, I'm convinced that it's as deafening as an alarm and that Enforcers are going to pop out of the shadows at any minute.

There are no signs to guide me on my way—probably because these tunnels are used so frequently, people don't really need a guide—so I use my instincts to lead me in the right direction. They've worked for me so far. Here's hoping they don't give up on me now.

Within ten minutes, I find myself thoroughly lost. I've gone down at least four flights of stairs and I quite literally don't know if I'm coming or going. Even when I sit down and try to get my bearings, it's useless. The tunnels all look the same and there are so many junctions, I don't know which one to take. The heat and humidity is making it difficult to breathe, and sweat is creating sticky trails all along my skin.

I close my eyes and picture where I came from and how I got to where I am. If I'd gone the normal way, I would have had to travel southwest. But I don't know where I am now. I don't even know if I'm still in the Residential Sector.

Guilt blooms again when I worry about being found and what will happen to Gavin if I don't return.

I decide to risk detection and take a peek to find out where I am.

Opening one of the doors carefully, I leave only a gap

large enough to peer through. It doesn't take me long to realize I'm near the Square and Festival is in full swing.

Apparently I've been heading in the right direction all along. After I close the door, I follow the tunnel until the next junction, then take it to the left, keeping straight until I hit a place where I can only go left or right. I take the left and continue down that path. When the tunnels get brighter and cleaner and cooler, I know I've made it to the Palace Wing. Only there would Mother care what the tunnels looked like. And that's only because she wouldn't want the servants tracking dirt all over the marble floors.

Since there aren't any turrets in the Palace Wing, I feel it's safer outside the tunnels than in them. I know my way around the Palace Wing a lot better than I know the tunnels and I can find a place to hide if need be. I step carefully into the open and breathe in deeply, inhaling the sweet scent that fills the air. Mother always insists that lavender flows through the oxygen recyclers in this area. It's so familiar to me, it instantly calms my scorched nerves.

I glance around to get my bearings and am happy to note I am not far from Mother's rooms, or mine for that matter. Just up a few flights of stairs and a decision to go right or left. I debate whether or not to just go to my rooms. I can do everything there that I can from Mother's computer and no one would be the wiser.

Except that I'm sure Mother is waiting for me to do exactly that. So Mother's rooms it is. Knowing Mother, she probably thinks I wouldn't dare try to use her computer.

I creep down the corridors, and at first I'm concerned with the lack of life. There doesn't seem to be anyone around. Then I remember it's Festival. Everyone should be at the Square, including Mother and Father. They've never missed a Festival and I'm sure they won't miss this one. Not now that a Surface Dweller has broken in and stolen the Daughter of the People. They'll want to present the illusion that everything is fine and just like it was before.

With that thought, I walk more confidently down the halls and up the stairs. I should be able to hear anyone coming before they can get to me.

Maybe I should stop by my rooms, I think again at the junction where I would go left for Mother's room and right to go to mine, but while I'm more confident I can sneak in and out without being caught, I'm still fairly certain going to my room is not a good idea.

It's only one more corner and then I'm standing at Mother's door. I place my hand on the door to open it, but then quickly yank it back. Memories of beatings for stepping into Mother's private quarters without permission swim in my head.

More Conditioning.

My breath hitches as my skin crawls and I'm bombarded by glimpses of other memories.

I swallow hard and take several deep, calming breaths before I'm able to push aside the terror and open the door. But even then, staring at it, I can't force my feet to take a step in a forward direction.

The room itself is fairly large—about twice the size of my own. The walls are covered in what I know is silk wallpaperings. All except the recess in the wall to the left that houses her computer and hologram equipment.

The large, canopied bed takes up a large portion of the other wall, with two ornate nightstands on either side. The bed is made up perfectly and there is nothing left out on the desk or nightstands. Mother doesn't tolerate any kind of sloppiness or mess.

The wall that is host to the door also boasts her vanity, complete with mirror. And like mine, hers is littered with perfume bottles. Unlike mine, however, all her bottles are beautiful, cherished treasures. There's no sign that she actually uses them or the vanity. There are no makeup pots or tubes, and while there's a silver brush, comb, and hand-mirror set, I'm sure they're all for show. The only thing that seems out of place is the picture tucked into the side of the large mirror.

Directly across from me is a sliding wall made entirely of glass that leads out to a balcony with a magnificent view of the lava flows and the ocean. The balcony is where Mother usually takes her breakfast. Alone, of course.

I don't have much time, so I force myself to take those initial steps into her room. When nothing happens, I shut the door behind me, leaving it open a crack so I can hear if anyone comes. Then I walk to her computer and boot it up.

Only the blue glow from the computer and the orange glow from the lava flows outside Mother's window light the room. The computer immediately asks for a password. At first

I panic. I have no idea what to do. One wrong move and I'll set off a chain of events that will give me a one-way ticket to those lava flows. I close my eyes and take a deep breath to relax, then open them again, letting my instincts guide me on what to do.

But still, I barely breathe while I fight the computer.

My fingers fly over the holographic keyboard and my arm aches like a bad tooth, but I don't dare stop. Even though I've never done this before, it's like the codes and sequences are all there in my mind just waiting for me to use them. Somehow I know how to peel down each wall of security as if it's an orange. Another lost memory? I don't take the time to think on it. With every step I take forward to break the code, the more concerned I am the computer will tell Mother what I'm doing. Finally, just as another drop of sweat dribbles down my back, the desktop appears on the holoscreen. I cracked the password.

Breathing a sigh of relief, I do a search for the DNA files. I expect them to need passcodes as well and, when I finally find them, I'm not disappointed. I stretch my fingers and pop my knuckles. This is going to take more finesse. If I know Mother, she's got fail-safes on them now. In case I find a way to get to them.

I start slowly tearing down each section of the security until finally—almost thirty minutes later and with stiff and aching fingers, head, and joints, including my shoulder that's back to feeling like someone's pressing salt into it—I'm looking at a list of every Citizen that has ever lived in Elysium. As

Daughter of the People, this is the same list I look at every request day, to verify credentials for coupling. The only difference is this is the master list and can be altered, while my file was always just read-only, which gives me an idea. I do a search on Gavin's and my names and put us back into the system.

Then I back out of the program, re-implementing the security around it, but changing the passcode. It's not permanent, but depending on when Mother tries to get back in here, it should buy me enough time to escape Elysium. Well, at least, I hope so.

Then, even though I know this could backfire, I go and re-approve Macie's Coupling License and stamp it. Then I even assign Nick and Macie new quarters. That way, by the time Mother figures it out, things will already be in motion and Mother will either have to go along with it or admit there was a clerical mistake. Something that *never* happens.

I smile. "Explain that one away, Mother."

Now, I go after the gold. To find out the reason I'm still being Conditioned and the real way out of here. Like I told Gavin, I know she's got to have a list of potential emergency exits. And baring that, maybe she has information on what exactly that EMF is at the exit and what it does, if anything. Maybe it's just another of Mother's scare tactics.

Finally, I find a folder labeled GENE MANIPULATION DATA.

I click on it. It brings up file after file after file of scientific jargon. Most of which is far above my head, but one of the files has my name on it.

Instincts humming, I open the file.

It brings up several more files. I click the first one dated several months before my birth.

SUBJECT 121:

Implantation of the female embryo, hereafter referred to as Subject 121, has proven successful. The host, while feeling the normal physical complications of gestation (i.e. morning sickness and fatigue), appears healthy. I will continue to monitor the host and embryo carefully for the rest of the first trimester, but if all goes well, we will continue medical exams as normal.

I know I'm not going to have time to read it all, so I scrounge around Mother's desk until I find a data cube, then slip it into the data slot and hit copy on the file. I'll read the rest later when I have more time.

While it's copying, I search the computer for more damaging files against Mother, clicking copy on everything I think is relevant. I pause when I see a map of the facility. The entire building that makes up Sector Three is red. Staring at it, I ponder what that means, before hitting copy on that as well.

I glance back at the computer. Just as it finishes the download, I hear the telltale click of Mother's shoes on the marble. I yank the cube out of the slot and then look for a place to hide. I've barely pulled my feet under the bed when she walks in. My arm is on fire and I can feel blood trickling down my arm, but I don't even look at it. I don't want to make a sound.

My heart pounds in my ears, but I'm still able to hear her muttering under her breath as her Maid flutters around her, telling her the details of the party she is to attend for Festival.

"Mr. Hummel will be there, and he's requesting an audience with you to discuss some more funding allocations for his new project," the Maid says.

"Yes, yes. That's fine. Just not tonight. Make sure to schedule something for tomorrow." Mother makes a sniffing sound and I wonder what she's doing.

"Yes, ma'am. Also, Ms. Blackner will be there with her daughter, Seri."

"And?" She sniffs again and pauses.

"You wanted me to invite them so you could look at the girl, in case . . ." She swallows audibly, and says, "She's the one who aced Med Spec exams."

"Oh right, right. Yes. Thank you."

After several more minutes of this, Mother stops, but apparently the Maid doesn't know because she slams into the back of her. A glass shatters on the floor, spilling red wine.

I stop breathing. It has landed just millimeters from the tips of my fingers. The Maid immediately bends to clean it up, apologizing.

Mother, obviously having had more than a few drinks, just laughs it off. "Leave it. Just fetch me a new glass, will you? And bring the bottle." She waves her away.

The Maid rushes out the door, still apologizing.

Mother, still chuckling, sits at her vanity. I'm able to peer up enough that I can see her reflection in the mirror glass. She brushes her hair—not surprisingly using the more practical brush that was in one of the drawers—and adjusts her makeup, also pulled from one of the drawers, before she touches a finger to the corner of her eye. Then she reaches the same hand out to the picture on the mirror. It appears to be a picture, but I can't see of whom.

"You left me, too. Why does everyone always leave?" she whispers.

My eyes widen when she pounds a fist onto her vanity, knocking down one of her perfume bottles. When it hits the floor, it breaks, sending the smell of lilies all over the room. She pushes up quickly, and kneels to clean it up.

She only picks up a few pieces of glass before she jerks her hand above her head and throws the handful of glass onto the ground full force. Most of it shatters on impact, sending shards flying in every direction. Then she stands and starts screaming, yelling words I can't understand because of the crashing and breaking of glass that accompany it, as she tosses stuff around her room.

She tosses another of her perfume bottles and it shatters centimeters from my head, nicking my face and arms. It burns like hellfire from the alcohol in the perfume, but I bite my tongue to stop myself from crying out.

When she finally stops, the floor is littered with what used to be the decorations and furniture in her room. My heart hammers so loudly I can't believe Mother doesn't hear it. But even over it, I can hear the sobbing gasps of her breath and I know she's weeping.

The Maid returns and stops short in the doorway. "Oh, my! What happened here?" She rushes to Mother and I wince, expecting Mother to freak out on her. She pauses and I hear her intake of breath. "Oh, no, ma'am, you've cut yourself."

"It's nothing. Just a small cut. From the perfume bottle." From my vantage point, I see Mother grasp the Maid by the upper arms and her voice cracks when she says, "Don't let anyone see this. I can't let anyone see."

"I won't, ma'am. I'll take care of this personally."

"This is Evelyn's fault. She left me for a *Surface Dweller*. Everyone *always* wants to leave."

"I know, ma'am. And after everything you've given that child. After you saved her from her failure. Gave her another chance to be something special. Let's get you to Dr. Friar. He'll know just what to do. . . ."

They walk out the door and the Maid's voice slowly fades away.

My mind whirls. What in Mother's name was all that about?

Chapter Nineteen

What was once just a spark of an idea in Mother's head became all that you see and know in our wonderful city. Mother created Elysium so that she, and those like her, could live in peace, far away from the greed and intolerance raging war on the Surface.

—HISTORY TEXT, YEAR FIVE

I lie underneath the bed long after they leave, my breath haggard. It's several minutes before I feel it's safe enough to risk venturing out. When I do, I'm astounded. Even though I heard the damage she'd done, I had no idea of the full extent of it.

Everything that could be lifted was broken. Broken glass and splintered wood litter the floor. Every single one of her precious jeweled bottles lay shattered on the dresser and floor. Bits of colorful glass are everywhere. Even in my hair. Her china dolls—her most prized possessions—are broken and strewn about the room like the victims of the footage of the Surface I was forced to watch in Mother's Daughter of the People lessons.

It hurts to see it.

With a glance at the door, I sneak a peek at the photograph. It's a picture of a blond woman sitting in front of some kind of stone wall with a hole in it—a fireplace, I think—and there's a young child sitting in her lap. Curious, I flip it over. Written on the back are the words, "Never forget."

With no time to figure it out, I shove the data cube I'm still holding into my bra. Taking a deep breath, I stick my head out into the hall, then sneak as quickly as I can back to the door I came in from. Festival is still going on, but I'm still pretty recognizable. Besides, I haven't made sure the turrets are completely turned off. No sense in testing it out where innocent people could get hurt.

I stick as close to the original path as I can, only taking a detour when I hear voices of workers. They seem to be in a hurry. I wonder whether they're late for Festival or looking for me.

Since I know my way this time, it takes only half the time to get back to Macie's as it did to get to the Palace Wing and I'm grateful for that. The episode with Mother weighs on my nerves. I can't wait to share this information with Gavin.

I push through the door and lean on it to close it. It's completely silent in the apartment, and my instincts immediately begin to hum. Why is it so quiet? It's not like I expected them to have a party while I was gone, but I did expect some kind of noise. Like talking.

Creeping toward the living room, I check every room along the way for something amiss. There aren't many to check—only a bedroom and bathroom. I peer around the corner to the living room and knit my brows together. Nothing appears to be wrong. They're both sitting and staring into space. Macie sits on her couch, her arms resting in her lap. She keeps glancing at the clock and wringing her hands.

Gavin sits in the armchair. There's a tick in his jaw, just a tiny flutter every few seconds. His hands keep fisting and then unfisting, crumpling the material of his slacks.

I step through the doorway and both of their gazes fly over to me. At first there is relief in both of them, but Gavin's quickly fades to anger. He shoves off the chair, stomps over to me, and grabs me.

My heart flutters a little, but I stand my ground. I'm not sure if it's fear or something else that causes the flutter.

"What the hell were you thinking? Have you lost your damn mind? Do you realize what you just put me through? You could have been killed. I thought we were in this together. We were going to get out of here *together*. Remember?"

When he finally releases me, I wobble. We stare at each other, then he spins on his heel and disappears down the hall. A few seconds later the bathroom door shuts. It's so close to a slam, I wince.

Macie clears her throat. She glances back at the hallway. "He was quite angry."

"I thought he would be," I say. Suddenly tired right down

to my toes, I sit on the couch and rest my head on the back of it, closing my lids. "But it needed to be done."

The couch squeaks when she sits next to me. "I take it you fixed the problem?"

"Yes." I open my eyes and look at her. "Yours, too."

She knits her brows together. "What are you talking about?"

"Your problem with the coupling. I fixed it. You and Nick are now re-approved for coupling. And I even assigned you quarters already."

She draws in a breath and her eyes start to water when she smiles. "Truly? You did that for me?" Then her euphoric expression fades and is replaced by a mask of anger. "You mean you spent time helping me!" she yells, standing and forcing me to do the same. "For Mother's sake, Evie! What is wrong with you? Gavin is right: You could've gotten yourself killed. You were just supposed to go in and fix the computer. Not play matchmaker."

Gavin runs back in. "What's going on?" He looks between the two of us.

We ignore him.

"I was right there! What did you expect me to do? Just ignore it and walk away?" I yell back, fuming. Here I'd risked my neck to fix something I'd broken and she was *yelling* at me?

"Yes. I did. It wasn't worth the risk." She places her hands on her hips and pins me with her eyes.

Gavin turns to her. "What wasn't worth the risk?"

Again we ignore him. "You're my best friend," I say. "One of my only friends. I caused that to happen and you're right. I was selfish. I didn't think of the risks you were taking. I only thought of Gavin and myself. Getting him out of here so he could leave us far behind. It's not exactly what best friends do. So I fixed it."

Gavin's eyes widen, but he doesn't say anything.

Macie looks down at her feet. "I was wrong to say that. You weren't selfish. You were desperate. Besides, that's what friends are for."

I shake my head. "I was going to leave you to deal with the consequences. It was selfish and wrong. And I'm sorry." I smile at her. "And now I've fixed it. Congratulations. You and Nick will be very happy, I'm sure. Consider this your coupling present."

She growls low in her throat. "You're so damned stubborn!" She spins on her heel and stamps off.

Well, that makes two for two. I'm on a roll.

"I guess you took the time to get her authorization for coupling back?" Gavin asks.

I look at him from the corner of my eye. "Are you going to lecture me, too?"

"She's right, Evie. What in the hell were you thinking?"

"You've asked that already. Are you going to let me answer this time?"

He pulls in a breath through his teeth and makes a hissing sound. "I don't know. Do you have an answer that doesn't use the words, 'I had to. You would have just hindered me'?"

"I could come up with something," I say, and try a smile.

He bangs a hand on the end table, making the lamp wobble back and forth. "Damn it, Evie. This isn't funny. You could have died and I would have never known."

"That's not true. Mother would have . . ." I trail off and look to my hands when his eyes flash.

"Oh, yeah. That's *exactly* how I want to find out you died. Don't you care about anyone but yourself?"

His words steal my breath. I feel like I've been punched in the stomach and I cross my arms around it. His words are so close to what Macie said.

"I care about you," I whisper, blinking back tears.

"Do you? Because you haven't shown it."

Haven't shown it? *Haven't shown it?* "I've risked my life to help you escape, haven't I? I'm giving up my home to help you. Isn't that enough?"

"No!" he says.

"What else do you want from me?"

"I want you to—" He cuts himself off and thins his lips.

"What?"

"I want you to . . . trust me. To let me help you when you need it."

I weave my brows together. I'm sure that's not what he was going to say, but he's crossed his arms over his chest and I doubt I'll get the real answer.

"I want to know I can trust you, too. That you won't leave me behind like some incompetent ass that can't take care of himself, let alone his girl."

His voice is quiet now and I can hear so much sadness behind it, I immediately feel ashamed for not trusting him, when he trusted me.

"You're right. I'm sorry," I finally say. "I trust you. I won't do it again."

He looks up at me, suspicion clouding his eyes. "Are you sure?"

"Yes. You and me. Together. Until the end. For better or worse."

He raises an eyebrow, and he gives me a tilted smile. "Until the end," he repeats. Then he's pulling me in for a shaky hug, squeezing so tightly I squeak when I try to breathe. When he hears the squeak, he releases me a fraction.

"I'm sorry, Gavin," I say. "I really am. I can't imagine what it was like waiting for me."

He pulls back and I'm sure I'm in for another lecture, but then his mouth crushes down on mine, his hands traveling over every available space on my body.

I'm so shocked I don't do anything. This kiss is different from our others. Way different. My heart thunders in my ears and kicks in my chest. My breaths turn ragged. My head spins, but this time there's no panic. Only surprise. And pleasure.

When he finally releases me, I wobble.

We stare at each other, until Macie clears her throat. "Touching by unCoupleds is against the law. Unless, of course, you'd like to share something with me."

I turn my attention to her. She's standing now, and

although her stance is wary, there's a hint of amusement in her eyes, and the corner of her lips quiver with a smile.

"You're one to talk," I blurt out, and then frown. How did I know that?

She only continues to smile, not even pretending to correct me.

Gavin flashes me a grin. "So, you going to show me what's under your dress?" he asks with a look toward my chest.

Huh? "Under my . . . Oh!" I laugh when I realize he felt the data cube in my bra. I pull it out and hand it to him.

"What is this?" he says, studying it.

"It's a data cube. It's got some information I think we can use." Finally, I say, "Have you forgiven me, then? For leaving you here?"

"No," he says bluntly, without even looking at me.

"Oh."

"But I understand why you did it." He turns to face me. "I suppose I would have done the same thing." He takes the hands I'm clenching at my sides and clasps them between his. "And you promised to never do it again. I trust you."

"You do?" I ask, completely shocked. "Still?"

"Yes. I do."

Macie clears her throat again and I look at her. Her eyes are red, and I'm sure it's from crying. In order to preserve her dignity, I ignore it and hope Gavin does, too.

I step back from Gavin and hold up the data cube. "I brought back some interesting goodies. Feel like doing some analysis for me?" I ask.

She sniffles, then nods and takes the data cube. "What is this?"

I gesture for her to sit, then tell them about what had happened with Mother in her quarters. They're both leaning forward by the end of it.

"Who was the picture of?" Gavin asks.

"I don't know. It was a woman, and she was holding a small child on her lap."

Macie pops the cube into her computer system and a section of her wall lights up to reveal a holographic display. Gavin's eyes just about pop out of his head.

"That is wicked!" he says. "I wish we had something like this, but we've only got these crappy things that don't work most of the time."

Macie and I share a smile before going back to look through the files. She takes half and moves them over to another screen and I stay on the first. We look through them for what feels like forever until I find what I'm looking for.

It's a diary. Mother's diary.

I almost shut it down, thinking it's too personal and probably of no use to us, when something catches my eye. It's an entry from when Mother was a child.

FEBRUARY 1
Daddy says it's time to go. He can't stand the thought of losing me, too, so he's going to go to the only place he knows is safe. We're going to move to his resort. Elysium! That's the

one under the ocean! Mother never much cared for that one.
She was much too afraid of being underwater, so I've only
been there once. But it's beautiful.

Daddy's asked me for a list of my friends and their
families to come with us, but I don't want anyone there but
Daddy and I. No one else deserves to live in such a lovely
place. They didn't care that Mother died. They didn't even
try calling to see if I was all right! Even when they knew I
saw those awful people shoot her just because she was wear-
ing some gold necklaces! They even took my favorite hair-
band! The one with all the diamonds on it.

I don't care that Daddy said my friends just didn't know
what to say or do. Mother always said that ignorance is no
excuse for bad manners. But he's inviting his friends and I
suppose I don't want to be around people older than me all
the time, so I'll make the stupid list.

The next eight years of entries talk about how much she
idolized her "perfect" father, how he could never do any
wrong, and reminiscing about her "perfect" mother. How
she's surprised about what Father allows to happen, and how
her mother would never have tolerated some of the goings-on.
And more and more rants about the Surface and the Surface
Dwellers as she's started calling them. Nothing all that important or surprising, just the incoherent ramblings of someone becoming increasingly hostile to the happenings on the
Surface, so I just scroll through them, scanning for important

information until I find what I was looking for: the day Mother took control of Elysium.

JUNE 6

Father has gone out of his mind. He actually wants to return to the Surface. He says they've changed. The people who live up there. The ones who started the War.

Even after it ended, they still tore apart the land with their manipulations, greed, and hostilities. Worst yet, he seems to have forgotten that they are the ones who took Mother from us.

He says he misses the sky and fresh air. That he wants to look at more than just the walls of this complex. How utterly ridiculous. What's prettier than the sea and its inhabitants? I asked him, but he just says it's because I don't remember the Surface. I remember the Surface, all right. It was filthy and disgusting and lawless.

How a civilized person is expected to live, let alone thrive up there, I have no idea, but I know that it's my responsibility to talk sense into Father.

JUNE 7

Father refused to listen to reason and insists that all his guests—and that includes me—must return to the Surface. I consider this nothing short of betrayal of Mother and myself and have rectified the situation in the only way befitting a betrayer.

JULY 1

I have taken official control of the city. There is much to be done to cleanse the taint of the Surface Dweller from my fair city. Elysium has remained mostly disconnected from the Surface and we have the capability to become fully self-sufficient with minimal effort and changes. All we need is the addition of a fully equipped medical center, agricultural sector, and a separate residential area. I refuse to live in the same space as those that Father deemed acceptable.

The taint from the Surface has infiltrated farther than I thought. However, the situation should be easily rectified with stricter rules and harsher punishments. I will rule with an "iron fist," as they say. This will no longer be a relaxing resort, but a thriving city. No matter the cost.

I'm certain there will be those who resist, but any further betrayals will not be tolerated. Dissenters will meet the same punishment as Father.

I must remain forward-thinking. And the first step into making this city perfect is to "purify" the city, by removing all carriers of unwanted genetics and preserving those that fit the model of perfection I'm striving for.

Chapter Twenty

Subject 121, Evelyn Winters: It appears she is resistant to normal Conditioning techniques. All methods have failed, seemingly at an increased rate each treatment. I believe a full medical evaluation will be needed to determine the cause.

—Dr. Friar, progress note to Mother

My gaze moves over to Gavin, shock rendering me mute. He was right. Mother lied about who founded the city, and why the city was founded. I guess I shouldn't be surprised he was right. The real question is, when has he been wrong?

He must sense me staring at him, because he turns and smiles at me. It slips when he sees my face.

"What's wrong?" He jumps up from his seat.

Macie turns and frowns at me. "Sweetie? What's wrong?"

I only gesture back to the screen. I can't make myself say the words. I'm not sure why this surprises me so much. It only makes sense. Her hatred for the Surface. Her obsession with everyone being perfect. Her words in her room. Gavin and Macie crowd behind me, and I know the minute they realize what they're seeing as their mouths drop open. It would be comical if not for the foreboding feeling I've got in the pit of my stomach.

"No way!" Macie says. "The city isn't that old. Our history teachers said so. We are the first children."

"Think about it," I say quietly. "You said it yourself. She's the one in charge of the curriculum. If I said the water was purple, she'd change it. She changed the lessons to state her truth."

"But why?" Macie asks.

I exchange a look with Gavin. "Because she didn't want anyone to challenge her authority."

"I don't understand." She tugs on her hair in a way I've seen dozens of times before whenever she's frustrated. I can't say I don't know how she feels. I want to pull my own hair out, but I know it won't do any good.

"Haven't you ever wondered why there isn't a Sector One?" I ask.

She shakes her head. "I always thought that was the Palace Wing."

Fair enough. "Okay, well, Gavin and I found an abandoned Sector. And it looks identical to Sector Two. I think that's Sector One."

Her eyes widen. "What?"

"There's no one living there. Hasn't been for a long time, if the dust is any indication. About thirty years or so."

"What happened to all the people?"

I open my mouth to tell her, but no sound comes out. I

can't force myself to tell her. I look down at the floor instead.

Gavin squeezes my shoulder. "We think they were killed."

She sinks down so she's sitting on the couch again. "Why?"

"Because they were trying to escape." I keep my attention focused on the tips of my shoes. "Even then, Mother had strict rules."

"From what we can gather," Gavin continues, "someone snitched, and they had to escape quickly, but we're not so sure any of them actually made it."

I go on to explain the journal entries in detail.

"Oh, Mother," Macie said. Her face is as white as her walls. Her blue eyes pop in contrast. "So, she just erased them? Like they didn't exist?" Then she sighs. "Of course she did. Hasn't she been doing that with the people who disobey her? Just on a smaller scale. I'll bet that's why she came up with the Enforcers."

I nod, pleased she is taking this better than I'd expected. "Exactly. In fact it says right here"—I point to further down on the screen—"the Enforcers gave her the idea for genetic manipulation. So, it all leads back to Sector One."

That reminds me about the files I found with my name on it, but I go back to reading Mother's journal. I'm hoping that maybe the answer to my problem is in there. If not, I can always dive into the other files.

The entries are full of fear and deep gratitude for the safety of Elysium. I can't make sense of it all. There seems to be entries missing, and sometimes she devolves into some kind of code. I think she was getting paranoid. And the more paranoid she got, the more she wanted total control.

She grew to hate free will. She believed she had a pure vision of a perfect society—a perfect family—but the Citizens did not comply. She saw the city falling apart before her eyes. The harder she worked to bring her vision to the city, the more the people rebelled against her rules. She wanted them to be more docile, so she worked with a scientist to experiment with gene manipulation.

At first it was only by controlling breeding, like cross-pollinating plants or breeding out the venom in bees as we've done. Then her experiments with creating the ideal secret police force began, and her experience in training the Enforcers showed her she could get even better results with Conditioning—an idea Dr. Friar had brought with him from the Surface.

There's a large section in her personal code around this time, but eventually she achieved her dream. The entries are filled with tales of her success and the development of the Citizen's Code of Conduct.

Then I reach another section in code. I can't make out much, but the dates correspond with the journal from Sector One. Finally, I find a blue hyperlink within the code and I know I have to see where it leads.

I sneak a quick glance over my shoulder and click the link. The screen shimmers, then another window pops up and shows me what looks like video footage of Sector One. At first there doesn't appear to be anything unusual. Just the normal wanderings of Citizens milling around the Square. But at two minutes and fifty seconds in, a man in a white coat dashes across the Square. It's hard to see him in detail, but he seems familiar to me.

He runs toward the wall where Gavin and I found the room, followed by a swarm of others. The man in the white coat doesn't make it far, though, when he grabs his head with both hands and falls to his knees. His mouth is open in what appears to be a scream, but there's no sound.

A nearby woman reaches out to him, presumably to help him, before she, too, grabs her head and falls over. The rest of the people gathered around quickly follow suit, and by five minutes and fifty seconds into the video, everyone in the Sector has collapsed and is lying on the ground.

I narrow my eyes when Mother steps into the camera view and walks over with a group of Guards behind her. She gestures to the bodies and one of the Guards kicks the woman hard in the ribs. She doesn't even flinch. Mother glances up at the camera, then says something and walks away.

The video continues for another few minutes while the Guards pack the bodies into black bags, proving what I already know. The Citizens are all dead.

Macie makes a small noise and, startled, I glance over. She's staring at the screen, her eyes filled with tears, her hand covering her mouth.

"She's insane!" Macie whispers.

"Well, yeah, that's nothing new," Gavin says.

"No, I mean, really, really insane. She should be locked in

a padded cell in the Medical Sector," Macie says. She moves her eyes from the screen to mine. "You guys need to get out of here, now. There's no time to waste." She's quiet for a moment as she glances over the screen, where the video has started to replay. She stares at it for a long moment, before meeting my eyes. "And I'm coming with you."

Gavin and I exchange a look before he shrugs and I nod. "Absolutely."

"Just . . . let me just go find Nick. I can't leave without him."

She tosses a few things into her bag, then saves the files on the data cubes to two more and hands one to me and one to Gavin. "In case we get separated," she says. "At least someone will know of all this."

She leads the way to the door and throws it open. Standing there is a tall man—taller than Gavin—with short, curly blond hair and light blue eyes.

"Nick!"

He grins back when he sees her. "Hey, there's my girl."

Before he can pull her in for a hug, she's tugging on his hand. "Oh, wow, thank Mother you came—" I can only assume she's trying to pull him into the hallway. "We've got to go, Nick. Now."

"Go where?" Nick asks, laughing, tugging back on her hand.

"To the Surface. It isn't safe here anymore." She tugs on his hand again, but he doesn't budge.

"Mace? What—" His voice trails off when he sees me, then Gavin standing protectively at my side. His eyes focus on the front of my dress . . . and that's when I remember I'm still covered with my own blood.

His fists clench at his side and his eyes swirl with anger. Little warning bells go off in my head. It reminds me of something, but I can't quite place it.

"What is *he* doing here?" he demands, staring right at Gavin. Then before anyone can answer him, he takes a step toward Gavin. "What are you doing here?" The veins in his neck bulge with each word and his face is turning red.

Gavin stands his ground, even moves slightly in front of me.

Macie seems puzzled by Nick's reaction, but she steps in front of him. "Nick. We have to leave. Mother is insane. She *murdered* an entire Sector. It isn't safe here."

Nick doesn't even spare Macie a look, he's so focused on Gavin. "Escape where? To the Surface?"

"Yes," she says slowly, and looks over to us, her eyes wide.

"You want to *leave* the safety of our *home*. To go to the Surface. A place filled with horrors we can only imagine. Because this *Surface Dweller* has made up some *lie* about Mother?"

"It's not a lie, Nick. I saw it myself. You can see it, too, if you want," she says, and starts to turn toward the screen.

He finally faces her. "Are you telling me I'm wrong?" he asks with his teeth clenched. "That *I'm* wrong and this Surface Dweller is right?"

Gavin looks at me, and I'm sure his face mirrors mine: eyes wide with shock and filled with a mix of terror and misery.

Macie turns back around. "Nick? What's wrong? Why are you so angry?"

"Why am I angry?" he asks. "You have to ask why I'm angry?"

She shakes her head and steps back, seeking the safety of our trio.

"Could it have anything to do with the fact that the woman I'm supposed to couple with trusts a Surface Dweller over me?" Nick yells, startling all of us.

"That's not it. We have proof, Nick," I say, taking a step forward. Gavin yanks me back toward him.

Nick ignores me and continues to glare at Macie.

"Surface Dwellers are manipulative and dangerous."

"Oh shit," Gavin says under his breath and exchanges a look with me.

Macie, however, takes another step back. "She's right. That's not—" She's cut off when he shoots an arm out and grabs her neck, his fingers wrapping around her throat.

In a flash, he's got her pressed against the wall with her feet dangling about a meter from the ground. Her head almost touches the ceiling. And she's clawing at his forearms. Blood oozes from the scratches.

"Nick!" I yell.

Nick growls at me and then squeezes harder on Macie's throat.

"His kind is the reason for the fall of man and our exile to

the ocean. *Surface Dwellers are manipulative and dangerous and should be shot on sight.*"

Macie's kicking the wall now, and her eyes are bugging out of her face. There's a blue tint to her lips, but Nick just keeps repeating the words I recognize from my own Conditioned responses.

Gavin stands next to me and I can practically hear the gears in his head as he frantically tries to come up with a solution. His eyes roam the room, but he doesn't act. He's probably just as afraid as I am to make the wrong move.

"Nick. Please listen to me. You need to put Macie down. You're hurting her," I say as if I'm talking to a toddler who's having a tantrum. I don't want to do anything that will set him off, but I can't just let him kill my best friend.

I slide my eyes to the side. Gavin's fists are clenching and unclenching again and that tick is back in his jaw.

Macie squeaks and I turn my attention back to them. Her whole face is a reddish purple and the blood on her fingers is not just Nick's anymore. Her struggles to tear Nick's fingers from her throat have caused her to break her nails back.

I walk slowly to Nick, still begging him to let Macie go, apologizing to him. Promising we won't leave. That it was just a bad joke. I'd say anything to get him to let Macie go. At first he doesn't listen, then his fingers loosen and Macie takes a large breath. Relieved, I stop walking.

When he turns around, the strange look is still in his eyes. It's a look that will haunt me forever.

Macie tries to get away from him, but he suddenly tightens

his grip on her. I start forward, automatically trying to help her, and he throws her across the room.

She hits the wall across the room with a sound like eggs breaking. She slides down the wall, leaving a trail of blood behind her, then crumples onto the floor like a rag doll.

Chapter Twenty-one

Enforcer Testing Requirements

In order to pass training, an Enforcer must:

1. *Lift 5 times her own body weight (bare minimum)*
2. *Have mastered at least 100 different forms of martial art techniques*
3. *Be able to name, dismantle, repair, and correctly use weaponry available to them*
4. *Endure emotional, pain tolerance, and healing tests*
5. *Possess varied computer skills, including but not limited to: extensive knowledge of all operating systems (past and present), coding, and software for the express purpose of "hacking," and forensics*

I stare at Macie, her pretty little doll's face still perfect, except for the trail of blood coming from her mouth and nose.

"No," I whisper.

A red haze funnels in from the sides of my eyes, and there's a click inside of me. Something I haven't felt in so long, but is as familiar to me as breathing.

Nick growls, his eyes still flashing and rolling with madness. Gavin yanks me behind him and tries pushing me toward the door, but I won't have it. Not from a Surface Dweller. How *dare* he touch me. But Nick must be taken care of first. Nick broke the law. There must be payment. And I'm just the one to exact it.

Before I can stop myself, I shove past Gavin, practically shoving him to the floor, and charge Nick, knocking him down to the ground near the kitchen door. He struggles to grab me, growling and snapping his teeth in frustration, but I don't give him the chance. I slide around behind him and grab a hold of his head. Before either of us can blink, I twist.

There's a sound like a branch cracking, then he lies still in my arms. Disgusted, I let go and his head hangs limply on his shoulders. He finally resembles the man he did when we first saw him at the door.

I look over at Gavin, intent on completing my duties, but I'm bombarded with so many memories that I'm forced to my knees by the tide of them. They surface so quickly I can't focus on just one before another is pushing it away.

"Congratulations! Evelyn has been chosen for the Enforcer program . . . She must begin her Conditioning immediately. There is no time to waste."

"Failure will not be tolerated again. You will do as you're told. Do you understand, Evelyn?"

An older man refuses to bow his head to Mother as she passes on her way to Sorting. I sneak behind him, then grab him by his arm and pull him into the shadows. Although he struggles, it's a simple matter of injecting him with the syringe of medication Enforcers use to calm the unwilling, then I place my hands around his head and twist.

"Very good, Evelyn. You've gotten a perfect score in martial arts. Let's move on to weapons training."

Bone-chilling sounds of screams and gunshots from the crowd ring in my ears, then sounds of sobbing replace the screaming in my head as the clouds of smoke clear, revealing dozens of men, women, and children lying in blood. But relief fills me as I realize that I'd kept my real father safe. He'd escaped in the confusion. Hopefully along with my real mother.

"Subject 121, Enforcer Evelyn Winters, will be undergoing yet another Conditioning session, due to her repeated resistance to previous attempts."

"Evelyn Winters, you have been accused of failing in your mission to protect Mother, resulting in the death of an Enforcer. Mother finds you guilty and condemns you to have your memories wiped until she decides on your final judgment."

"I was an Enforcer," I whisper to myself, bile threatening to rise and choke me. Then I see Macie lying on the ground across the room.

I rush to her, but Gavin is already there. The expression on his face as he looks up at me tells me it's already too late.

"No, no, no," I moan.

I kneel next to her and pull her limp body into my lap. The face is a lie, I think. It's perfect, giving the resemblance of life, but she's broken. Gavin stares at me, his hands shaking where they rest on Macie's arm, but I don't look at him.

Oh, no. No, no, no, no, no. I killed Nick. Because he killed Macie. I was going to kill Gavin. And that's what Enforcers do. I'm an Enforcer. A trained killer. I killed my best friend's betrothed.

Everything about me is numb now. The click that had fueled my need to kill Nick is gone, leaving an empty space—and overwhelming exhaustion. The pain in my shoulder flares like I've been shot again, but I ignore it. Macie is gone. My best friend. Who is as close to me as any sister. Who I had almost carelessly tossed aside. The one who'd loved her boyfriend more than anything, who would never see her dreams come true. And it was my fault.

All my fault. That's what had happened before. Why I was punished. I deserve to be punished. Innocent people are dead because of me. And now I know it isn't the first time. How many other deaths are on my hands?

Gavin suddenly grabs my arm and tugs. "Come on. It's time to go."

I stare at him, uncomprehending. "Go? Why? Where?"

"People are coming. They must've heard something." He tries yet again to pull me to my feet.

At first I resist. I won't leave Macie. She needs me. Then I hear the banging on the door.

"Evie, come on. Please. We have to go."

"We can't just leave her!"

"There's no time! I'm sorry. I really am. Please! Don't make me throw you over my shoulder and drag you out the door."

The door to the apartment crashes in and my instincts, my Enforcer instincts, kick back in. I jump to my feet and pull a surprised Gavin toward the servant's tunnels. Unfortunately, people are already coming through that way, effectively cutting off any escape. Now we're stuck in the middle of the hallway, surrounded.

Again I hear the clicking sound in my head and my whole body calms. My heart rate settles. My breathing evens. Even the pain is gone. I smile at the Guards as they jam into the small hallway. I take a quick head count. Six to my front. At least twice that to the rear.

"It's them," one says. "The Surface Dweller and the Daughter of the People."

"She's covered in blood," another says.

"Where did it come from?"

"Why is she protecting the Surface Dweller?"

Their voices swim in and around one another, making it impossible to differentiate who's talking.

Gavin is tensed, ready to spring, but I think he's waiting for me to make the first move. I'm torn. Fighting the urge to side with the Guards and take Gavin down, and calculating what it'll take to escape with Gavin, without killing anyone else. There's only one way to go, and that's back out the way we came in: the front door. There seems to be fewer Guards that way, which will make it easier for us. Chances are they sent the majority through the maintenance tunnels.

When someone gasps and a whisper rises up about the

two forms lying broken in the living room, one lying in a pool of blood, I realize that's my chance. I smile, but it's more like baring my teeth.

Still, they don't seem scared. I can change that, I think.

"Move," I growl, startling them with the hate in my husky voice. I know what they're thinking and I have every intention of playing on it. I don't care what they think of me. I have nothing keeping me here anymore.

I growl again. And watch them jump. "Leave us."

Even when I step forward, they don't budge. They aren't afraid of me. They're watching Gavin. The manipulative Surface Dweller.

I shake my head, clearing the hateful thoughts from it. I'll have to find some way to force them to move. I pull out the Reising from the bag, slam a magazine into it, and hold it to my shoulder.

The Guards tense, but still don't move. One even snickers at me. "Hand over the gun, sweetheart," he says, "before you hurt yourself."

With narrowed eyes, I squeeze the trigger, releasing a spray of bullets into the ceiling.

Bits of concrete rain down on our heads and the Guards take a step away from me, pulling out their side arms and aiming them at me.

"Do you really think you worry me? Now get out of the way."

They don't move.

"I'd listen to her, if I were you," Gavin says.

The Guard directly in front of us sneers. "Shut your mouth, Surface Dweller. Hiding behind a girl. You should be ashamed of yourself."

Gavin steps forward, but I don't give him the chance. I aim the gun right at the Guard's heart and squeeze the trigger.

The gun slams into my bad shoulder, but I don't even feel it as I watch the bullet tear through the chest of the first Guard, then the one directly behind him.

There's a look of shock on the first Guard's face as he topples to the floor.

"Anyone else care to argue with me?" I ask, stepping forward.

The rest take a step back. With each step I take, they take another until finally our backs are toward the broken door. Gavin watches our exit over his shoulder as we back toward it. Just as we get to the opening, I reach into my bag and pull a grenade out of my pack.

I yank the pin out with my teeth and toss it directly at the remaining Guards. There's no choice, we have to get away and we won't be able to if they're at our heels.

As soon as we clear the threshold, I spin around, then run through the hallways. The blast from the grenade blows out the doorway and slams us against the wall, knocking our breath from our bodies.

Before we even land, Gavin's yanking me back up and pulling me down the hall. I have no idea where we're going because I've let Gavin lead the way. I don't even know where we could go. I'm hoping he's thought of something, because my mind is suddenly blank. I don't even realize I'm crying until the tears welling in my eyes blind me.

Voices follow us, and every once in a while someone stops us to ask if we need help. My heart trips each time, but Gavin keeps his head down and says, "Got caught in the turret malfunction by the Tube. I'm just taking her to the Medical Sector."

Unfortunately a trio realizes we're heading in the wrong direction, and tries to stop us from going farther. One of the women says, "That's Miss Evelyn!"

Like before, the click sounds in my head, and everything but the people in front of me disappears.

I straighten and kick out with a leg, knocking the woman into the two men behind her. Before any of them can regain their footing, I'm on top of them. I yank the woman up by her arm as she tries to cower from me.

My plan is to break all three of their nosy necks, but when I glance at Gavin, he's staring at me in horror. When he notices I've hesitated and I'm looking at him, he shakes his head.

I shove the woman off to the side and she hits the concrete wall and crumples to the ground. I watch her chest for a moment, confident she's only knocked out when I see it rise and fall.

The other men are still trying to untangle themselves. I quickly bang their heads together. Their eyes cross, then they slump over each other.

There's a crunch behind me and I whirl around and drop into a crouch, prepared to defend myself from whoever it is.

Gavin tosses his hands up. "Whoa. It's just me."

Again I'm filled with suspicion and hate directed toward Gavin.

After several tense moments, I force myself to drop my hands. I glance over to where the woman lays against the wall and it reminds me so much of Macie. . . . The next thing I know, I'm collapsing to the ground.

Gavin wraps his arm around my waist and pulls me up, then leads me down the street, glancing behind us every few steps. It surprises me we haven't passed anyone since I attacked those people, but I'm not going to complain.

I don't want to hurt anyone else. For Mother's sake, I almost killed those three, and they'd just been unlucky enough to run into us.

Finally we get to a wall that looks familiar. But it isn't until he presses a block and the wall swings open that I realize we're back in Sector One. He shuts the door, but doesn't stop. He follows the path we made just a few hours before and then forces me into the secret room.

After crawling into a corner, I curl into a ball and sob into my knees. Within moments he's next to me, pulling me into his lap, much the same way I'd pulled Macie's body into mine.

At first I fight him. How can he want to touch me after what I've done? After finding out what I really am? But he just holds me tighter to him and I give in, letting him gather me into his arms and then sobbing into his chest. Tears are useless. I know that. But I can't help myself. Everything I thought about myself was wrong. I'm a monster.

To my relief, Gavin doesn't say anything. None of those useless words people always use when they don't know what to say. Instead, he just holds me tight and lets me cry myself dry. Finally the sobbing subsides, yet I cling to him. Despite the overwhelming exhaustion, not to mention the agony in my arm, I can't bear to let him go.

It's quiet in the room, the only sound the occasional hiss from the recyclers. Then I hear voices. I should have known our escape had been too easy. And with the mess I left, it's not surprising they found us.

I stiffen and Gavin brushes my hair with his hand. "It's okay," he whispers.

I look up and place my finger over his lips. He narrows his eyes, then they widen and I know he's heard the voices as well. We both crawl over to the small door.

"Are you sure they came in here?" a female voice asks. The sound of her voice brings a flood of memories and I recognize it as one of the friends I'd trained with. She's an Elite Enforcer. I stare wide-eyed at Gavin. What have I done? Killing all those Guards . . . and now an Elite is after us. We'll never escape.

"Well," a male responds, "witnesses say they ran this way, and there's nowhere else they could go. Besides, this is where they were earlier."

"People see a lot of things. *I* don't see anything," the Enforcer says. "This trail is fresh, but you said they were here earlier. There isn't any blood, and if she was covered in it, like you said, there'd be blood somewhere."

"Then where do you suggest they went?"

"Probably into the tunnels. They could be anywhere now. Send your men to search."

"What about you?"

"I'm going to search this place just to prove you're wrong."

There's silence, then the scrape of shoes against the concrete, and he mutters, "Bitch."

I'm sure she hears it, but she doesn't respond. It's entirely too quiet for my tastes. Then she mutters, "Come out, come out wherever you are!" There's silence again and I dare not breathe, for fear she'll hear it. "Now that you know what you are, where are you going to hide? Do you really think that Surface Dweller is going to accept you now that he knows?"

More silence. Then there's another scrape and her shoes click against the concrete as she walks away. We wait, frozen in our spot, too afraid to move even a centimeter, until long after we hear the squeal of the hinges of the wall door. Then we sneak out and make our way back to the apartment we stayed in before, watching our backs the entire trip.

Gavin double and triple checks the apartment before securing the door.

I'm a mess, covered in blood and Mother knows what else, and I just want to wash everything away.

My feet drag and I know it's not only the exhaustion that

has finally caught up with me; it's mind-numbing depression. Not only did I watch my best friend die while I did nothing, but then I went psychotic and killed her boyfriend.

I go straight to the shower, but sit on the floor of the stall and let the freezing water wash over me. I'm hoping the water will wake me up, but even when I'm completely clean and shivering, I still feel weighted down. The water soaks my bandage and burns the wound, but I can't make myself get out. I just sit in the corner of the granite stall and bury my face in my hands. I've cried myself dry, but that doesn't stop the sorrow.

Eventually, Gavin comes to check on me. He knocks at first, but I ignore it, hoping he'll just go away. I should have known better, because when he receives no answer he pushes into the room. Then rushes across the bathroom, practically ripping the curtain from its hooks in his hurry to check on me.

His expression changes from worry to sadness when he sees me curled into the corner. He turns off the water with a flick of a wrist, then bundles me into a fluffy white—and dusty—towel and carries me into the bedroom. Then he starts chafing me with the towel, trying to rub warmth into my freezing body.

Even when I stop shivering, I still feel cold. I wonder if I'll ever feel warm again.

"How are you feeling?" he asks after several minutes.

I jump. I hadn't expected him to talk. "I don't know," I say. "She was my best friend. And she died because of me."

"Not you. Never you. Mother. She's the one who started this."

"I'm an Enforcer," I say without any emotion. "A monster."

"No, Evie. Not a monster," he says quietly.

"I killed those people. I've killed lots of people. All in the name of Mother's 'peace.'"

"Because Mother programmed you to do it. And Nick. Apparently." He takes my chin in his hand and forces me to look at him. "You also saved me. And you tried to save Macie. You only killed the Guards in self-defense and you stopped yourself from killing the innocent people in the hallway. That's not a monster."

There's nothing to say to that.

"You're not afraid? Of me?" I ask finally, averting my eyes.

He waits until I look back up at him before he shakes his head and smiles at me. "No. Never."

Gavin pulls me into his arms again and kisses me. Gently at first, then more aggressively. As if he can't help himself. And the minute of panic fades as if it was never there. The kiss has the effect that nothing else has—it warms my blood and soothes my soul. I don't want it to stop.

Winding my arms around his neck, I pull myself into his lap. I shiver when his mouth trails down my neck.

My hands impatiently race over his body. Every hard line and ripple. His body trembles as I splay my hands over his chest. He pulls me closer and deepens the kiss.

I lose myself along with my breath and my heart.

Chapter Twenty-two

Unauthorized coupling is punishable under the law
and will be dealt with most severely.
—Citizen's Social Code, Volume VI

When I wake, my face is pressed into a pillow and there's a light flutter on the back of my neck. I swipe my hand at it and my fingers catch in my tangled hair. I suck air through my teeth, making a hissing sound when I yank a few of those hairs from my head.

The fluttering happens again and I realize it's Gavin's breath on the side of my neck. I slowly turn so I'm facing him and watch him sleep for a few minutes. He looks like a little boy lost in dreams. Well, except for the shadow of hair growing along his jaw.

I smile as I remember last night. Shortly after he'd kissed me brainless, weariness overtook me. I must have been lulled into sleep in his arms. The only true solace I can ever remember.

Tentatively, I brush back some hair that's fallen over his face. His eyes fly open, wary at first, but then they lock onto my face and clear instantly.

He smiles. "Guess we fell asleep," he says, his voice husky. It makes me shiver. "I guess so. Good morning," I say, even though I'm not exactly sure what time it really is.

He leans forward and kisses me gently, just a light press of his lips against mine. When he pulls back, his eyes are worried again. "How are you feeling?"

He doesn't mean my general health. He's asking how I'm handling Macie's death. The one thing I don't want to remember.

I roll onto my back and stare at the ceiling. I stick to the one part I'm willing to talk about. "It's hard. Knowing I'll never hear her voice again. But you were right. It's not my fault." My whole body tenses and my voice hardens. "And I swear I'll make Mother pay. No matter what, she'll pay for taking Macie from me."

Gavin leans over and peers into my eyes. "Evie, I know how you feel. But it's not worth losing your life over." I shrug and look away. He takes my face in his hands and makes me look at him again. "Don't do something stupid, Evie. I can't lose you now that I found you. I need you. We need each other."

"Found me? When were you looking for me?" My voice is still hard. Harder than I intend it to be, and I try to soften it with a laugh, but Gavin doesn't seem to care about how I said it.

"I didn't know I was looking until I found you," he says

seriously. He looks deep into my eyes, his thumb caressing the side of my face.

My heart gives a little thump and my breath catches, but I don't say anything.

"Promise me you won't do something stupid." I still don't say anything and he gives me a little shake. "Promise me!"

I sigh. "All right. I promise."

His eyes search mine and, after a few minutes, he smiles again and kisses me. Slightly angry with him for making me promise, I don't kiss him back, but he doesn't give up. He just changes the angle and takes my breath away. It doesn't take me long to give in and try to pull him closer to me.

We both tense when Mother's voice emits from the speaker above our heads.

"Attention Citizens of Elysium: Festival is cancelled until further notice."

Gavin and I exchange a look. What is she doing now?

"I know you are all asking yourselves why. It is my deepest regret to inform you that for the first time in the history of our city there has been . . . a murder."

She pauses here and I know it's for dramatic effect, not to give people time to let that news sink in.

Gavin whispers in my ear. "What is she talking about? She murders people all the time."

"Yes, but it's in the form of punishment. People don't see it as murder. Besides, most people don't realize what happens to the people who are being punished. They think they just vanish."

"And they don't question where they go?" His voice is incredulous.

I tilt my head to the side. "Would you?" He opens his mouth to answer, then promptly closes it.

Mother finally continues. "I'm devastated to say that it appears the murderer is none other than my own daughter. Evelyn." Again she pauses, but it's shorter this time. "I know how you all must be feeling, but let me just say that it appears she is being coerced by the Surface Dweller. There is evidence he has seduced her into helping him." She sniffles and I narrow my eyes. "I blame myself. If I hadn't been so lenient with her, she would have already been Coupled and this would not have happened."

"What? Lenient? She had you *brainwashed* whenever you disagreed with her. She turned you into an Enforcer, then breeding stock. What's lenient about that?" Gavin's eyes flash and his hand clenches, fisting into the sheets beside my head.

I shush him so I can hear Mother, who has lost all trace of her "tears."

"However, I cannot be wholly responsible. The majority of the blame rests squarely on this Surface Dweller's shoulders. He has invaded our home, and enticed Evelyn with his savage and destructive ways. He must be stopped. At any cost. We must take precautions to keep innocents from being hurt. Therefore, I am closing Festival and instituting a city-wide lockdown."

"Lockdown?" Gavin mouths.

"House arrest," I say. "She's shutting everyone up in their

quarters, but I doubt it's to keep them safe. It's more than likely to keep them out of the way." Then I lay my finger over his mouth to keep him quiet.

"Due to the leak in Sector Three, Citizens from that Sector should report to the Square for reassignment. This is a terrible inconvenience and I apologize. But they have already shown they lack restraint." She pauses again, but this time I sense glee in the silence. I shiver because I know what she's going to say next, and I know the only reason she's saying it is to hurt me. "Because, besides the dozen or so Guards she took out when they tried to arrest the Surface Dweller, the victims are none other than Evelyn's closest friend, Macie Beaumont, and her betrothed, Nick LeFavre." She makes a clicking sound with her tongue. "It's such a shame, as these two were approved to couple and were preparing to cohabitate. I had approved the paperwork a few hours before their deaths. This is a great loss for our city and for their families. Our hearts and prayers go out to them. Before I conclude and let you return to your homes, let us have a moment of silence for these two unfortunate souls."

Gavin gathers me into his arms, and it's at that moment I realize I'm shaking—but not from sadness like yesterday. Pure, unadulterated hate and anger rages through me. She hadn't approved anything. I did. Me. How *dare* she use Macie like that? Like she was nothing more than a . . . a pet!

My blood boiling, I shove away from Gavin to stalk around the room. He watches me for a bit, then grabs me and forces me to sit with him again.

"I know what you're going to say," I say when he opens his mouth.

"Good," he says. "Then I can save my breath. But it's true and you need to listen to it."

"I know. I know." I throw my hands in the air. "She makes me so angry—using Macie like that."

I glare at the speaker when Mother continues. "Now, please calmly and safely return to your homes. And under no circumstance are you to engage Evelyn or the Surface Dweller. If you see them, report them immediately. Thank you for your understanding."

The speaker crackles again and all is silent.

"How long before they clear out?" Gavin asks, and I know he's thinking what I'm thinking. That now's our chance. If we're ever going to escape, it has to be now, while the city is in chaos.

"Probably less than fifteen minutes."

"Then we'd better hurry."

Before he leaves the room to change clothes, he tosses me something from the closet. I glance down at the material in my hand. It's another dress. It's only then I realize I'm not wearing any clothes. Slightly embarrassed, I laugh as I look at the dress, hoping we don't run into any more ladders.

That reminds me of the wound on my shoulder. I glance over and see more blood has seeped through the still sopping-wet bandage.

I wish I could shower the blood off again and change the

bandage, but there isn't time. Unsure what to do, I bite my lip. If I leave the wet bandage, the wound could get infected. If I take the time to change it, we could miss our chance to get to the trains and to the other side undetected.

Gavin walks back in with my bag slung over his shoulder. His face is hard, and I wonder if this is what he looks like when he's hunting. It's sexy and scary at the same time.

His gaze follows mine and lands on the bandage, before flickering away and resting just a few inches above my head. That's when I remember, again, I'm not wearing any clothes. I cross an arm over my chest.

"We'll fix it when we get to this other Sector. We have plenty of bandages. But we should hurry," he says.

I nod. Of course that's what we should do. I knew that. So I toss on the new dress, hissing at the soreness and tightness of my shoulder, before following him out of the apartment to the wall-door that will get us back to the Square and eventually to the Tube station. It surprises me no one is guarding the Sector, but then, the Enforcer was quite certain I wasn't there. And it had been several hours. If there was anyone waiting, they probably were removed—or got bored and left. The Guards can have an annoyingly short memory if there's no one around to supervise them.

"Evie, wait." Gavin places a hand on my shoulder, stopping me from bolting out the opening. "If Mother was able to see that you fixed Macie's coupling thing, wouldn't she have just removed us from the computer again?"

I give him a thin smile. "No. I made it 'read-only.'"

He stares at me for a minute, before he barks out a laugh. "That had to burn her ass. We'd better hurry anyway."

We hurry through the opening, and I run to the left only to be stopped again by Gavin who frowns at me.

"The Tube's this way, right?" He points to the right.

I stare that way for a few seconds, blinking.

"Yes. Of course. Sorry, got turned around."

He continues to watch me for a second, then shrugs and we dive back into the crowd, ducking our heads and hoping no one will notice us. Thankfully my dress strap covers the bloody bandage.

But it seems we have nothing to worry about. Everyone is too busy talking about the murders in hushed tones. They don't even look at anyone. It's as if they're afraid they'll find us and don't really want to.

We follow the crowd making its way to the Residential Sector, then break off and follow the much smaller group heading to the Tube station, where we slip into an empty car of the train that's heading to Sector Three.

I'm not sure if it's a good thing or a bad thing about the leak in Sector Three. But then, I suppose it doesn't matter either way. If Mother is watching through the cameras, she'll react anyway, whether there are innocents around or not. The bloodstain on the floor of the Tube station is proof of that.

We hold our breath until the doors slide closed and the train leaves the station with an automated announcement about holding on to the handrails set throughout the car. At first the tunnel is dark, but it lightens up when we leave Sector Two and head into the open water between Sectors Two and Three.

The water glows with an orange color from the lava tubes. Gavin gets up and touches a hand to the glass of the windows.

"Why is the water orange?"

I sit on the floor and lean back against the wall, letting my eyes close. "Lava flows."

"Lava flows?"

"It's amazing, really, that such a deadly thing is the only reason we're able to live down here. The geothermic energy it produces is used to heat the boiler, which in turn creates steam, which turns the turbines to create electricity and provide heat throughout the facility. We use the steam engines to power everything, from the lights to the Tube and everything in between. How Mother got this city to function like that . . . well. I guess it really wasn't her. It was her father."

He's quiet for a moment, then asks, "How does the train work when we're underwater?"

I open my eyes to look at him. "The train is in a tube, hence the name, which is made of reinforced glass. The tracks use magnetism to keep the train moving in the right direction."

"Magnets?" He whistles softly and turns back to watch the water out the window. Without warning, the train stops, sending him crashing into the wall on the other side of the car. I rush over to him and help him to a sitting position.

"Are you okay?" I ask, looking for injuries.

He rubs the side of his head. "Yeah. I think so. Ugh. What happened?"

"I don't know."

I help him stand. Then a holograph flickers to life in the center of the car and Mother stands in front of us. Gavin immediately pushes me behind him. I know it's useless—she's not really there—but I let him try to protect me. I peer over his shoulder.

Mother laughs. "Well, well, what is this? So the hunter is a protector, too? Very interesting." She shakes her head and gives me a disappointed look. "I thought you were smarter than this, Evelyn. What a shame it has come to this. You know, I don't have to wait. I can just press the button now, if I want to." She focuses her attention back on Gavin. "It's useless to protect her. You have nowhere to go."

"What are you talking about, Mother?" I make a show out of examining my nails. Inside, though, I'm getting nervous. What is she planning?

Turns out I don't have to wait long to find out.

"Why don't I just show you?" she says with a wide smile. The hologram shuts off and the doors open, revealing the tunnel.

Gavin turns to frown at me. "What's going on?" he asks as my veins turn to ice.

I don't need to hear the screams from the passengers in the cars up ahead to realize what's happened.

"She's flooded the tube," I manage to say before a wave of freezing water rushes into the car.

Chapter Twenty-three

Caution: For your safety, Sector Three is under quarantine until further notice. There is a possible biohazard situation due to leaks in labs and mechanical areas. Failure to follow instructions could result in injury or death.

—sign located in Tube station, Sector Two

It takes no time at all for the freezing water to fill the car. The saltwater sears my eyes and the wound in my arm, but I bite the inside of my cheeks to prevent myself from screaming out. I need to get to the rebreathers. I know they're around here somewhere. It's not like I haven't done countless emergency drills for just this occasion, but I can't remember where they are.

The cold water has made not only my limbs and body cold, but seems to have frozen my brain, too. I spin around in circles, little bubbles of air foaming around me as I look for anything that resembles storage. I refuse to even look at Gavin and see the panic and fear in his eyes. It won't help me find the rebreathers, and will only remind me how hopeless things are.

Finally I see it: a little door on the floor. I swim down and start tugging on the silver handle. Gavin quickly realizes what I'm doing and swims next to me to help me pry open the door. Finally the whole door pops off and he tosses it to the side, where it slowly drifts back to the floor.

Inside are several rebreathers. They look like black vests, but there's a tube that juts off to one side and has a mouthpiece attached to it. There's a large red button on top of the mouthpiece.

Lungs screaming, I grab one and shove the mouthpiece into Gavin's mouth, pressing the red button. Instantly, I doubt myself. It was the red button, right? But what's that gray one? Red and black spots form in front of my eyes and I can hardly see to grab my own rebreather.

I have to breathe. Just one little breath. That's all I need.

As I open my mouth to do just that, something is pushed past my teeth. I taste rubber and saltwater and only instinct prevents me from choking by shoving my tongue into the mouth piece when Gavin presses the purge button and a rush of saltwater tries pushing into my mouth, but when I inhale through my mouth, sweet, sweet oxygen pours into my lungs.

I greedily gulp in air, gently kicking my legs to keep me buoyant. When the spots recede, I see Gavin is watching me. He gives me a questioning look and a thumbs-up. I return it and he hugs me, his strong arms pinning me to his chest.

That's when I remember the other people in the other cars. I yank on his arm and swim down the tube outside the train as fast as I can. My arm screams with the movement, but I don't stop. If those Citizens didn't get to the rebreathers, we may still have enough time to help them. With a mixture of relief and horror, I see there is only one car with people in it, and even then it's only a handful. Unfortunately, none of them got to the rebreathers in time. They're all just floating at the top of the train, their eyes glassy with death, the rebreathers floating next to them.

I share a horrified look with Gavin. How could she do that? How could she just kill people without a thought? These people had done nothing except get on the wrong train at the wrong time.

Gavin pulls me out of the car toward the end of the tube. I'm relieved for his help. My arm protests each time I try to use it to swim. When we get to it, the huge metal doors are locked tight. I don't know how to open them.

I signal for Gavin to look for some sort of release on the left side, while I swim to the right, but it doesn't really matter, I don't know how Mother flooded the tunnels. Water could still be pouring in. And if it is, what happens if we do open the doors? Will we flood the Sector, killing more innocent people? And if we can't open the doors, what happens? The rebreathers won't last forever.

After a few minutes of swimming up the side of the main door, my fingers find some kind of lever. It shows a picture of a filled tube on the top of the lever and an empty tube if I pull the lever down. I yank the lever. And even though fire erupts in my shoulder, the lever doesn't budge. Not so much as a millimeter. Then I notice the scanner on the side of the lever. Hoping Mother hasn't gotten past the new security I placed in her computer and I'm still in the system, I place my hand on it. The pad blinks red as it scans my palm, then green.

I try pulling the lever again and this time it slides easily. The water slowly drains until I'm no longer able to swim and am standing on the tracks next to Gavin.

He pulls the mouthpiece out. "What's going on?"

"I think we're waiting for the tube to drain completely. Then the doors should open."

As if to prove me right, the doors stutter open with the sound of grinding gears and clinking metal. Using the tracks as leverage, we climb up the slight embankment toward Sector Three's Tube station.

When we get to the station, I collapse onto the platform. No one is around. Probably already in their new quarters, ushered there by Guards and Enforcers. My eyes and arm are on fire. I just want to curl into a ball until the pain goes away, but Gavin has other ideas.

"We should refill the tunnel," he says, staring into it as if expecting monsters to crawl out at any moment.

Then again, it wouldn't surprise me if there *was* something crawling through the tube. When Mother figures out we escaped without dying, she'll send people to finish the job.

"Right. Mother won't be too happy when she realizes we

outsmarted her, which won't take long. So, this will at least buy us a little time." Though I'm pretty sure she already knows we're out of the tube anyway. Something doesn't feel right about how easy this has been, but we don't have any choice but to keep going. We'll just have to deal with whatever Mother's planning when we get to it.

He holds out a hand to help me up and at first I reach for it. But then a wave of anger pours over me and I yank my hand away.

"Don't touch me," I say with clenched teeth.

He raises his eyebrows and slowly withdraws his hand. "Sorry," he mumbles, hurt and anger pooling in his eyes.

I close mine as the anger fades. Where in the world did *that* come from? "No," I say, holding out my hand to him. "I'm sorry. I . . . I don't know what came over me."

"It's okay. We're both under a lot of stress." There's something in his eyes when he says it, but he helps me up and into the booth, where I study the control panel.

Since I know what I'm looking for this time, it doesn't take long. I press my hand to the glass plate and wait for it to do its thing. Then press the lever up. The doors close with a clang, and then there's a silence that's almost as deafening.

Exhausted from the pain and everything else, I lower myself back to the ground and Gavin kneels next to me. "You okay?" he asks.

"Yes. There's a manual lock on the doors. It's a red switch. It's there in case of a Surface Dweller attack." I laugh at the irony. "Just press the button. It'll ensure Mother can't send anyone through the tunnels."

When I hear him step away, I glance at my shoulder. For some reason, it hurts even worse when I see the blood soaking the bandage. Turning my head away, I close my eyes again.

Gavin returns and kneels next to me.

I keep my eyes closed. "I don't think we need to clean the wound now."

"What do you mean?" he asks. I can hear the frown in his voice.

"The saltwater," I say.

"Oh, shit!"

He yanks off my rebreather, pushes the dress strap down my shoulder, then slowly removes the soaked bandages. Even though he's being gentle, I wince and have to bite back a scream.

He grabs the antiseptic bottle from the first-aid kit on the wall, then pours it over the wound. This time I can't hold the scream back. I look over to make sure I still *have* a shoulder—it feels like the lava flowing over it dissolved it. The wound bubbles with pinkish-white froth.

Gavin watches the wound and pours more antiseptic over it when the froth turns dark red.

"Why is it still bleeding?" he mutters. "It should have stopped by now. It's been almost twelve hours."

"Well," I say with a forced smile, "it's not like we've given it time to heal."

After what feels like forever, but is probably only a few minutes, the pain ebbs until it's only a dull ache.

He studies the wound carefully before rebandaging it. "You okay?"

"Yes."

"Good. Let's get going. I want to get the hell out of this living nightmare."

He helps me to my feet and I bristle, nearly snapping at him that at least it's better than the Surface, but I swallow the words and the irrational anger.

Knowing it doesn't matter what we do to hide from this point forward, since we're soaking wet and they'll find us by our trail, we stay in the open and make our way through Sector Three's vestibule. This Sector has several floors and there are several stories above and below us, so there is no view of the ocean in the ceiling. We have to settle for floor-to-ceiling windows.

But something is wrong. Everything is deserted. We should have run into *somebody*. Even with the leak and even if everyone was evacuated, there should still be Enforcers and Guards to make sure no one comes back here until the leak is fixed. And what happened to the workers fixing the leak?

We turn the corner that will take us to the elevators. And stop in our tracks.

Littering the ground are bodies. Women, men, children. About fifteen or so.

Slowly walking forward, I examine each body we pass.

There's a bullet hole dead center in each of their foreheads. Each and every one.

A memory flashes in my head: Me, aiming a gun. Pulling the trigger.

"Enforcers," I whisper.

"What? How can you tell?" Gavin asks, kneeling beside a woman who's holding a child to her chest. Her eyes are open and staring. He closes them before gently touching the downy hair of the toddler.

It breaks my heart to watch him. How careful he is with them. And they aren't even his people. It was their own people who did this to them. It's obvious now Mother was wrong about Surface Dwellers.

"One shot to the forehead. This is an assassination. They were ordered to kill and do it quickly."

It was quick. For that much, at least, I can be grateful. Most of them probably had no idea what was going on. No time for fear or pain.

We continue walking through the pile. Gavin insists, in case there are any survivors. It doesn't take long to figure out there aren't any.

Suddenly, there's laughter from my left, and I whirl around to see the holograph of Mother standing there. I didn't even know Sector Three had holographic capabilities. I do a quick scan for the cameras and holograph projection unit and sigh when I see the shine of lenses in the upper right corner.

There it is.

Mother claps her hands in that slow way people do when they're mocking you. One side of her mouth is twisted into a smile. It makes me shiver.

"Smart girl. Getting out of that tube alive. Not that I had any doubt you would." She spreads her hands out. "Like your welcome gift, honey?" she says, with a little tinkling laugh that makes me want to shudder.

"What do you want, Mother?" I ask. I make sure my voice doesn't reflect any of the outrage, guilt, or disgust I'm feeling. I keep it as emotionless as ice.

"Long life, beauty, power. A daughter that listens to me. You know. The basics," she says.

Gavin snorts, but it's filled with derision. Mother doesn't even spare him a glance.

I glare at her. "Well, it appears you've got three of the four. Isn't that enough?"

Mother lifts one of her shoulders. "In normal circumstances, I suppose. But I cannot let you leave with the Surface Dweller."

"Why?"

"Because you are the Daughter of the People. The Citizens look up to you."

This time I'm the one who snorts. "No one looks up to me, Mother. Especially now that you've told the whole city I'm a murderer."

She narrows her eyes at me. "That is no one's fault other than your own. No one told you to kill all those Citizens."

"You know very well I didn't kill Macie."

"You don't deny the others? I'm surprised."

I don't say anything. I only cross my arms over my chest.

She huffs out a breath. "Besides," she says, "if you escape, what will prevent the others from trying to do the same? A society only functions if all the parts work together toward a common goal."

"What goal? Yours? Where you experiment on your own people?"

Her face turns hard. "I'm making them better. I'm helping them rise above themselves."

"Right. That's why Nick killed Macie. Because he rose above himself." I roll my eyes toward Gavin.

She spreads her hands out in front of her. "He was not an appropriate subject. I'll admit that. His testosterone levels were too high. Occasionally, a subject's response to Conditioning is . . . unpredictable." She shrugs. "However, all great discoveries require sacrifices. And there is always collateral damage when ruling."

"Is that what Macie was? All these people? Me? Collateral damage? How very forward thinking of you, Mother." This time some of the disgust seeps through.

She must hear it, because her face becomes drawn and pinched and her eyes flash. "Sniveling little brat. I gave you the gift of being an Enforcer, spent precious time and resources on making you better than the rest—making you *perfect*—making you my own when you failed and this is how you treat me? Running off with the first man who crooks his finger?"

Gavin surges forward. "If you're so perfect, why did you

have to adopt Evie, huh? Why didn't you just have your own daughter? Wouldn't the child you created be more perfect than someone else's? Can't do it, can you? You infertile? Missing your girl parts? What?"

Mother's face turns dark with rage, but I have to wonder if he's right. Is Mother infertile? Is that why she adopted me instead of making her own child? Either way, now is not the time to pick a fight.

I push him back. It surprises me how hard it is to force him to stop. "Leave it alone! She can't hurt me," I say to him, then turn back to Mother. "Did you hear that, Mother? You can't hurt me anymore. I'm not under your thumb anymore. I don't care that I was an Enforcer. He doesn't care. You can't brainwash me and you can't threaten me. I've made it this far. We'll make it the rest of the way."

Mother starts laughing and I stare at her, baffled.

"You think so, do you?" She smiles, and it gives me chills. "Well, then I guess you won't worry that I've *let* you get this far. That I've known every move you've made and every move you will make. That I'm completely unconcerned about this little . . . escape attempt. That I know you will fail."

Gavin and I exchange another look. "What are you talking about?" Gavin demands.

Again she ignores him. "Darling, you didn't expect we'd just let an Enforcer walk out the door. You had to know there were fail-safes in place."

"Fail-safes? What fail-safes?" I ask.

Mother smiles again. "Little tiny instructions set far inside that dense brain of yours. If you don't turn Gavin over to us and do what we tell you to do, including being a good little girl and coupling, you'll have no choice."

"I won't do it."

"Yes, you will. Didn't you hear me? You'll have no choice."

"I don't understand."

She gives an exasperated sigh. "Haven't you noticed it yet? Like when you killed Nick? Or when you got by the Guards? Those other Citizens? Just a tiny little click."

I don't say anything, but that's all the affirmation she needs. Gavin's gaze burns into me as Mother's smile widens.

"It's already started, hasn't it? You're already starting to hate him. It's just tiny lapses now, but it won't be for long. And there's nothing you can do about it. If you value the life of your little boy toy, you'll return him to me. I'll even let you keep him. All he has to do is go through Conditioning and he'll be all yours."

"Never," I say.

She shrugs. "Suit yourself. Then he'll die by your hands."

"What do you mean?"

"Your training. Must I explain everything?" She smiles that awful smile at me. "The closer you get to escaping, the more you'll forget who you are. The more you'll revert to your Enforcer Conditioning. And the harder it will be to resist killing a Surface Dweller. After all, that was what you were programmed to do."

The hologram flickers and shuts off as her laugh echoes around the empty Sector.

Chapter Twenty-four

SUBJECT 121, EVELYN WINTERS:
Failure to follow a direct order, resulting in the unnecessary deaths of 10 Citizens and 1 Enforcer. Evaluation shows Conditioning has failed yet again. Recommend immediate disposal. ETA: Mother has taken over control of said subject.

—DR. FRIAR, INCIDENT REPORT
FOLLOWING MASSACRE AT FESTIVAL

I stare at the spot where she just was. I wish I could say that it surprises me, but it doesn't, not really. How stupid and naïve I've been to think Mother would just let me walk out the door with a Surface Dweller.

Despite how awful things have turned, our escape *had* been too easy up till now.

Gavin gently touches my arm. "I don't think I understood what she just said."

"She means I'll succumb to my programming before we can escape." I pause, my voice getting quieter. "My memories weren't coming back. I was . . . reverting, the longer I was escaping with you. And because I was trained to eliminate Surface Dwellers, I will kill you." Each word I speak causes another fissure to open in my heart. "She has a point. It's probably best if you go by yourself. And that I return to Mother."

She won't be happy I let him escape, but since by then he'll be on his way to the Surface, there won't be anything she can do about it. What she'll do to me, though, that's another thing altogether.

He shakes his head. "I'm not leaving without you. We haven't come this far for me to abandon you at the end. We're almost there. You've broken through your Conditioning before." He touches my rose charm. "You'll do it again."

"I know, but this is different—"

Gavin places his finger across my lips. "Don't. It's no different." He takes my hand. "And I'm not turning my back on you, and I'm not letting you turn your back on me. It's all or nothing now, Evie. For better or for worse, right?"

My stomach flips and my heart lodges in my throat. "But your family. They need you."

He smiles his lopsided grin and cups my cheek. I melt when he looks into my eyes and says, "*I need you.*"

Closing my eyes, I lean into his hand. "All right, but if I kill you, you have no one to blame but yourself."

"You won't kill me. It'll never happen," he says so confidently, I almost believe him.

He leads the way down the hallway toward the elevators that will take us to the floor the submersibles should be on.

I don't follow, wishing I had as much confidence in myself as he has in me.

He turns when he realizes I haven't followed. "Coming?"

When he first turns, the red glow from the emergency lights floods over him. He looks like he's covered in blood. Then he steps back into the white lights and the vision fades in a blink. I hope it's not a premonition.

With a nod, I hurry to catch up.

It seems that we've both lost any fear of Mother that we may have had in the beginning, but I wonder if my lack of fear is the Conditioning taking over. The farther into Sector Three we get, the less my nerves bother me and the more assured I am that I can handle anything.

But I'm worried about what Mother said. Especially now when, trapped in the elevator as it shoots us up to the topmost floor of the Sector, with nowhere to go—nowhere to escape—Gavin touches me on the shoulder. Another wave of hate for him threatens to drown me. I want to strangle him for touching me. For making my nerves wriggle like snakes under my skin.

I force myself to face away from him. To remember everything we've been through together. That it's only Mother's programming that's causing this. It's not my real feelings. But it's hard to remember what my real feelings are at this point.

The worst part is how often it's happening now—the feeling of intense hate that overcomes me for Gavin. It lasts only seconds, but it's stronger each time.

But that's only one of my problems. The other is that I think I'm starting to forget things. It started before we left Sector One, when I couldn't make up my mind about showering or leaving, when the answer should have been obvious. When I went the wrong way trying to leave Sector One. Then again when I couldn't remember where the rebreathers were or if it was the red button or the gray one that activated them. Now I don't remember which way to go to get to the submersibles. I'm going to have to rely on Gavin's memory.

I don't want to concern him, though, so I just pretend I'm letting him go ahead so he can protect me. Of course, some of my confusion might be due to the fact I've never really been over to this side of the city. It's *nothing* like my part. It's dirty and grimy. The concrete walls, normally a pewter color, are dark with something that looks like soot.

My finger comes back covered in the black stuff when I run it down one of the walls. The stuff is slippery and grainy, grease of some sort. I sniff it and wrinkle my nose. It smells like oil.

The smell reminds me of someone. A boy, about my age. Blond hair and blue eyes. Hard, rough hands. Strong. *The perfect Suitor for me.* I'm sure I know him. A name floats in my mind, then flits away before I can grasp at it, but the vision of wind chimes appears before my eyes.

My smile falls when another vision replaces the chimes. A vision of pain and blood. Lots of blood. I stare at my hands and instead of the greasy dirt they're covered in blood.

I gasp and wipe them over and over on my dress, but it's no good because it's covered in blood, too.

Gavin turns around from farther down the hall. "Everything okay?"

The vision fades and I lift my gaze to him. What was I doing again?

He frowns and steps toward me. "Evie. You okay?"

I nod, slowly. *"My life is just about perfect."*

His eyebrows wing up. "That's good." He takes my hand, and kisses my palm. The contact clears the fuzziness in my head.

I frown at him. "What's going on? Why did we stop?"

He sighs. "You had a small episode."

I groan. "Again?" Then I panic. "What happened? Did I try to hurt you?" I pat my hands over his body, looking for damage.

He pulls my hands away and holds them by the wrists with his hands. "I'm fine. I'm just worried about you. Are you really okay? You looked terrified and in pain."

I pull a hand away and press it to my forehead. It feels like someone is trying to dig their way out of my head. "I'm fine. I can't remember what happened."

He watches me for several seconds. "Okay, well, let's keep going, all right? We're not too far from where the map said the subs are."

I nod and follow behind him again. When we turn the corner, I notice a metallic scent. That click goes off in my head again and every muscle in my body tenses, ready to spring into action. Gavin's body stiffens, too, so I know I'm not imagining it. We walk cautiously ahead. Our senses are tuned to every noise, every shadow.

Without warning, the lights flicker and go out throughout the complex. The red emergency lights stay lit, but ahead the hallway is dark. I reach into my pack and pull out my flashlight pin.

When I click it on, the light cuts through the darkness. It's actually brighter than the lights that would have lit the hallway, but it isn't big enough to dispel all of the gloom.

We keep our guard up, sticking close together. Our arms brush together, and at first I have to fight the urge to jerk my arm away. I bite my tongue, hoping the pain will be enough to distract me from my homicidal thoughts, but it isn't until he squeezes my hand—a simple gesture of his promise to protect me—that I'm able to push the thoughts to the side.

I can't fight this much longer. I hope we reach the submersibles soon.

After a few minutes, he releases my hand and I have to resist the urge to grab out for him again. It's the only thing grounding me from going crazy, but we can't take the chance of holding hands. We don't know what's ahead.

Suddenly my foot slides in something wet and I almost fall to the ground. I throw my hands out to the side to catch myself with the walls.

When I lift my foot, my shoe makes a sucking sound. I

tap Gavin on the shoulder, then point to the floor. "There's something here," I say.

He nods and stands watch over me, while I kneel to shine the small light onto the floor, careful not to let my knee dip into whatever the sticky mess is. It's a puddle of something dark red, almost purple. I tilt my head, then stick my finger in it and bring it nearer to me to study. It's slightly tacky, like wet glue or drying paint.

Bringing it to my nose, I sniff at it. It has a metallic scent, like rust. Then it hits me. I know exactly what this is. It bothers me that it took me that long to figure it out.

When I turn to show Gavin, he's already staring at the puddle with a look of horror on his face. "Blood?" he asks.

"I think so."

"What from?" He pulls out an antiseptic wipe from the first-aid kit in one of the packs and wipes my whole hand down, then helps me to stand, pulling me away as far from the puddle as he can.

"I don't know. But it's a lot."

As one, we both look down the hall. I shiver and Gavin, wordlessly, takes his gun out, making sure it's loaded. There's a click when he releases the safety.

While I know I should do the same, I don't trust myself not to shoot him if I have another episode. I leave them in the packs Gavin is carrying. I even consider emptying the chambers, but don't want to risk having the guns in my hands at all right now.

We continue forward and it isn't long before we find more blood. This time it's in the form of handprints along the floor. They move up to the walls, as if the person was using the wall to help them stand, then lead down the hall. It's like they're luring us somewhere.

Chills chase up and down my spine, but we have no choice except to continue. I don't remember if there are any other ways to the submersibles, and Gavin only knows this one route.

Suddenly the handprints stop. Gavin and I exchange a look, his eyes barely visible, but then continue forward. Hurrying now, because there's red light ahead. We stop at a junction. Ahead it's still pitch black. The lights are all out. But on either side of us, the hallways are lit with the eerie red light, and I can make out different doors. It looks like living quarters or maybe labs.

The calm that came with the click is gone now and fear creeps back in, making thought difficult.

Does Sector Three have labs? I press a hand to my forehead. I think so. This is the Engineering Sector, after all. It would make sense for them to have labs for the creation of those things, right? Then again, the Engineers and their families need somewhere to sleep. What did the map say this section was?

Is it even important? The real question is which way do we go?

Gavin looks at me. "The notes said straight until we end

up at a dead end, then left." And even though he sends me a questioning look, I can't help but think he knows I don't remember.

I decide not to confirm his thoughts. "Yes. That's right. Straight, then left."

He gives me an odd look, but turns and continues down the hall. Soon, we're drenched in darkness again. The light is behind us, reminding us there's safety there.

I start to think that maybe leaving isn't such a great idea after all. That maybe we should just break into one of the quarters down that lit hallway. Surely we'll find an empty one, and we can just hide in there. Mother won't be able to find us.

Then I shake myself. That's a stupid idea. Mother won't give up until she does find us. And we'd be trapped in those quarters. Gavin would be trapped. Besides, now's not the time to give up.

We're almost there. Just a few more turns and then freedom.

Straightening my shoulders, I step up my pace, catching up with Gavin, who had just slowed to match mine. He turns so I can shine the light on his face. "You okay?" he asks for what seems like the hundredth time. I force down the anger it creates. I know why he's asking. It's a test to see if I'm myself.

I nod and smile at him. "Perfect."

He grins, relief flooding his eyes. "Great. Let's keep going," he says.

I'm about to turn away when I glance at the wall behind him and gasp. Behind him, on the wall, is another bloody handprint trail. I follow it with the light and find a splatter; this one has bits of gore in it. I shine the light on the floor and see another trail of blood, thick pools of it, leading us down the hall. Without thinking I follow it, practically running, trying to avoid stepping into any of it.

Gavin follows without asking any questions. I know what we're going to find at the end of the tunnel, and I'm not going to like it, but I have no choice. If there's even the chance of saving the person whose blood this is, we must try.

The handprints are small. A woman's. I shudder, thinking how terrified she must be, running alone and in the dark.

When we get to the end of the trail, there's a body lying on the floor, surrounded by the light of my flashlight, just as I expected. But what's there is far worse than anything I was anticipating.

There's a man leaning over the body of a woman, who is most certainly dead. Or at least I hope so, because the man is ripping her apart.

Chapter Twenty-five

Relocation of affected parties from Sector Three to Sector Two to commence immediately. For record-keeping purposes keep audio/visual recording on at all times while in Sector Three.

—ORDERS FROM MOTHER TO GUARDS

Bile threatens to come up my throat when Gavin pushes me behind him. I don't know if it's to protect me from the man or the sight. Either way, I'm grateful. I press my forehead against his back. There is no click or its accompanying calmness. My stomach rolls and I really want to retch, but I'm too scared to make a noise.

Gavin gestures for me to walk backward, but I'm frozen in place. I can't move. I recognize the man. He is one of the Guards from the Palace Wing. He used to help me carry flowers to the Science Sector before he was relocated to Sector Three.

Gavin reaches blindly behind him and grabs my arm, then he pinches me. Hard. I bite back a squeal, but the pinch has done its job. It clears my head and I slowly turn around to walk back the way we've come. Maybe the Guard won't notice if we just go back the way we came and find another way around.

But when I turn around, there's another man right behind me. I don't recognize him, though it doesn't help my fear any. And I almost squeal with fright again when I realize how close he is.

Gavin, unaware of what's in front of me, bumps me and pushes me forward, almost knocking me into the blood-covered man.

"Evie. Back. Up," Gavin hisses.

"I can't!" I whisper back.

"Why no—" He turns his head while he's talking and catches sight of the man. He swears.

Since that pretty much sums it up, I don't say anything.

The man in front of me continues to smile, but he's singing now. Softly under his breath. And what he's singing chills me to the bone.

"Way down yonder, down in the meadow,
There's a poor wee little lamby.
The bees and the butterflies pickin' at its eyes,
The poor wee thing cried for her mammy."

"What is he saying?" Gavin whispers.

"He's singing," I say, even though I know he's more in shock at the words than not actually being able to hear what the man is saying.

"Singing? Singing what?"

"A children's song. Does it really matter?"

"That's a freakin' creepy children's song! Why in the world would you teach that to children?"

"We really don't have time for explanations, but it's a song to symbolize what the Surface Dwellers do to their own children. The lamb is a child who, even though he's crying for his mom, has just been tossed aside to die. Happy?"

"Uh, no. I guess not. So? Got a plan?"

"There's a poor wee little lamby."

The singing is really distracting and I can't think. I don't know what to do. Gavin asks again, but I can't really hear him over the buzzing sound in my ears.

"The bees and the butterflies pickin' at its eyes."

"Evie, what do we do?"

I start shaking and my head threatens to explode as the singing seems to grow louder and louder and Gavin's voice rings in my ears. This time I can feel the change, the slight wavering in my vision and the burning in my nerves that signals my Enforcer programming is trying to take over. I can't let it. Not this time. It's stronger now and I know, if I give in, I could kill Gavin.

But if I don't . . . he could die anyway.

I don't know what to do. Either way could result in death.

But I've been fighting my Conditioning almost my whole life. Maybe I can control myself enough.

I can do this. I *can*. I have to. There's no choice. It's the only way we can escape the monsters that have us trapped.

Taking a deep breath, I close my eyes and let the programming take over. The click in my head goes off and I know just what to do. I'm calm again. And I have to admit the calmness is welcome compared to the mind-numbing terror from just seconds ago. I'd much rather have this control over myself than the constant fear I've been living with.

"Evie?" Gavin has apparently noticed my change.

"Just don't get in the way," I say.

The man in front of me is bigger than me and possibly stronger. But, while he's staring straight down at me, his eyes are blank. As if there's nothing there anymore. But he's still singing.

The man has obviously killed before, so I don't know why he hasn't attacked us, but I slowly reach into my pack for my gun and raise it to aim at the man's chest. He doesn't budge. Doesn't even blink.

Gavin places his hand over the gun and pushes down, before whispering in my ear, "He's not really there, Evie. He's harmless. Just let him go."

I don't really trust that he's harmless, but Gavin's probably right. The man didn't make any move to stop me from killing him.

So I nod and lower the pistol.

The sounds of grunting and tearing flesh let me know

the man behind us is still busily attacking his victim and most likely hasn't noticed us.

Even with the Enforcer programming running through my system, I shiver at the sounds surrounding me: Gavin's gasping breaths. The thunder of my heartbeat. The ripping of flesh. And, making it all worse, the man's rasping voice as he sings.

We turn slowly so our backs are pressed against the wall and then shuffle sideways down the hall, hoping the man tearing the woman to pieces won't see us. But just when we get behind the man, he stops.

We immediately do the same.

He slowly turns, so he's facing us, then tilts his head to the side, watching us.

A shiver runs down my spine, and Gavin's breath catches. I tighten my grip on the pistol, preparing to raise and fire if need be.

"It is my privilege to follow Mother's orders. We don't question Mother." Then he leaps toward us and I have no time to think before I'm raising the gun and squeezing the trigger. A ball of blue light emits from the gun and the man in front of me bursts into flames.

Before I can even think, I'm already turning and dragging Gavin along behind me. We rush down the hallway until we get to another junction that's lit on both sides. The state of the hall is evidence that those two Guards are just the first of many.

I skid to a stop and spin around to face Gavin.

"Grab the plasma pistol. It has less of a kick and will be easier to handle."

"You think there's more of those . . . things?" he asks, and although I'm sure he's scared—I would be if not for my training—his eyes don't waver from mine.

"I don't think. I know." I gesture to the bloodstained walls on either side of us.

He stares wide-eyed at the corridor to our left. "What are they?"

"More of Mother's victims, I think," I say, turning to face him, then stumble back as a huge black wave of hate flows over me. I give myself a mental shake. "The one tearing up that girl was spouting off Conditioned responses. Apparently Nick wasn't the only failed experiment. She must be experimenting on all the Guards." I pause as another idea comes to me. "That's why she wanted to shove that Guard on me to couple with. He must have been the only one who hasn't gone crazy!"

Gavin gives me a sad look and I clench my teeth as rage rolls around my head.

He's a manipulative, dangerous Surface Dweller, my mind screams at me. *Why am I trying to save a Surface Dweller? His kind destroyed the Surface. He hunts for fun. Life means nothing to him.* You're *nothing to him. Kill him. It's your duty.*

I close my eyes and take deep calming breaths. No. That's not true. He's not like that.

Surface Dwellers are all the same.

I squash down on the thoughts. My fists clench and I bite down so hard on my bottom lip I taste blood.

Finally the voice inside my head quiets and the only things I hear are my somewhat uneven breaths and the sounds of metal clinking against metal.

When I open my eyes, Gavin is kneeling next to his pack and digging through it.

"What are you looking for?" I ask. He glances up and suspicion surges through me. I struggle to ignore it.

"Ammo," he says after a second. "I want to make sure I'm prepared."

"Plasma ammo is in the things that look like small air tanks." I press a hand to my now-aching forehead.

He quickly grabs two of the silver cylinders. They're the size of his hand, but fit in his pocket. Then he grabs his Reising and slings it over one shoulder and an ammo belt over his other.

He looks just like the pictures of the Surface warriors that were part of our training, and I suddenly want to shoot him. To attack him with my bare hands. Anything to bring down the threat my body is convinced he poses before he does the same to me.

"The plasma is probably more than enough," I say through clenched teeth.

He gestures for me to hand him my pack. "It's better to be safe than sorry," he says, and hands me the Reising from my pack without even looking up. He doesn't realize how hard I'm fighting with myself.

Knowing he's right, I take it and dig through my bag for my own ammunition. I slip a gun belt out of the pack, hook it around my hips, and fill the pockets full of ammunition for both guns, before shoving a fresh clip into the Reising and hooking it around my shoulder.

When we're both finally ready to go, I make him stay behind me. I can protect him easier if I'm in front . . . and it's easier to forget he's a Surface Dweller if I can't see him. Not to mention I don't need the light anymore. Somehow the click has made it so I can see easily in the dark. And I figure it's safer not to use the light in case we run into more of Mother's experiments.

We continue down the darkened hall and little noises make my ears twitch. There's a scuttling noise ahead of us, as if there's a large rodent infestation in the walls. I'm not particularly surprised when I realize it's another of the failed experiments; this one is by himself but covered in blood like the others. He seems even worse, though, scrabbling on his hands and feet instead of walking, and his tongue keeps flickering out.

He tilts his head when he "tastes us," and Gavin and I come to a wary stop.

"Help me," he whispers. "Mother promised . . . to make me smarter . . . pain . . . so much pain. . . . please." He looks at Gavin and alarm crosses his face. "Surface Dweller . . . protect Elysium . . ." He crouches lower to the ground.

Without warning, he springs up, growling with his teeth bared.

I don't hesitate. I raise my gun hand and bring him down with one shot of the plasma.

Then we're running from the screaming mass of fire-soaked flesh.

"He wanted to be smarter," Gavin says.

"Only whatever they did, it obviously didn't work," I finish for him.

"So, Nick went ballistic because she messed with his head."

"They *all* went crazy because she 'messed' with their heads."

There's silence behind me, and the only proof I have that he's still with me is the slap of rubber against concrete and the wheezing of his breaths.

"I heard about soldiers going crazy during Vietnam. Collecting scalps and teeth and stuff like that."

"Vietnam?" I ask.

"Never mind. I'm just saying people can do a lot of crazy shit if you put them under enough pressure. I bet the Conditioning makes it easier for these people to go crazy like this," he says, almost to himself. "Like your brain is made of clay and it can be shaped into anything. Even a monster."

We finally reach the dead end and turn left. Both sides are dark, but that's not what stops me in my tracks. It's the pile of bodies littering the floor. More bodies. Wonderful.

After a quick study, I realize that most, if not all, of the bodies are no longer living, and we walk quickly through the mess. It looks like another massacre, but this one was not merciful. Most of the bodies are torn to pieces and their parts strewn about as if a child has had a temper tantrum and torn apart her dolls.

Remembering Nick's reaction, I'm pretty sure that's exactly what happened.

Gavin starts gagging behind me, but surprisingly my stomach is like steel. I feel nothing. Not even sadness.

Enforcer training, I think. I guess I should be grateful for it this time.

"Just close your eyes and hang on to me," I say.

Gavin grabs the back of my dress and lets me lead him to the other side of the pile.

When we do, he collapses to the floor and rests his head on his knees. "I've never seen anything like that."

I tamp down my irritation. "Yes, it's unpleasant, but we have to keep moving. Sitting here and crying isn't going to help us."

He looks up, surprise widening his eyes. "Excuse me?"

No matter how much I want to, I can't swallow my reply. It's like someone is speaking through me. "Get up, Surface Dweller. Keep moving. We don't have time for theatrics."

"Theatrics?" He starts to speak, but cuts himself off.

The look on his face makes my hand go to my plasma pistol. I draw it out and point it at him, my finger itching to squeeze the trigger even as I wish I could take back everything I said. My voice won't cooperate, so I just glare down at him.

He lifts an eyebrow, and I see so many emotions whirling

in his eyes that it finally breaks the hold my training has over me. I drop my hand to my side and shove the pistol into the belt. "I'm sorry," I whisper. "I'm trying . . . I just . . . can't. Okay? I can't control this. You should just leave. Now. Without me, before I really can't control myself."

There's a scratching sound as he stands and I squeeze my eyes closed even tighter. My heart breaks at the sound of his footsteps.

He's leaving. I finally pushed him away.

Instead, he pulls me against him. I struggle to pull away, but he holds on tightly. "No, I'm sorry, Evie. I know that's not you talking. And I'm not leaving you. We're in this together. Remember? I'm not leaving you and you're not leaving me. Got it?"

"This is so bad. Horrible," I say, my voice cracking. The Conditioning is pulling at me again. "I can't do this without my training. I have to let it take over."

"I know. We need to keep going. There's nothing we can do about those people. They're dead. We're not, and we have to remember that and keep going. The sooner we get out, the sooner we're safe." He squeezes me again, before letting me go. "You can do this. I trust you."

His words chill my blood, but I nod and open my eyes. Even in the dark I can tell he's pale, but I have to give him credit. There's not even a tremor in his legs. He palms the plasma pistol again and says, "Ready?"

I straighten my shoulders and let the Conditioning in again. "More than ready. Let's get going."

There are more bodies along the way, but no one is ever alive. The farther we go and the more bodies we run into, the harder it is to keep my emotional side in check. To keep the Enforcer part of me going without giving in to my programmed distrust of Gavin.

We finally reach the dead end that should be where the subs are. There's a small double sliding door with a sign that says, AUTHORIZED PERSONNEL ONLY. TRESPASSERS WILL BE PROSECUTED.

Since "prosecuted" is Mother speak for executed, I'm not surprised no one has tried to get in here.

There's a flat glass panel on the side for handprint access. I don't want Mother to know where we are, so I open the back of the panel.

Less than thirty seconds later I'm replacing the panel and there's a soft snick as the bolt unlocks. I nearly smile in relief when the doors slide open. I want to be safe—to go slow—but a sudden scream behind us propels me through the door. Whatever's on the inside can't be worse than what is outside.

I'm wrong. The door shuts behind us with an ominous clang and we look out over the submarines' bay . . . which is filled with Enforcers.

CHAPTER TWENTY-SIX

Way down yonder, down in the meadow,
There's a poor wee little lamby.
The bees and the butterflies pickin' at its eyes,
The poor wee thing cried for her mammy.

—CHILDREN'S SONG, PART OF PRE-SCHOOL CURRICULUM

So, this is where they've all been. No wonder they haven't stopped us.

Gavin groans. "I don't suppose *any* part of this escape could be easy."

I have to laugh. "What's the fun in that?"

Veronica, the apparent leader of the Enforcers, steps out of the group.

"We have been waiting for you," she says.

Time to bluster. I spread my hands out to encompass the room. "Obviously. I can't imagine why you would stay in here otherwise. Though the view is lovely." I gesture to the clear glass door that leads to one of the submersibles.

Gavin snickers, but the Enforcer only bares her teeth.

"This is not a joking matter. You've caused enough trouble and Mother has had quite enough of the both of you."

"Oh, I'm sorry." I exchange another grin with Gavin. "We didn't mean to keep you waiting. We didn't know you'd be here. If we had, we'd have gotten here sooner."

She laughs, and it has this hollow sound to it that sends chills racing up and down my spine. "You don't *really* remember me, do you?" she asks, but gives me no time to answer as she continues without pause. "I was recruited after you." Her fist clenches and then unclenches. "Every training exercise I had to hear how I should look up to you. How *all* the girls should look up to you. That you were the best. The Governess's little *pet,* and everyone else had to follow in your shadow."

"What are you *talking* about?" I ask.

"Oh, stop playing stupid. I know you're not as dumb as you want everyone to think. I should know. You were constantly upstaging me. The child prodigy. You aced all your language classes. Broke all the training records. Had your first kill at the age of six. You were Little Miss Perfect."

Gavin looks back and forth between the two of us. He doesn't say anything, but I have to wonder what he's thinking. If he's questioning how much I know. How much I remember. And, if I do remember, why I haven't said anything to him.

I give a small shake of my head to tell him I don't remember any of what she's saying.

"But you weren't perfect, were you? You were a *failure.*"

She gives me a smug grin. "Which left me to take your place. And I did. *I* became Mother's new prodigy. And I'm better than you ever were."

I don't say anything. I don't know what she wants from me.

"Aren't you going to say anything?" she snarls.

"Say what? That I'm scared? Or surprised? Angry? What?"

"I've waited years for this moment." She presses her fists to her eyes. "And it isn't going at all how I wanted it to. You don't care. Just like always. *You've never cared about anyone but yourself.*"

Her words remind me of what Macie said. *"Mother and Father adore you. You can do no wrong in their eyes. . . . You've never cared about anyone but yourself. . . . But now this Surface Dweller comes and you show what you really are. A selfish, flighty, and foolish little girl."*

Are they both right? Am I really so selfish I never noticed this girl?

Then I remember what happened to Nick. What Mother did to him. What she's done to the men we killed. What she did to *me*. It's all because of the Conditioning.

"You're still not *listening*!" she yells, pulling me back from my thoughts.

"You're right," I say. "I am selfish."

Gavin gives me a quizzical look with his brows knit together. The girl, however, tilts her head as if not understanding what I said.

"But so are you," I continue. "And it's because of Mother that we're this way. It's the Conditioning. You think you're her new prodigy? Her pet? Think again! She's using you. Just like she used me."

Veronica laughs. "Nice try. Is that what *he* wants you to think?" She jerks her head toward Gavin. "It's more like he's using you. And you expect me to fall for it, too?" She laughs. "Mother explained everything to me. How your training failed and your true self is coming out. That without the Conditioning *you're just a stupid, flighty, foolish girl.*"

". . . But now this Surface Dweller comes and you show what you really are. A selfish, flighty, and foolish little girl."

My eyes widen as I begin to understand. Why the two sound the same. Macie was Conditioned. Just like Veronica. Like Nick. Like me.

". . . And you can't even see that Mother isn't using you. She's had only the best intentions for you. It's the Surface Dweller who is."

I glance over at Gavin, who is glaring at the girl. He shoots me a worried look, but I turn my attention back to her.

"No," I say. "He isn't. But Mother is using you. And me. She's destroying the city. She's experimenting with Conditioning, and it's failing!"

She shakes her head. "That's what Mother said you'd say. It's not destroying anything."

"We've seen it," Gavin blurts out. "Everyone in this Sector is either dead or some kind of experiment gone bad. People are *killing* one another."

Veronica raises her brow. "Then you must feel right at home, Surface Dweller. Your people are nothing but savages and murderers." She dismisses him and turns back to me. "No one here was killed by anyone other than us. They were traitors, just like you."

It's no use arguing with her, and we're wasting time. Gavin nudges me and then tilts his head toward the left. I follow his gaze to see he's gesturing to the control panel for the submersibles.

Obviously, he wants to get over there so we can open the doors to one of the tiny little ships. I give a slight incline of my head, gesturing to him that I understand and agree.

"They were innocents," I shout, startling everyone but Gavin, who creeps toward the panel.

Veronica glares at me. "They were not. They were helping you escape. Once they found out you'd murdered your best friend. They were coming to your aid."

"What? No they weren't." Why would they do that? *After* I killed Macie? It doesn't make sense.

"Yes. They were Timothy's friends and family." She tilts her head. "Remember him?"

I don't say anything. I'm too shocked. That was his name. The boy with all the blood.

"Oh, of course, you don't," she snickers. "Why should you? He was nothing. Just a commoner. A Third that was never good enough. Just. Like. You."

"He wasn't a nothing. Not to me. I thought I loved him," I say quietly, as the memories of all the times we'd snuck out together collide in my mind. Gavin stops and stares at me, his eyes a storm of emotions.

All those twisted memories make sense now. The dark recesses. The rough touches and gentle kisses. *The plan.* One night plays in front of my eyes. We'd decided we'd couple. I'd chosen him.

Then Mother had him killed.

Veronica laughs. "You loved him? Well, look where that got him. Two shots to the chest and a permanent resting place at the bottom of the sea." She glances over at Gavin—who pales—with a grin. "Better hope she doesn't love you, Surface Dweller. Or you'll never make it out. Oh wait. That isn't going to happen anyway."

Anger bubbles up in me, then just as suddenly it's gone. I grin at the girl, whose smile fades when I say, "I'm not *nothing*. I'm more than you'll ever be."

I lift the plasma pistol up and aim at her.

Nothing happens.

Veronica bursts out laughing. "Out of ammo? See? You *are* a failure."

"First rule," I say, swinging the Reising up to my shoulder. "Always come prepared." I pull the trigger slightly so only a single bullet leaves the chamber.

It's a perfect shot, and the sound echoes throughout the tiny room. But I'm not prepared for what happens next.

The bullet tears through her chest and hits the Enforcer behind her, but Veronica remains standing.

"Ow," she says. "That hurts!" Then she sprints forward, coming straight at me.

I shoot again. This time a three-round burst. They rip

through her and blood sprays everywhere, but it still doesn't stop her. She tackles me to the ground and my head slaps the concrete. Stars dance in my eyes and compete with the wave of pain.

But I don't have time to wallow in it. She's trying to tear me apart. It takes everything I have to wrangle my legs between us. I set my feet on her chest and kick as hard as I can.

She flies backward into her group of Enforcers. I don't understand why they aren't attacking me. Why didn't they kill us the minute we stepped in here?

I shove myself to my feet and glance around for Gavin. He's over at the control panel, but he's facing down two Enforcers. While he looks like he's fighting with everything he has, they're not even breaking a sweat.

What is going *on* here?

Hearing a shout, I twist my body just in time for Veronica to pass by. When she turns back around, she's covered in blood, but the wounds on her body are closing. I don't understand what I'm seeing.

She grins. "I asked for better healing. I was already perfect at everything else."

Wonderful.

I glance over to where Gavin is still fighting with the girls. They're just slapping away his advances like he's an annoying fly.

Even Veronica is just standing there in front of me. Grinning.

"You're wondering why you aren't dead yet, aren't you?"

I nod.

"We have orders to try and take you alive. Both of you." She smiles wider. "But what Mother doesn't know won't hurt us and I'm done playing games."

She pulls out her gun and aims it at me at the same time I slap in a canister and pull out the plasma pistol, taking aim at Veronica. "Last chance, Veronica. Stand down and let us by, or I shoot you and your girls."

She laughs. "Haven't you learned anything? Bullets have no long-term effects on me."

"They don't have to." I sigh. "These aren't bullets."

I aim and fire. The surprise on her face quickly morphs into fear, then pain. But before the flames can engulf her face, the rest of the Enforcers are pulling out their own guns. Gavin yanks the plasma pistol out of his pocket and shoots the nearest one. My eyebrows lift when he manages to get not only the first girl, but also the one nearest to her with the single blast. They drop to the ground, fire encasing them, and even though they're still trying to get to him, it isn't long before they're a pile of ash on the ground.

Two more Enforcers aim and fire at me, and I spin just in time to avoid getting a bullet to the head. I fire again, this time not taking a chance. Apparently it's me and Gavin or them. So I continue to shoot until there's no one in the room except Gavin and me, several piles of ash, and one or two who died when I shot Veronica with the Reising.

Emotionally exhausted, I stare at what's left of the group,

but Gavin has more worries on his mind than how we've destroyed girls who had no choice.

"Evie, are you hurt?"

I shake my head.

"There's blood all over you."

"It's not mine. It's Veronica's."

I stumble over to the control panel and try to figure out how it works. We're interrupted when Mother's voice comes through the speakers in the ceiling.

"For the last time, Evelyn, I won't allow you to leave. It's only a matter of time before your own Conditioning takes over. You can't fight it forever." Her voice wavers and there's a ferocity to it now. Obviously us prevailing over her Enforcers wasn't part of her all-knowing plan.

"We're at the submersibles dock, Mother. There's nothing you can do," I say.

There's a long silence, and I wonder what she's doing. Then the speakers hiss again. "That's what you think," she says softly. "You know? Killing those girls was not very smart. How do you expect you'll find the power room now? Though I doubt they would have helped you anyway." She laughs, and it isn't just me that hears the madness behind it.

Gavin looks at me and narrows his eyes. "We're getting to her," he finally says.

"It's such a shame, really," Mother says, either not hearing Gavin or ignoring him. "Because you were right about his eyes. And his genetics. The child you would have made together would have been perfect for my plans. An indestructible Enforcer."

"Indestructible? What are you talking about, Mother?" It comes out as a sigh. I'm over all this nonsense. I just want it to end.

"Didn't Veronica tell you?" She clicks her tongue. "Your genetics are superior to anyone in this city. You were the perfect Enforcer. Your body was quite literally designed for it. A wunderkind, so to speak. I should know; I made sure of it. You did everything perfectly your first time out. Sadly, your brain is constantly rejecting the Conditioning, but that's easily fixed. In your children. A few modifications and we would have had the perfect Enforcers."

Rage tears through me. "Is that why you kept me alive, Mother? When it would have been easier to kill me?"

"Yes. But once we were quite sure the children were what we wanted, you would have been destroyed. Just like anything defective."

"Sorry to upset your plans, but that's not going to happen," Gavin says.

"Oh, it will," Mother says. "Her Conditioning will take over, then she'll kill you and return to me and we'll put all this nasty stuff behind us." She pauses. "Oh, and Evelyn, do be safe, will you? I'd rather you not get killed by those defectives running around Sector Three."

CHAPTER TWENTY-SEVEN

The War has corrupted the Surface Dwellers. They have been consumed with hate and violence, and should be considered extremely dangerous. Any Surface Dweller who attempts to break into Elysium should be shot on sight.

—ENFORCER STATUTE 104A.1

The speaker crackles, then cuts off. I glare at it before moving my gaze to the console.

Gavin rubs a hand on my shoulder. "Don't worry, Evie. I won't let anything happen to you."

I don't say anything because I'm still staring at the console. There's not a single light on it. Just like in the corridors. Apparently the emergency power doesn't extend to these.

"Damn it!" I pound my fist against the glass.

"What's wrong?" Gavin demands.

"There's no power," I reply with a sigh.

The news doesn't surprise him. He only shrugs. "Well, that's easy to fix, right? I mean, we're in the Engineering Sector. Didn't you say that the power control room is in this Sector?"

"Yes, but I don't know where it is." I look at the ground. I'm having trouble looking at him again. Partly from embarrassment, partly because just looking at him makes me want to snap his neck.

Unaware how hard I'm fighting, but obviously sensing something is wrong, he rubs a hand up and down my bare arm. Unable to control myself, I grab his hand and toss it aside.

"Don't touch me," I growl. "Don't you realize what I want to do to you?"

"For God's sake, Evie! You're hurting. I can see it. Do you expect me to just do nothing?"

"Yes. Yes I do. Because I want to kill you. I want to take my hands and wrap them around your neck and watch as you die." Gavin blinks and takes a step away from me. "Now will you please stop touching me!"

"I'm sorry," he says quietly.

Seeing the fear in his eyes, I curse and pull at my hair. "No. *I'm* sorry. It's just getting harder and harder for me to be around you."

"Do you want to split up? Will it help you not kill me?" He grins, but I only shake my head.

"No. I can— I *will* control this, and we shouldn't split up. Not with those . . . *things* walking around. All in all, you're still probably safer with me." This time I force a smile. "We're in this together, right?"

"For better or worse," he says. "Besides, I suppose if anyone was going to kill me, I'd rather it be you." He kisses the side of my cheek, just to the left of my lips, and watches me as he pulls away, as if to see what my reaction will be.

Surprisingly, the kiss and his words make the haze of hate fade. Just a tiny bit.

"We need to find out how to get to the power room. Any ideas?" he asks.

I slowly shake my head. For the life of me, I can't remember anything about this Sector. It seems the harder I fight the Conditioning to kill Gavin, the less I remember.

Gavin purses his lips and for just a moment he reminds me so much of Mother, my hand is at my plasma pistol before I realize it. It takes every ounce of self-control I have to pull my arm back.

I want to kill him. *He's a dirty, filthy Surface Dweller. He means nothing to me. He's not my friend. Why am I helping him escape?*

The voice in my head doesn't sound like mine. It sounds like Mother. I wonder if she has a direct path into my mind.

I shake it off. Because he's your only hope, I tell myself. If you stay, you will die like everyone else. The Surface is worth the risk, if it means you'll live.

I force my hand away from the pistol.

Gavin continues to watch me for a moment, before asking, "Are you okay?"

My life is just about perfect, I want to say, but another surge of anger overtakes me as I fight the programmed response. After just a few seconds I say, "Yes. Fine."

He breathes a sigh of relief, then searches the remaining

bodies for something we can use. Suddenly, his face brightens. He reaches into a pile of gore and pulls out a thin piece of glass.

I frown. I have no clue what it is.

He hands it to me. "Macie had something like this. She tried to find the route you'd take when you snuck off to the Palace, but it didn't show the maintenance level."

I shake my head. "I don't know what it is."

His brows bunch together. "You don't?"

I lift my shoulder. "I'm sorry."

He studies it for a few minutes, then says, "Can I see your hand?"

Grudgingly, I hold it out. He presses the cool glass against my palm. A green light shoots out of the glass, then it beeps. A whole slew of words pop up onto the glass.

"I thought so," he mutters. "Recognize it now?" He holds it out to me.

I don't. I shake my head again.

He groans. "I really, really hate your mother."

I don't know what to say to that. He continues to study it and then starts pressing different things on the glass.

"Aha!" he says after a few minutes, and then a picture is projected from the glass. It's a 3-D rendering of the facility.

"A map?" I ask.

"Yep, and I think this here is where we are." He points to a blinking red dot. "I don't really know how to work it. Do you?"

I know this. I know I do. I hold out my hand and he

hands it to me. The contact with the device gives my memory a little boost and I'm able to locate the find feature. Then I pause. I can't remember where we were going.

I look up at Gavin, who says, "Power control room."

Right. I type it in, using the holographic keyboard, and it brings the map up again. This time there's a red dot: us. And a flashing orange dot: power control room. Small pink dots lead from the red dot to the orange dot.

It appears to be several levels below us and on the opposite side of the Sector. I hand the map back to Gavin. "Probably safer for you to have it," I say.

He takes it without question, reloads his plasma pistol, then hikes the backpack onto his shoulder. I do the same, and we cautiously slip out the door and start down the path.

It's quickly evident that following behind him isn't a good idea. The urge to shoot him in the back is too great. I'm still in control—so far—but I decide to take the lead. He'll just have to direct me.

It doesn't take long to make it to the elevator that will take us down, but I hesitate when Gavin opens the gate to the car. He stops, realizing I haven't followed him.

"What's wrong?" he asks, adjusting his pack.

"There's no power to run it."

He half laughs, half groans. "Right. I forgot about that." He looks back down at the map. "It looks like there's a set of stairs over there." He points a few feet away to a door.

Being as quiet and careful as possible, I open the door.

My Enforcer senses are running on double time as I creep through the door and gesture for Gavin to follow.

Despite how quiet we are, the slap of our feet echoes around the small area and I'm surprised we aren't met by any more of Mother's experiments. It bothers me that we haven't run into anyone. There should be hundreds of people in this Sector, but we've only encountered a few dozen.

We finally get to the bottom level and slip into an even darker corridor. It's so dark I can't see my hand in front of my face. But I don't need to see to know why we haven't met anyone. I can smell it. Something fleshy. And blood. Lots of it.

"Evie," Gavin whispers.

"I'm fine," I say, and flick on the flashlight attached to my dress.

"Oh my God," Gavin says, and starts gagging.

Even I can't blame him. The hallway is covered with dead bodies. The floor is sticky with partially dried pools of blood. The walls and even the ceiling are covered in sprays of red. And it drips from the ceiling like sprinkles of rain.

Laughter from farther down the hall sends chills running up and down my spine. But the light doesn't reach that far. I can't see anything.

Taking a deep breath, I move forward, trying hard not to step on anyone. My feet make sucking noises as they lift from the puddles. There are so many bodies it takes nearly ten minutes for me to cross.

Gavin uses the light from the holographic map to guide

his way. I'm dizzy and sweating by the time we're across, but I can't let on that anything's wrong. *Weakness is unacceptable. Shameful. A flaw that must be eradicated.*

The laughter echoes through the halls again, but this time I can make out other sounds, too. The scraping of feet against concrete. Talking. More than one person? And I think I hear singing.

I keep the light pointing straight ahead and my eyes and ears open. Whoever is down here isn't sane. And if the people behind us are any indication, I'm sure they aren't friendly, either.

With Gavin tapping me on the shoulder each time we need to turn, we finally find another room. The door is partially ajar. Lucky, I think, until I see what is holding it open.

The body of a girl in Enforcer garb is lying in the doorway. Blood puddles around her body. She's young, younger than she should be. Is Mother getting so desperate she's bringing them in earlier? Which begs the question, is she skipping parts of their training? Or just training them faster?

Trying not to gag, I step over her. Gavin does the same, but I notice he doesn't even flinch when he sees her.

For some reason, that makes me livid. She looks barely old enough to be an Enforcer, and she's already dead. He should be as shocked as I am.

I bite back the urge to yell all this at him. It's just the Conditioning making me feel this way, I remind myself. He's not saying anything because it won't help us. It will only make things worse. And he probably doesn't want to set me off again. But I can't help but glance down at the girl one more time before I straighten my shoulders and follow Gavin to the power console.

There's a series of levers, dials, and switches and I don't know which does what. I stare blankly at it. Gavin seems to understand how it works, however, and quickly starts turning knobs and dials, and flipping switches. Then he goes to a big metal box secured to the wall and lifts a lever on the side.

I narrow my eyes. How does he know how to do that?

I'm distracted when light floods into the compartment, blinding me. There's a *whoosh-thud-squish* sound and I realize with horror that it's the door. It's opening and closing on the girl. Every time it closes, it tries to latch, but can't. Because of her head.

I rush over and try to pull her out of the way. But I can't, because an experiment has decided now that he can see, he's got himself a feast.

He makes a high-pitched scream when I yank her away and swipes out with a knife. The first swing catches my bad shoulder, tearing the skin. I scream and he lashes out again, just barely missing my stomach. Again I try pulling her out of the way, but another experiment rushes through the open door and plows into me. We both slam into the ground and he knocks the breath out of me.

Gavin pulls out his plasma pistol and shoots both men. They disappear in a burst of flames. Then Gavin sweeps me up and over his shoulder. He runs with me down the corridor, while I fight to get down.

Anger swiftly flows into me as another horde of Mother's mistakes file into the hallway, instantly giving chase.

Trying to channel the anger into something other than shooting Gavin in the head, I pull my pistol out and start shooting behind him. One by one, the experiments fall, but for every hit there's a dozen more chasing after us.

Gavin jumps nimbly over the piles of dead bodies, somehow making sure to avoid stepping on anyone, or slipping on the slick floors.

I don't know where all this is coming from, but I'm not complaining, since he's saving my life.

Gavin flies into the stairwell and up the flights of stairs. By the time we reach the top, he's winded and wheezing, and I can tell his legs are weak and shaking, but he doesn't stop to catch his breath. He continues down the corridors the way we came until we're back in the submarines' bay.

All in all, we've only been gone maybe thirty minutes. How did he know how to work the power generator? What else hasn't he told me?

I shake my head furiously. It's only the Conditioning. He saved me.

There's shouting and running feet from the corridor and I know it won't be long before those things find us.

Gavin sets me down on my feet, then goes to the control panel. "Evie, I need your help. We need to lock ourselves into the room until we can get in the subs. Do you remember how?"

I try, but I can't. "No. I'm sorry."

The shouts come closer and I panic. We'll be trapped if I don't remember how to work the controls.

My heart careens around in my chest and I can't catch my breath as the entire room spins.

I stare at Gavin in horror. He's going to die if I don't do something. I rip off the bandage, shove my thumb into the wound in my shoulder and twist, hoping the pain will help clear my head. Then, suddenly, I hear that click again. The click of my Enforcer training. And I *do* remember. I remember *everything* Mother taught me. I walk to the control panel and lay my palm flat on the hand plate, then flip the switch for the doors to lock.

Gavin exhales in relief. "Can you work the subs? We need to get the hell out of here." His eyes are wild with fear, but all I see is a dirty, manipulative, and dangerous Surface Dweller. *One who killed your best friend and her boyfriend,* a voice says in my head.

No, that's not right. I did it. Nick killed Macie and *I* killed Nick.

No. He did. You remember. He killed them—he only made sure you thought he did. And he let that little girl die. He could have saved her, but he didn't.

"No," I whisper, pressing a hand to the sharp pain forming above my right eye.

Yes. He's the one who let that poor little girl die in the power control room. She couldn't have been any older than seven. A promising young Enforcer snuffed out by a vile Surface Dweller. He'll kill you next. He's been lying to you this whole time. He was sent to destroy Elysium. That's how he knew how to work the generator. He's just manipulating you.

"Yes, of course," I say out loud. "I remember now." The pain disappears as I listen to the voice.

"Evie? We have to go," Gavin says, turning to face me.

I slowly raise my plasma pistol and aim it at his heart. "No. We don't need to go anywhere," I say. "The only thing that needs to be done is my duty."

His eyes widen and I see myself in them. I see the hate I feel for him as I tighten my finger on the trigger.

Chapter Twenty-eight

Now I lay me down to sleep, Elysium, my heart to keep. If I should stray from Mother's eyes, I pray my mind erase its lies.

—CHILDREN'S BEDTIME PRAYER

The gun clicks and I realize the plasma cartridge is empty again. I quickly pull it out and slam in another.

"Evie," Gavin says, his voice calm. His eyes and face are blank. "Don't do this."

"Why not?" I spit out. "You caused all this. Just like your people ruined the Surface. You're the ones who forced us down here, now you're trying to destroy us again. You've brought your hate and misery with you and it's contagious."

His eyes narrow and he takes a step toward me. I lift the gun higher.

"No, Evie, I didn't come here to destroy you. The only one doing this is your mother. Remember? She Conditioned you. She's controlled you your whole life. Not me."

I pause. Something rings true about that. But my head

keeps telling me it's a lie. "You're just saying that so I'll help you. *Surface Dwellers are manipulative and dangerous.*"

He takes an imploring step forward. I pull the hammer back on the pistol. "Don't. Move."

He stops immediately, but his hands are still out. "You know I'm not just saying it. You saw it with your own eyes. Remember, Evie. Remember what happened to Macie."

I frown at him. "Who's Macie?"

His eyebrows wing up. "She's your best friend, remember?"

I shake my head rapidly as contradictory memories collide in my head. "No. I don't have any friends. I'm an Enforcer. All I need are my sisters." But a tear trickles down my cheek as a memory forces its way to the surface. She took me into her quarters one night after my failure. She wasn't supposed to, but I needed a friend more than anything.

Another memory, of us going to Festival together last year. Her telling me all about the fun things she'd done with Nick and how she thought she was falling in love and it was all thanks to me.

Of her lying on the floor, surrounded by her own blood, with her boyfriend meters away, eyes glassed over with death.

"No," I whisper.

It's a lie, Evie. All a lie. He's tricking you. *Surface Dwellers are manipulative and dangerous.* He deserves to die for what he did to your city. Your people. Macie, Mother's voice screams in my head.

Macie's the lie. She didn't exist. She wasn't real, I think.

No, she's real, but he killed her. Not you. Not Nick. It was him the whole time. He's just made you think it was you.

He did?

Yes. *He's just a Surface Dweller; he deserves to die.*

"Yes," I repeat after the voice in my head. "You're just a Surface Dweller and you deserve to die."

I put pressure on the trigger, pulling it toward me with my fingertip, just as I was taught.

Do it now, Evelyn! Now, before he tricks you again. Before he can get it away from you. *Surface Dwellers are manipulative and dangerous.* Do it *now*!

I pull the trigger, but my hand jerks down at the last second, as if someone is pushing down on my arms, sending the plasma ball into the floor. It melts a small divot into the floor by my foot, startling me.

I curse and line up my next shot, but before I can wrap my finger around the trigger again, Gavin is wrapping his hands around mine, and the gun. "Don't listen to her, Evie. She's lying. Not me. Not you."

I fight to pull away from him, but it's no use. Even my own body is fighting me, and I feel so weak. Something wet trickles down my arm. The wound on my shoulder is bleeding again. A lot this time.

Dizzy, I sway. Gavin tries to catch me, but I push away. "Don't touch me," I slur.

His eyes are worried, but apparently he doesn't think I'm a threat anymore. "I can't help it, Evie."

I struggle to remain standing. I'll kill him before I go down. Again, I raise the gun, aiming for his head. I won't miss this time. I won't fail again.

He closes his eyes and steps forward, pressing the gun to his own head.

"What are you doing?" I ask. Panic is tearing through me and I don't know why. I should be grateful he's doing my job for me.

"Making it easier for you. With that arm, you wouldn't be able to hit the broad side of a barn."

"Are you crazy?"

He nods and there's a small ghost of a smile. "Yeah. I think maybe I am. I've fallen in love with a girl who's programmed to kill me. Not a very sane thing to do, is it?"

My jaw drops. "What? What did you say?"

He looks straight into my eyes. "I love you, Evie."

He's lying. He doesn't love me. *Surface Dwellers are manipulative.* He's just using me, I think, as Mother's voice continues her rant inside my head.

I fumble back the hammer with shaking hands. *I have to kill him. That's my job. To protect the city from filthy, dirty Surface Dwellers. Surface Dwellers are manipulative and dangerous. Nothing more than heathens who'd just as soon kill you as look at you. He's the worst of them all. Why am I protecting him? He means nothing to me.*

The words come to me in a voice that's so different from mine, I suddenly know they're programmed responses.

But the answers to those questions are so simple I can hardly argue with them.

He isn't a manipulative and dangerous Surface Dweller. He's smart. And kind. And nothing like what Mother said a Surface Dweller is. He means much more than nothing to me. And that's why I'm helping him escape. Because he means everything to me. Because I love him. And he loves me. And I've done everything I can to protect him.

My fingers fall from the pistol, which clatters to the ground as pain rips through my head. It feels like hundreds of bees stinging my brain. I gasp and scrunch my eyes closed, grasping my head as I fall to my knees.

The bees fill my head with a buzzing that blocks all other sounds, then it slowly dies down and Gavin's voice turns from a soft hum to clear sentences as he holds me tightly to his chest.

I push myself up to a sitting position and he slowly pulls away, but stays within reach, his eyes filled with concern as he watches me.

Tears pour from my eyes as I collapse into his arms. "I love you, too," I choke out as the final twinge of pain fades away like it was never there in the first place.

I touch him everywhere, as if to reassure myself he's really there before pressing my lips to his. "You're insane. I could have shot you from shock alone." I press kisses all over his face.

His mouth finds mine. "It was worth it," he mumbles against my lips.

Suddenly a bang sounds behind us and we turn to see the door to the rest of the Sector is being hit by something. Another bang and we see it bend inward.

"They're coming," I whisper.

"Quick." Gavin turns back toward the console. "I need you to work the sub controls. How do we get the door open?"

I stare at the console, filled with blinking lights and levers, knobs, and buttons. I close my eyes and try to recall my training, but something's wrong. The Enforcer memories that were so clear just seconds ago are fading.

Hand plate. Hand plate. Hand plate, my mind screams at me over and over, but I don't know what that means. Hand plate?

I shake my head. "I-I don't know." I slam my hand down on the console. Lost. Defeated. We're going to die here, because I can't remember. Mother's last trick has succeeded.

Mother's voice is no longer in my head, but the victory has come at a terrible cost. My memories.

Bang! I turn to see fingers work their way through the gap that's been opened between the two doors. They grab the sides of the doors and slowly start to force them open the rest of the way.

"Hurry, you idiots, they're going to escape," Mother's voice shouts, and I shudder.

She's here. Directly on the other side of the door. And those must be her Elite Enforcers. They'd be the only ones strong enough to force those doors open. From the sounds, she probably brought what's left of them.

With two on the door, how many is that? Five? Six? Dozens?

I can only stare in horror as those fingers yank the doors wider, allowing slim, muscled arms to slip through the opening. They manage to shove the doors enough that through the crack I see Mother standing in the middle of at least half a dozen Enforcers.

Despite the fear piercing through me, part of my mind is already cataloguing their exact positions, calculating the angle of attack, the distance between us, which weapons they'll use in this small area.

When Mothers sees me, she smiles, replacing the scowl. "Come now, Evelyn, you've had your fun, but playtime is over. You don't want to go to the Surface." She steps forward, and lifts her arm, extending her hand into the gap for me to take. "There's no need to fear me, Evelyn. The Surface Dweller has manipulated you into thinking I'm the monster, when it is he and his kind. I saved you, Evelyn. Made you my own. Because I love you. Just take my hand and I'll help you. You can trust me."

I can trust her? I tilt my head to the side. *Of course I can trust her. Mother loves me. She has had nothing but my well-being in mind. It is my privilege to follow her orders.*

I step toward her and lift my arm to take her hand.

Suddenly I'm being picked up and spun around. I scream and fight and kick, trying to do anything to escape from the real monster.

"Shh, it's just me," Gavin says in my ear. He hugs me

tightly and kisses the side of my head, and the fog that started when Mother started talking lifts and I remember exactly why I can't trust her.

"Gavin," I whisper.

"Evelyn, don't listen to him."

My head throbs as a series of those deep clicks go off in my mind. My visions strobes as my Conditioning turns on and off. I grit my teeth against the pain, and the vertigo.

Suddenly, Gavin lets out a whoop and hauls me toward the submarine.

"No!" Mother screams. "Get those doors open now! Evelyn must not escape!"

"Let's go!" Gavin says as he lifts me over the side and drops me into the seat of the submarine.

He got it open, I think. Somehow he got it open.

I immediately twist around and watch in horror as the first of the Enforcers finally push their way through the opening. The doors to the sub slam close just as Mother and the rest push their way through.

She's yelling again and her eyes and face are dark with rage.

I glance over and see Gavin at the controls. "Just hang on tight. I have no clue what I'm doing, but I've played a few video games in my lifetime. Either way this is probably going to be the thrill ride of your life."

I laugh, but this time the movement pulls on my shoulder and I end up gasping and clutching at my chest.

Gavin shoots me a worried glance, but stays where he is. He pushes a series of buttons on the console and then I'm being shoved into my seat as we blast away from the city and toward the Surface.

Even as the submarine's computer voice warns us to buckle our seat belts, I quickly turn around to watch as, for the first time in my life, I can see the whole of Elysium laid out along the trench walls and ocean floor like a great mechanical octopus. To my shock, it's brown, covered in overgrowths of the plant life I've always seen through the windows. Nothing like the shining silver beacon in the painting in the Palace dining room. It looks so old.

Soon, I can see only the shine of its lights, before it finally disappears in a curtain of bubbles.

I don't know how I feel about leaving everything behind. It feels bittersweet. Macie, my gardens, Father. It hurts knowing I'll never see anyone or anything I cared about, but after everything I've learned, it's also a relief.

I glance over at Gavin and can't help but smile. At least one good thing came from all of this. Gavin. My knight in-not-so-shining armor.

He keeps glancing behind him. Even when we can no longer see my underwater city and I continue to watch him.

A voice jolts me out of my daze. "Warning! Angle of ascent is not recommended for current cabin pressure equalization protocols. Course adjustment and slower ascent is strongly recommended."

Gavin frowns at me. "What does that mean?"

"We're going up too fast for the submarine to automatically equalize the pressure. If you continue to go up this fast, you'll get the bends."

His face pales and he immediately slows the submarine.

The pressure from the blast lightens up, but now there's a terrible pain in my chest and shoulder. Something is wrong. My head is buzzing again, and I can't understand what the computer voice is saying. I hope it's nothing important.

My hand is warm. And wet.

I glance down and see the entire front of my dress covered in blood. I pull my hand away and see there is a glove of blood from my fingertips to my elbow.

Too much blood, I think, my head growing foggy. There's entirely too much blood.

"The pressure . . ." I murmur. "Why aren't the nanos working?"

I glance at Gavin, but he's staring straight ahead now, entirely focused on getting us to the Surface. My head lolls back to the center and I stare ahead. I can't tell him. There's nothing to be done anyway.

I can't quite recall what I meant to tell him.

I feel a sharp pain in my shoulder and glance down. There is blood all over the front of my dress. How did that happen?

Inside my head, I hear lovely violin music and I smile. I do love the violin.

The fingers of my left hand begin to finger imaginary strings in time to the melody and a pain shivers along my arm. I glance down. There is blood all over the front of my dress. How did that happen? I wonder.

The music gets louder, but my fingers can't keep up anymore. How odd.

I turn to the left and catch sight of the person beside me. Gavin.

The nanos.

She barely tried to stop us.

"Gavin," I gasp out, trying to reach for him, but my body won't cooperate and I only jerk uselessly. He turns. "We have to go back. The electromagnetic fi—" I cut off when a sharp pain tears through my head. I gasp and slump forward. I hear my name as I'm pulled into the blackness.

"Evie . . ."

I fight to open my eyes, but my sleep is so deep and so seductive.

"Evie, please. Answer me."

There is so much light pouring through my eyelids. More light than I can bear. I try to pull a hand up to my face, but I can't seem to move. The whole world seems to move around me. Rocking me.

Even through my closed lids, the light scorches my eyes. Even if I want to look, I can't, but I can smell air. I don't know where I've smelled air like this before, but it's familiar and it's mixed with the scent of salt and something else I can't identify. The warmth on my skin feels so good from the chills I'd felt before.

I let myself be soothed back into sleep by the rocking, the comfort of whatever is holding me, and the warmth on my skin.

Blood and pain. That's what fills my dreams. A voice screaming that I failed. Someone whispering he's sorry. Another voice screams for me to run.

I wake slightly when I'm picked up from my seat, but a familiar scent and the strong arms that hold me soothe me. I know that scent. I know I do. I try to open my eyes, but it's too much effort. So I stop fighting and curl into whoever's holding me.

Then there's a jarring motion when whoever is carrying me jumps from the steadily rocking platform we were on, to something soft and crunchy. The jar tears at my shoulder and I want to scream, but no sounds escape me. It's all echoing in my head.

Soon, the steady sound of footsteps and the new, different rocking motion put me back to sleep. Back to the dreams of pain and blood.

I wake when a sharp pain in my arm tears me from my nightmares. Mother! is all I can think.

There's some type of glasses over my eyes. Everything is a shade of gray. I try to claw them off, but my arm won't cooperate.

"You won't want to take those off yet, Miss," a deep voice says. "Your eyes haven't adjusted to the light here and we don't want you to go blind on top of fixin' up this here wound."

I turn my head and the first person I see is a withered old man with dark skin and silver hair. I start thrashing around, trying to get away. I won't let him get me. I have to get away. Find . . . someone, and get away.

"Shh. Evie, it's okay. He's a friend. He's going to help you," a familiar voice says.

I look around to find the source of the voice. The room is familiar, yet not. The furniture is all strange and metal. The room scares me more than the strange man. I stop searching when I see a face I recognize. A young man with dirty blond hair and gray eyes.

He smiles when my eyes latch on to him. He reaches out and cups my cheek. "How are you feeling?" he asks. He kisses my lips and pulls me closer into a hug without waiting for an answer. "Oh, thank God. I thought I was going to be too late."

I don't say anything. I've no idea what to say. He hugs me tighter and his mouth sends tremors throughout my body when he leans in close to my ear.

"I love you," he whispers.

My eyes widen. He loves me? My stomach flutters, but I don't know why. How could he possibly love me? What does he want from me?

I stutter out the only thing I can think of to ask. "Who are you?"

Chapter Twenty-nine

I've been here for a few days now, yet I still can't remember anything from before then. Flashes now and then, but nothing substantial. Nothing that I can say I know is the truth. The only thing I know for sure is that here is not my home.

—FROM EVIE'S JOURNAL

I'm on the Surface. I finally made it. I try to look at the sun as it sets, but the bright orangey yellow is still too painful, even with my dark glasses. It's beautiful, though. Like nothing I've ever imagined. More than I could ever have dreamed. I like sunset best, when the light doesn't hurt my eyes so much, and the heat of the sun is bearable on my pink skin.

The doctor says my sunburn would fade faster if I stopped going out into sunlight, but how can I? It's fascinating and wonderful and irresistible.

Mother was wrong.

I let the wet sand dribble through my fingers, enjoying the rough wetness. Then I tilt my head to the side and wonder who Mother is. I picture a woman with honey blond hair and a pretty smile, but I know that's not who I'm thinking of.

I sigh. Why can't I remember anything?

I glance down at the clean white bandage on my shoulder. It has something to do with this, I know, but all I can remember is getting shot and then hiding inside some kind of ticket booth.

It hurts like crazy. I have to have it packed every few hours. Not exactly an enjoyable experience, but if I don't do it, I could get an infection. That's what the doctor tells me.

So I do what he says and hope it heals soon so I can go home.

Home? I don't even know where that is.

It surely isn't here, where all the people save one are unfamiliar. Where even the sea and sand is strange. I have visions of glass and metal walls. Hard, concrete floors. Not the wood and metal structures built haphazardly a few meters from the shoreline.

Right now I'm stuck sleeping in what I'm told is the hospital. When I heal completely I'll be allowed to live elsewhere, but for now I need to stay near the doctors. It's not much of a hospital as far as I can tell, just a few small, worn rooms. But the people who watch over and take care of me are kind. I've been here only a few days, but they already count me as one of them.

"You're Gavin's," one girl told me this morning when I asked her why everyone was being so nice. "That makes you ours."

I don't know exactly what that means, but I have to admit it's been on my mind since she said it, and it makes me happy.

The sound of footsteps crunch behind me and I jump up and spin around, half afraid the monsters from my nightmares are coming for me. But I relax when I see Gavin walking toward me with his hands in his pockets. He comes every day, but only when I'm sleeping. At least that's what I've been told by one of the girls who takes care of me. Apparently he doesn't want to pressure me.

But I've missed him, somehow, and I wish he had come to see me when I was awake sooner. It gives me tingles in my stomach just to see him.

"Hi," he says, and kicks some sand with the toe of his shoe.

"Hi," I say back. Although I'm enormously pleased to see him, I'm shy as well. I sit back down and clasp my hands together in my lap.

"Can I join you?" he asks.

I gesture to the spot beside me. "Of course. I hear you saved my life."

He sits and extends his fingers toward mine before curling them into a fist. "Yes. But you saved mine first," he says softly, and then looks into my eyes.

"Really?" I smile. "I'm glad. I only remember bits and pieces, but what I do remember isn't very nice." The smile fades.

"What do you remember?" He watches me, his hand clenching and unclenching into the dirt.

I stare into space. "Running. Getting shot. Pointing a gun at you." I look back at him. "Lots and lots of blood."

"Do you remember anything else?"

I shrug. "I've tried. It only gives me headaches."

"You don't remember anything else . . . about me?"

I shake my head again. "I remember your name now, but no. I'm sorry."

He nods, then stands and starts to walk away.

Panic fills me and I know if I don't do something right then, I'll never see him again. "Wait!" I jump up.

He stops and spins around, a hopeful look on his face. I slowly walk to him, not sure what I want to say, but I know I want to—have to—say something.

When I reach him, I still don't know what to say, so I just reach out and take his hand, keeping my eyes on his. They widen and the hope grows brighter.

I lift his hand to my face and nuzzle into it. "I don't remember you, yet. But I do know you're important to me. I can't stop thinking about you. And just the thought of you, or the sound of your name, or your voice, gives me flutters . . . here." I lower his hand to my stomach.

He swallows, but doesn't say anything.

It doesn't matter though, because I have more to say. "And I don't want that to stop. Ever." I look back into his eyes. "I know this isn't fair to you, but"—I take a deep breath—"but if you'll wait for me, I know I'll remember you. Soon."

He smiles and caresses my cheek with his thumb. "I would wait forever for you."

I smile and push up on my tiptoes to press a kiss to his lips. He tenses and I lower myself back to the flats of my feet, staring at the ground as a blush creeps into my face. I have no idea why I just did that.

"I-I'm sorry," I say.

Without any warning, he snakes his arm around my waist and tugs me to him. Then his mouth crushes mine. Mindful of my shoulder, I carefully entwine my arms around his neck, dragging my hands through his hair.

We're both gasping for air when we pull back from each other. He smiles and brushes the back of his fingers down my cheek.

We turn and stare out over the gorgeous blue water. It sparkles as the sun catches the ripples. And the sun! Even though it hurts, I don't want to turn away. It's turned the most beautiful reddish orange. The sky glows like coals, and the clouds around it are the same fiery orange.

"It's so beautiful," I say.

"Yes," Gavin says, but when I glance over, he's looking not at the sunset, but at me.

Pleasure flows through me and for the first time, in what feels like forever, I'm truly happy.

Acknowledgments

Writing is an epic journey. A journey filled with ups and downs, wrong ways, detours, and dead ends. Sinkholes and quicksand. One with oceans, whirlwinds, and rainbows. And, ultimately, one that cannot be done alone.

First I'd like to thank my wonderful agent, Natalie Fischer Lakosil, whose unwavering faith, perseverance, support, and patience was the lighthouse in the rainstorm I needed. Thank you for cutting back the vines of publishing, talking me off ledges, and generally just going above and beyond the call of duty time and time again. And, of course, thank you to Laura Bradford for her insightful advice and for making *Renegade* even better.

A *huge* thank-you to my awesome-sauce editor, Mel Frain, for being my navigator, despite her hatred of bananas. Thank you for guiding me with your fantastic ideas and fabulous eye for uncovering *Renegade*'s true potential. This story wouldn't have been as great without you—high five. Thank you to the entire Tor Teen team. And of course, thank you to *Renegade*'s art director, Seth Lerner, and the fantastic cover artist, Eithne O'Hanlon, for giving me such a beautiful cover. It exceeded my expectations and I couldn't be happier.

To Liz Czukas, my very first crit partner and "harshest" critic, thank you for being my sounding board, shoulder to cry on, brainstorming partner, and, above all else, my best friend. Without you, I'd have gone bald long ago and I'd probably be talking to myself while rocking in the corner. Thank you for making my manuscript bleed more times than I can count, for lending me your ear and brain for hours on end, and for sending me mountains of horribly fantastic ideas and one-liners, such as "Oh my jellyfish." One day, I hope to do the same for you.

To Larissa Hardesty, thank you for being my friend and listening to all my griping and whining, for being my cheerleader when I needed one, and for tearing up my manuscript when it needed it. Your feedback and advice was priceless and I'll never forget it!

To Leah Crichton, thank you for being my first fan. Your never-ending support helped keep me going more times than I can count.

Of course, none of this would be possible without the never-ending support of my family.

My husband and the love of my life, Ben, who I've been in love with since he was the only boy in my health class my freshman year and who took me to see a chick flick with three other girls, just so he could take me on my first date. Thank you for listening to my incessant rambles about my story and the problems I'm having with it, for helping me shore up plot holes, and for helping me research the science behind my world. Thanks also for reminding me it's not the destination that matters, but the journey, and that love always conquers all. I love you now and always.

To my children, Charles and Aurora. Both of you know how much I love you and how much better my life is now that you're in it. No matter how frustrated I get with you and you with me, I hope you'll always remember and know how strong my love is for you. I hope you know that anything worth doing is hard, but to "never give up and never surrender." And, of course, a huge thank-you, Charles, for helping me come up with the title. I doubt anyone could have come up with a better one.

To my mom, for showing me the gift of reading by giving me her well-worn copies of *Nancy Drew* and everything Louisa May Alcott. And my dad, for giving me the ability to fight for what I want.

Thank you, also, to my other family, my sisters at Oasis for YA. All you beautiful ladies have kept me going with your amazing talent and love for YA. And to the wonderful writers of the debut group, The Apocalypsies, for helping me navigate these rough and treacherous waters.

Thank you to my brilliant photographer, Jessica Grimm, with whom I share a name and a talent for the arts.

Thank you to Taylor Swift, Marianas Trench, Avril Lavigne, and Evanescence for creating the brilliant music that poured through my speakers as I wrote this book.

Thank you to God for giving me the talent and perseverance to see this project through to its end.

More thank-yous to my wonderful group of blog readers and Twitter followers and other online friends. You all are fantastic. Please don't stop what you're doing. Keep it coming. And last but not least, thank you to *you,* wonderful reader. I hope you enjoy my book. I'm grateful you chose this book from all the other wonderful ones swarming the shelves.